Paul Burston was born in Yorkshire, raised in South Wales and now lives in London. A journalist and broadcaster, his work has appeared in *Time Out*, the *Sunday Times*, *The Times*, the *Guardian*, the *Independent* and the *Independent on Sunday* and on Channel Four. He is the author of several books, including *Queens' Country: A Tour around the Gay Ghettos, Queer Spots and Camp Sights of Britain*. *Shameless* is his first novel.

PAUL BURSTON

Shameless

An *Abacus* Book

First published in Great Britain by Abacus in 2001

Copyright © Paul Burston, 2001

Author photograph © LaurenceJaugey-Paget.com

The moral right of the author has been asserted.

A CIP catalogue record for this book
is available from the British Library.

ISBN 0 349 11479 X

Typeset in Berkeley by M Rules
Printed and bound in Great Britain by
Clays Ltd, St Ives plc

Abacus
An imprint of
Time Warner Books UK
Brettenham House
Lancaster Place
London WC2E 7EN

www.TimeWarnerBooks.co.uk

For Toni Duval
and Stewart Who?

part one

Pride

Chapter one

The boy serving behind the bar oozed confidence the way most of the predominantly twenty-something crowd oozed 'CK One' or 'Escape For Men'. He was cute in that silky, sulky, vaguely Latin way that promised a career modelling underwear for Calvin Klein, or at the very least a job behind a gay bar in Soho. He was also absurdly, enviably young – certainly no older than twenty. Martin felt attracted and resentful in roughly equal measures. What was it John always said, about yesterday's trade becoming tomorrow's competition? Well, there was little danger of that happening in this case. Martin knew from years of experience that boys this young and this pretty rarely performed sexual favours for anyone who couldn't match them in the beauty stakes – pout for pout, muscle for muscle. And at thirty-two, Martin was in rather a different league.

Not that he was looking too bad for his age. He had always been considered fairly handsome (usually by straight women, admittedly), and unlike many gay men on the scene, he didn't run around like some strange teenage impersonator, squeezed into outfits designed for someone half his age. He also knew that thirty-two wasn't exactly old – not in real terms. But, as John was also fond of saying, it was practically fifty in gay years. If John's theory was correct, then gay men aged at about the same rate as dogs. In fact, the only people who aged faster were Greek women, which was why John swore blind that in all his years as an air steward he had never once met a Greek woman between the ages of twenty-five and fifty – by the time they reached their mid-twenties, their body clocks switched into fifth gear and suddenly they were swathed in black robes and riding a donkey. According to John, a similar thing happened to gay men, only they swapped the black robes for black leather and the donkey for a dildo.

In his weaker moments, Martin worried that there might actually be some truth in all of this, even though it was exactly the sort of thing a sourpuss like John would say. Theirs was one of those gay friendships that developed quite by accident (they used to frequent the same bar), rather than growing out of some mutual interest or even a one-night stand they both immediately regretted but felt strangely sentimental about. It was a friendship Martin maintained more out of habit than anything else. They'd had some great nights out together, and had even supported each other through some difficult times – when John had his HIV scare for instance, or when Martin's first proper boyfriend revealed six weeks into their relationship that he had a long-term lover in Paris who was about to move back to London. But really, they couldn't have been more different. John was only two years younger than Martin, but in the nine years that they had been friends, he had never held down a relationship for more than a few months. Martin, on the other hand, had been with

Christopher for almost four years now. So what if this bar boy was the prettiest thing in the room? That didn't make him a better person. He was probably arrogant, not to mention stupid. Boys like that usually were – body by Nautilus, brain by Fisher Price. Martin had met enough of them over the years to know that. He ordered a Red Stripe, and felt a tiny pang of guilt when the boy smiled as he placed the chilled can on the bar, together with a saucer containing the change from a five-pound note. He smiled back, hesitated before leaving a small tip, and squeezed through the crowd to a vacant space near the door.

Where did they all come from, these boys who packed the bars night after night? Each time another bar opened, the ruling queens of Old Compton Street shook their perfectly gelled heads and predicted that this would be it, that there wouldn't be enough punters to go around. And each time they were proved wrong. There were at least a dozen gay bars in the heart of Soho now, and not one of them showed signs of going out of business. It never used to be like this. Martin remembered a time, not all that long ago, when the only bars worth visiting in the West End if you weren't a '70s clone or a Northern rent boy with dodgy highlights were Compton's or the Brief Encounter – and they were never this busy on a Thursday night. Either every gay man in the country had migrated to London during the past couple of years, or the Soho boys had discovered a way of defying the laws of nature and multiplying like rabbits. At least that would explain why so many of them looked so similar. Looking around, Martin found himself wondering if maybe there was such a thing as a gay gene after all.

There was a mirror behind the bar, cleverly positioned so that customers could admire the bar staff from every possible

angle. The management at The Village were shrewd like that –
always looking for new ways of 'giving something back to
the community'. Martin caught a glimpse of his own reflection, and ran a hand over his newly cropped hair. It felt
strange, prickly, sexy. He had worn his hair in a dozen different styles over the years – slicked back, spiked up, floppy at
the front, shaved at the sides, bleached blond, dyed black. He
had even sported a footballer's perm once, when his mother
ran that hairdressing salon on the outskirts of Cardiff all those
years ago. But he'd never had it cut this short before. He
wasn't entirely convinced that it suited him, but that was
hardly the point. All the boys had their hair cut short these
days. Of course for many of them it was simply a way of dis-
guising the fact that they were receding. Still, it was definitely
considered sexy. You only had to flick through any of the gay
bar rags to see that. Once it was only arty Derek Jarman types
and the roughest gay skinheads who went for the severely
cropped look. Now even the rent boys who advertised in the
back of *Boyz* were at it. Of course they weren't actually called
rent boys any more – they were all 'escorts' now. Each week
their photographs were there – all smouldering looks and
brutally shorn heads, together with the promise of 'Nine
Inches Uncut and Thick' and 'Satisfaction Guaranteed'.

Christopher would like it – Martin was confident of that at
least. He'd hinted at it often enough. Barely a week went by
without him explaining in his fading West Coast accent how
the one thing British guys had over the hunks back home in
LA was their sexy haircuts, or how much more practical it
was to have short hair because then you didn't have to worry
about drying it when you went to the gym. The gym was
another of Christopher's passions. It had all started about six
months ago, when an old high-school friend of his flew in for

the weekend and insisted they all go to Trade. Martin had hated every minute of it. The music was too hard, and he could never see the attraction of clubs where everyone was off their face on drugs. If you needed to fry your brain with Ecstasy in order to have a good time, then surely there must be something missing somewhere? Christopher, on the other hand, had loved everything about it – the pounding music, the druggy atmosphere and the seething mass of half-naked, hard-bodied, wide-eyed men. The night ended in a blazing row, with Christopher and his high-school friend disappearing into a sea of bodies and Martin storming off.

A week later Christopher joined the gym. He'd been going regularly ever since. Even Martin was forced to admit that the results were impressive. Christopher had always had fairly beefy legs, which was a definite advantage. Most of the gym queens you saw around had great pumped-up upper bodies supported on tiny twiglet legs. They reminded Martin of the bulldog from *Tom and Jerry*. Maybe they assumed that nobody would be concentrating on their legs when they stripped off their shirts on the dance floor, but they looked pretty silly anyhow. John said it was the responsibility of every self-respecting gay man to refuse to have sex with any man whose biceps were thicker than his thighs. It just wasn't natural.

Martin had tagged along to the gym with Christopher a couple of times, but he soon lost interest. He tried justifying it to himself by saying that it was better to develop your mind than your body, but secretly he was slightly envious of Christopher's determination. He certainly thought that Christopher had started to get a bit obsessive lately, disappearing off to the gym four, sometimes five times a week. He put this down to the fact that Gay Pride was coming up.

There was a part of Christopher that craved constant attention. Being able to strip off at Pride, secure in the knowledge that his body would be admired – that was what this gym thing was all about. Martin told himself that he really shouldn't be too bothered by the idea. After all, having your boyfriend lusted after was a compliment in a way.

He looked at his watch. 7.55 p.m. Christopher was almost half an hour late. Typical. He wouldn't have minded, only it wasn't his idea to meet for a drink in the first place. If it had been up to him, they'd both be at home in Stockwell by now, curled up on the sofa watching *EastEnders* and eating a low-fat meal (Christopher only ate low-fat these days, ever since his personal trainer told him that the only way to achieve a washboard stomach was to drastically reduce his fat intake). Martin couldn't see the point in hanging around gay bars with your boyfriend – not unless you were looking for a threesome, which he and Christopher certainly were not. They'd tried it once, just over a year ago, but it didn't really work out. Christopher and the guy they picked up took ten minutes to decide that they were quite capable of having a good time on their own, and Martin ended up sitting in the bathroom, crying quietly to himself and feeling more possessive than he had ever thought possible. It seemed that most gay bars were geared towards cruising these days, unless they were designed for people to actually have sex on the premises. He had no strong moral objections to any of this, but he did find it a bit irritating that there were so few places you could go as a couple without feeling that someone, somewhere in the room would like nothing better than to see you split up.

He lit a Marlboro Light, took a swig of Red Stripe, and scanned the room. There was a guy over in the corner he recognised. He wasn't sure where from at first, until suddenly he remembered that they'd had a one-night stand together five or six years ago. The guy's name was Tom. Or Tim – something like that. They'd met at Substation, one night when Martin was out with John, both of them pissed as farts. He was a nice guy, Martin seemed to remember. He lived in this amazing flat somewhere off Tottenham Court Road. He worked for an investment bank, and was really impressed when Martin told him about his job as a graphic designer. He said he'd never met someone so creative before, which Martin thought was rather sweet considering that the most creative thing he'd done at the time was design a box of teabags for Sainsbury's. The sex was good, too. They'd even swapped numbers afterwards, but of course the guy never rang. The nice ones rarely did. That was why Martin felt lucky to have found someone like Christopher. He wasn't the perfect boyfriend, not by any means. He was moody at times, and he could be extremely selfish. On the other hand, he was the first man Martin had slept with who could still turn him on after four years. And he was dependable – most of the time anyway.

Martin looked at his watch. 8.10 p.m. This was getting ridiculous. Why were some people always so late? Was it something they just couldn't help, like dyslexia? When they looked at their watches, did they see the numbers arranged in a completely different order? Or was it simply arrogance, a way of showing the world that they knew they were worth waiting for? It would serve Christopher right if he arrived to find that Martin had been and gone, or that he was being chatted up by some good-looking guy with a posh flat in the West End. That would teach him not to take people for granted. He looked over to where Tom or Tim was standing, only he wasn't on his own any more. He was deep in conversation with some muscular young thing in a white ribbed vest and baggy jeans. Something about their body language told Martin that this wasn't the first time they had met. He wondered if this guy had seen the inside of Tom or Tim's posh flat. He wondered if they had swapped numbers afterwards. He wondered if Tom or Tim had been the one who had bothered to phone.

Just then, Tom or Tim looked up and caught Martin's eye. He looked at him quizzically for a moment, and then broke into a grin. It wasn't a friendly 'Nice to see you again' grin. It was a grin that said, 'Yes, I remember you. We had one night of meaningless sex a long time ago. I charmed the pants off you by telling you how creative and interesting you were, when really I was only interested in making use of your body for an hour or so. Of course you were too stupid to realise that at the time, too naïve to understand that there was never going to be any more to it than that. And now look at you, standing there all alone while I'm being adored by this gorgeous man. Serves you right. That's what you get for not knowing how to play the game.'

Martin turned away, gulped down the remains of his Red Stripe, and headed towards the bar. One more beer, then he was definitely leaving.

Caroline never knew what to do with her knickers during sex. Sometimes she would peel them off slowly, until they ended up in a tiny ball at her ankles. Then she would slide one foot over the other and grasp the little lacy bundle between her toes, like a magician performing a vanishing trick. Other times, usually when she'd had a bit too much to drink, she would just yank them off with both hands and hurl them across the room, where they would land delicately draped on the dressing-table mirror, or dangling from one of the wall lights. Of course there was one major drawback with this technique. Assuming the man didn't know her all that well, he might mistake her for an amateur stripper. Caroline wouldn't have minded being mistaken for a stripper, but she couldn't bear the thought of anyone thinking she was amateurish. She was a professional woman, the only woman in her family to have carved out any kind of decent life for herself, and she had the fat salary, the company car and the platinum American Express card to prove it. She was also the sort of woman for whom 'girl talk' invariably meant talking about sex. She had discussed the knickers situation with one of the girls at the advertising agency, who advised her that the best solution was to leave them discreetly tucked into the leg of your trousers. But this wasn't much use to Caroline. When she wasn't handling key accounts or attempting to woo potential clients, she never wore trousers.

Thankfully, Caroline's knickers hadn't presented quite so much of a problem since she'd met Graham. That first night together, he had insisted on removing them with his teeth. Darling Graham. Not only was he the best-looking man she had dated in a long time – tall and wiry, with a mop of curly brown hair and bright hazel eyes. He was also the kind of man who didn't turn his nose up at cunnilingus. In Caroline's experience, men with that many physical attributes were pretty thin on the ground. Martin had told her once that he was finally forced to admit that he was gay at the age of fifteen, when his girlfriend at the time asked him to go down on her. Try as he might, and desperate as he was to convince himself that he was really straight, he just couldn't go through with it. Caroline had told him that if eating pussy was the only thing that separated straight men from gay men, then there were a hell of a lot of men out there who were gay and just didn't know it yet. Before Graham, she had only ever known one man who knew the first thing about pleasuring a woman this way. The others merely snuffled around a bit, half-heartedly, like dogs sniffing a lamp post. And people wondered why girls like her learned to pleasure themselves from an early age. If she had waited for a man to bring her to orgasm, she would have been dry for twenty-seven years!

Yes, Caroline had had more than her fair share of bad sex. Men who squeezed her breasts so hard it hurt. Men whose idea of foreplay was to stick their tongue so far into her ear they practically burst her ear-drum. Men who came so quickly it was all over before she'd even begun to feel any kind of pleasure. Men with dicks so small she could barely tell when the point of penetration occurred. It wasn't their fault, of course. But if they only knew the lengths she had gone to, clenching her vaginal muscles in order to massage their fragile male egos, reassuring them that, oh yeah baby, it felt really good when really, she felt nothing. There was that guy she met at the Met Bar the Christmas before last – gorgeous body, sports car, the works. The only problem was, his penis was no bigger than her little finger. She tried so hard to compensate for it, clenching away for all she was worth. 'Oh, it's so big! It's so big! Is it in yet?' That was the difference between gay men and straight women. A gay man would have just dumped him on the spot, or wanked him off in a doorway. Women would lie back and clench for England.

Still, whatever indignities Caroline had suffered in the past, she had certainly made up for it in the past year. Sex with Graham was the best she'd ever known. He was so sensitive, so attentive, so athletic. There wasn't any position they hadn't tried. That boob job had turned out to be a really sound investment. Not having to worry about her tits disappearing under her armpits had freed Caroline up in ways she could never have imagined. There were no inhibitions when she was with Graham, no games she couldn't play, no fantasies she couldn't explore.

Finally, after years of envying gay men for their lack of sexual boundaries, their ability to act out their desires, their appetite for experimentation, Caroline was having the kind of sex her gay friends boasted about. In fact, had she not spent every waking moment being so thoroughly conscious of her own femininity, she might have suspected that Graham was really gay. Which was kind of funny, when she thought about it. And she did – fairly often.

Martin arrived home drunk, and lurched angrily into the living room. He was fully expecting to find Christopher sprawled out in front of the television with a slightly bored look on his face and an excuse already prepared. 'I was delayed at work.' 'I sprained my ankle at the gym.' 'I thought we said The Edge, not The Village.' Only the lights were off, and there was no sign of Christopher.

Martin reached for the light switch, and stared around the room in disbelief. The sofa had vanished. So had the CD tower. And the video. And that mirror Christopher's mum had given them as a house-warming present, that had gone too. Martin dimly remembered the girl downstairs telling him she had been burgled a few weeks ago. Apparently, there had been a spate of break-ins recently, all in the Stockwell area. They had taken practically everything, right down to her clothes. He ran into the main bedroom and flung open the wardrobe. All of his clothes were still hanging there – even the more expensive things like his Helmut Lang suit, his

Schott combats and his ever-expanding collection of Diesel tops. The only clothes missing were Christopher's, everything down to his underwear. Martin couldn't understand it. What sort of burglar would steal someone's underwear? And why take one person's clothes and leave another's? Something clicked and he hurried into the smaller second bedroom, the one that doubled as a guest room and a space used mainly for storage. Sure enough, everything belonging to Christopher had vanished. And next to the spare bed, propped up against the original '30s deco lamp Martin had discovered one Christmas at Greenwich market and Christopher had never really liked, there was a neatly folded piece of paper with his name written on it. He picked it up and read.

'Dear Martin', the note began. 'I guess you'll have worked it out by now that I've moved out. Sorry if this comes as a shock to you, but I can't see the point in dragging this out any longer than necessary. I've made my decision and it's time to move on. I could lie to you and say that it was a case of us wanting different things, but the truth is that I just don't want you. You'll probably think this sounds harsh, but I think it's best to be upfront about these things. I've taken what's mine, plus a few of the things we bought together. Everything else you're welcome to. Try not to think too badly of me. It was fun for a while, but all good things come to an end. Christopher.'

Martin sank onto the bed and struggled to hold back the tears. How could Christopher just pack up and leave like this? Things hadn't been going that badly, had they? They hadn't had sex in a while, but lots of couples went through difficult periods, and it wasn't as if he hadn't tried to spice things up a bit. He'd even gone to bed wearing a jockstrap one night, knowing how Christopher used to fantasise about the school jocks as a teenager, but even that had failed to ignite any interest. What was he supposed to do now? They'd been together so long, he'd forgotten what it felt like to be alone. The pain in his chest was so strong, it was almost physical. He'd heard people compare sudden break-ups to waking up and discovering that they had a limb missing. Now he knew what they meant. The feelings he had for Christopher were still there, the way people described still feeling a missing arm or leg. Only now there was this terrible pain too, and the awful realisation that a part of him had been removed and that there was nothing he could do about it.

He needed a drink. He went into the kitchen, fixed himself a large vodka and tonic, and stumbled into the bedroom. What time was it? The alarm clock said just past midnight. Caroline would probably be asleep by now. Maybe John would still be awake. Wasn't he due back from Florida tonight or something? Martin reached for the phone next to the bed and dialled the number. The answerphone clicked on immediately, which usually meant that John was at home and was either asleep or didn't want to be disturbed.

'John, it's Martin . . . Are you there? Christopher has left. I don't know where he is. He's taken his stuff. Can you come over? Call me back.'

Martin hung up the phone and stared at his reflection in the bedside mirror. He was such an idiot. He was an idiot to think that Christopher loved him. He was an idiot to think that a friend like John would be there when he needed him. And he was an idiot to think that having his hair cut this short would make him more attractive. It made his ears look enormous.

He felt a lump rise in his throat, and realised he couldn't

choke back the tears any longer. It was time to let it all out. Then the room started spinning, and he threw up.

A few miles away in Earl's Court (not quite Chelsea but handy for the airport) John heard the phone ring, saw Martin's number flash up and waited for the answerphone to click on. He'd been expecting this call – if not tonight, then sometime soon. It had been obvious to John from the start that Christopher and Martin would never last. Everyone knew that the gay world was arranged into pecking orders – or, as John preferred to think of it, pec-ing orders. Someone blessed with a face like Christopher's was always going to be out of Martin's league, and once he'd acquired a body to match it was only a matter of time before the rules of attraction tore them apart. John had never said this to Martin directly, of course. They were friends after all, and it wasn't exactly the sort of thing you said to a friend. Similarly, when John discovered that Christopher was having an affair he had kept it to himself. Well, unless you counted Shane, one of the gay cabin crew he had started to get friendly with. But Shane hardly even knew Martin anyway, and how else was a boy supposed to pass the time during those long hauls and drunken stopovers? No, all things considered, John had been the soul of discretion.

Which was more than could be said for Christopher. It was bad enough that he was having an affair with a whore. Rent boys weren't exactly the most low-key queens around – these days they were treated like celebrities. But to work out together at the gym? That was tantamount to taking out a full page ad on the back of *Boyz*. It was a well-known fact that muscle Marys were the biggest gossips in the world, never happier than when they were hovering around the bench press and ripping some poor queen to shreds. That was how John had learned about Christopher's secret liaison. He'd gone to the gym to work on his abdominals and had overheard two queens gossiping in the changing room. This rent boy (Marco he was called – weren't they all?), well he wasn't exactly the first. It seemed that Christopher had been putting it about quite a bit. They hadn't all been full-blown affairs. According to these two gym queens, it had mostly been quick tricks in the showers. In fact, John was surprised there wasn't a plaque on the wall in the changing room, in recognition of all the men Christopher was reputed to have serviced there.

Martin must have been blind not to have worked it out by now. Poor, stupid queen. For a moment, John considered calling him back, but decided against it. He felt sorry for Martin, he really did. But sympathy was a bit like cocaine – offer someone a little bit and before the night was out they'd be back begging for more. For John, friends came in two varieties. There were the Low Maintenance Friends, or LMFs – the kind of people who were fun to be around, but who didn't demand much in the way of emotional support, and who were always able to pay for their own drugs. And then there were the High Maintenance Friends, or HMFs – the kind of people you could enjoy the occasional night out with, but who had a nasty habit of unloading their problems on you, and who were always short of money. For the past couple of years Martin had been an LMF, which suited John down to the ground. Now, with Christopher gone, there was a strong possibility that he might suddenly mutate into an HMF. And as much as he liked Martin, John had no intention of becoming a shoulder for him to cry on.

Besides which, he'd had a bitch of a day today. Flights to

and from Orlando attracted some of the worst people on earth, people who shouldn't be allowed to set foot outside Croydon, never mind fly to America and back. He could tell that stupid cunt and her meathead husband would be trouble the minute they had turned up with all that extra hand luggage and their shining pink sprogs in tow – her screaming at the kids to 'shut the fuck up', him stinking of lager and complaining about the number of queers on board. John wasn't sure which was worse – the breeders who radiated hostility at any crew member who wasn't wearing a skirt, or the queens who snapped their fingers to gain your attention and assumed that gay cabin crew were all part of the in-flight entertainment. If there was one thing John hated more than being referred to as a 'trolley dolly', it was the assumption that he was some sort of flying mattress.

Thank God Shane had been on the same flight today. Shane was always so good at dealing with difficult passengers. He always knew the right thing to say to wind them up without ever being seen to be obviously rude or deliberately unhelpful, and giving them grounds for complaint. And when words failed him, he always knew how to get back at them in little subtle ways – the wrong meal here, the spilt drink there. Really, he was a man after John's own heart. It was a pity he only went for Oriental types. That was partly why Shane had become an air steward in the first place – all those stopovers in Bangkok. John couldn't see the attraction of Oriental boys, and he certainly couldn't understand rice queens with Shane's level of devotion. It just didn't make any sense. Walk into any gay sauna or backroom in London and you were guaranteed to find an Oriental on their knees. Why fly halfway across the world for a taste of the Orient when there was plenty going begging at home?

No, John had definitely been through enough today.

Besides, it was already past midnight, and he was expecting company. That guy he'd met on the internet would be arriving shortly. He went into the bathroom and studied himself in the mirror. His hair was looking good – blond and floppy at the front, kind of like David Beckham before Posh got her hands on him and he started looking too processed, like some suburban queen let loose at the cosmetics counter. His skin wasn't looking too bad either, which was a miracle considering the punishment it took with all that air travel. Still, the job did have its compensations. The bathroom shelves were piled high with the fruits of his travels – cut-price Clinique For Men skin products in their reassuringly masculine grey packaging, and an assortment of pharmaceutical drugs from around the world. Everything a gay man needed when he was feeling frazzled, inside and out.

John popped a Valium, applied some Clinique Non-Streak Bronzer to his cheeks and some John Freida Blonde Ambition Dual Action Mousse to his hair and vowed that he would phone Martin first thing in the morning. Unless his new friend stayed for breakfast of course.

Chapter two

Martin woke with a start and promptly wished he'd hadn't. His head throbbed, the whole room stank of vomit and the bed felt horribly empty. No wonder really. This was only the twenty-second time he had woken up alone in almost three years. Of course it felt strange. And cold, since there wasn't a warm body lying beside him. Christopher was a heavy sleeper, and barely stirred before the alarm went off. Some mornings Martin would lie awake for ages, just watching him sleep, before tiptoeing into the kitchen and bringing them both a steaming mug of tea. He wondered whose bed Christopher was waking up in right now, and whether they were drinking tea together. Maybe they were too busy having sex. Christopher liked a quickie before work – or used to anyway.

He'd have to start thinking about work himself. Just the thought of it made him feel ill, but if he didn't go in he wouldn't get paid. Three years designing packaging for groceries at the same supermarket chain, and he was still on a freelance contract. No holiday pay, no sick pay, nothing. He couldn't afford to take the day off, especially not now. There was the rent to think about, and the bills, and all the other household expenses he and Christopher used to split between them. He wished he was still at art college, and could spend the day avoiding lectures and discovering ever more inventive ways of running up his overdraft. He wished he was still young and free, instead of just painfully single. He wished he was still twenty, and looked like that bar boy from last night. He probably had potential boyfriends lining up around the block.

Christopher would love it if he could see him now. He always prided himself on knowing that he had the upper hand. It had been that way right from the moment he and Martin first met, that night at John's party. Christopher had gate-crashed, naturally. He was that sort of person. Always confident that he'd be welcome in any social situation, whether he'd been invited or not. Always sure of himself. Never embarrassed. Never apologetic. Martin had spotted that straight away. If he was really honest with himself, it was partly why he was drawn to Christopher in the first place. That, and the accent. Americans were an exotic breed in London, and always highly prized boyfriend material – except for that brief period during the mid '80s when AIDS first began making headlines in Britain and 'safe sex' meant snubbing the advances of American tourists who tried to chat you up in Earl's Court. Things always seemed to come so easily to Christopher – charm, self-confidence, good hair days. Not like Martin, who had been known to wash his hair three times in one evening, before finally summoning up the courage to walk out of the door. Oh well, at least he wouldn't have to worry about that any more. His mother had once told him that the average human hair grows a centimetre each month, so it would be baseball hats from now until the end of the summer.

He hauled himself out of bed, padded barefoot into the kitchen and swilled down some paracetamol while he waited for the kettle to boil. Maybe John was right after all. Maybe gay relationships were doomed to fail. How many gay couples did he know who were really solid? Two? Three at most? Most gay men didn't seem to know the meaning of commitment. They were too busy sleeping around, always on the look out for the next conquest, the next piece of trade to boast about to their friends, the next bit of meaningless sex that was somehow supposed to give their lives some meaning. He had kidded himself that Christopher was different, that he was serious about settling down. Obviously he'd been wrong. Perhaps it was better that he had found this out now, before they had entered the next phase of their relationship and taken out a joint mortgage. That was one commitment he could do without.

He was in the shower when the phone rang. He grabbed a towel and bolted into the living room, leaving a trail of soggy footprints. He was half hoping it was Christopher, calling to say that he'd made a terrible mistake, that he was coming home. But it wasn't.

'Martin, it's me. Are you okay? I called as soon as I could.' Martin's heart sank. All the declarations of concern couldn't disguise the note of excitement in the voice on the other end of the line. Martin could tell immediately that John knew something he didn't. As soon as the conversation was over, he called the office and explained that he wouldn't be coming into work today.

Caroline's mind definitely wasn't on the job. The day had started pleasantly enough. Graham had stayed over last night, and they'd woken up in a tangle of limbs, his morning stiffy pressing against her thigh in a cute yet still mildly titillating way. There wasn't time for sex, but they had cuddled for a bit. Caroline had even got to the stage now where she would kiss him good morning before rinsing her mouth out with Listerine and brushing and flossing her teeth, which for her was quite an achievement. It meant that they had reached the point where they felt comfortable with one another, which made the row that followed seem all the more ridiculous.

For some time now, Caroline had desperately wanted Graham to move in. Of course she hadn't said as much. That would have sounded far too clingy, and the only thing clingy about Caroline was her wardrobe. But she had dropped enough hints. She had also gone out of her way to make the flat seem more inviting. This had been difficult, since domesticity wasn't really her style. But she knew from experience that men were more inclined to settle down with women who seemed nurturing and house-proud. Even so-called 'New Men' preferred a woman who was equally at home in Habitat as she was in the kitchen, and who could rustle up something healthy and appetising at a moment's notice. With the best will in the world, Caroline knew that she would never live up to Nigella Lawson's shining example of a 'domestic goddess'. But God knows she had made a concerted effort. She had bought some cook books, and arranged them decoratively on a shelf in the kitchen, right next to the tea and coffee jars, where Graham would be certain to spot them. Just the other weekend she'd taken the curtains off to the dry cleaners, and had all the rugs shampooed. Bowls of pot pourri had suddenly appeared in every room. And she had even invested in a dozen glossy houseplants from Marks & Spencer, though keeping them alive had proved more of a problem.

Graham hadn't noticed a thing. Or if he had he certainly hadn't commented. So this morning, while he was shaving, she had casually mentioned that perhaps it might be more convenient if he started leaving a few of his things over at her place. And since he spent so much time there anyway, maybe it was time they talked about something a little more permanent. The look on his face should have been enough to warn her off. She had closed enough deals in her time to know when things weren't going her way. But something about his reaction provoked her. For a brief moment she found herself resenting him for all the things he hadn't noticed, all the things he hadn't said. She felt she deserved some kind of explanation, and so she pushed.

'I'm not asking you to marry me for Christ's sake! I just thought it was time we started thinking about where this relationship is going, that's all. But if that's your attitude, fine!'

She had definitely misjudged the situation, she knew that now. Her father had willed himself into an early grave to escape his wife's constant nagging. The death certificate said lung cancer, but even at fifteen Caroline knew what drove him to smoke so heavily. At thirty-three, she hated detecting echoes of her mother in her own voice. What made matters worse was that Graham had left without saying a thing, so her own words were still hanging in the air long after the door had closed.

She had driven into work in a foul mood, more angry with herself for making such a mess of things than she was with him for storming out like that. Graham flew off the handle quite easily, especially if he was feeling pressurised. It was just his way. The important thing was that he tended to cool down just as quickly, and was usually the first to apologise. She fully expected him to phone as soon as she arrived at the office, if only to say that they could talk about it tomorrow night when they met. But he didn't. Then her boss had called her into a management meeting which lasted the entire morning. When she checked her messages at lunchtime there was still no word from Graham. Martin had called, probably just to see what she was doing over the weekend, but that was all. The afternoon had been an endless succession of meetings with clients. She had been obliged to keep her mobile switched off, which only added to the anticipation. When she checked her messages again at five-thirty there was another message from Martin but still nothing from Graham.

Now it was after six, and some of the girls from the office were making their way to the local wine bar for their regular Friday night piss-up. She decided to join them, for an hour at least. As she left the office, she reached into her handbag and switched her mobile phone on, just in case.

'Have you thought about going for an HIV test?' John asked. It was later that evening and he and Martin were hovering next to the bar at Kudos, waiting to be served. 'I mean, I don't want to worry you, but this Marco guy he's run off with . . . Well, he is a rent boy after all. You can't be too careful.'

'Keep your voice down, John,' Martin hissed. 'I don't want the whole world knowing my business. Anyway, I don't need to go for an HIV test. We were safe, always.' Actually, this wasn't strictly true. Christopher could be very persuasive, and it was true that sex without condoms always felt more intimate somehow. Still, the last time they'd had unsafe sex had been over a year ago, and they had both tested negative shortly after that. There was no point worrying about it now.

'He could still have given you crabs though,' John said in a stage whisper. 'I think I've got a bottle of Qualada somewhere. Let me know if you need it.' Then, raising his voice until he was practically shouting: 'Christ, the service here is useless! I wonder who she sucked off to get a job behind the bar. Nice arse though. I couldn't help but notice, seeing as she's had her back to me for the past ten minutes!'

John had a tendency towards outbursts like this. He was the kind of scene queen who liked to cause a scene, and despite his rather lofty claims that he was making a solitary stand against the poor levels of service that were the scourge of every gay man in London, the truth was that he simply enjoyed the attention. When John walked into a gay bar, he liked to think that his reputation preceded him. In reality, the only thing that preceded him was his voice, which had the haughty tone and high volume of someone blessed with a complete lack of self-awareness.

The barman wasn't impressed. Unaccustomed to finding himself the target of such a torrent of abuse, least of all from someone visibly older and less attractive than himself, he turned and scowled. Embarrassed, Martin retreated from the bar and waited at a safe distance while John ordered two Red Stripes and made a point of pocketing his change and giving the barman one of his looks. John had a vast arsenal of looks, and he wasn't shy with any of them.

'Quick, there's a table over there,' John said, handing Martin a chilled can. 'Let's take the weight off our legs. I'm sure I pulled a muscle in my thigh yesterday. It's like I was telling this queen at the gym earlier. You don't need to spend hours on the Stairmaster to keep your legs in shape. Just try pushing a trolley up and down a 747 for ten hours.'

Martin nodded and took a swig of beer. 'I'll have to change

the message on my answerphone,' he said as they sat down. 'I really don't want to hear Christopher's voice every time I phone home to pick up my messages.'

'If you ask me you're better off without him,' John said, lighting a cigarette. 'I never thought he was right for you. Americans are far too full of themselves. And they talk too much during sex. All that, "Yeah, suck that big cock", like they're starring in a porn film or something. And half the time they've only got four inches! I remember the first time I went to New York. I got laid twice in one weekend, and they only had six inches between them!'

'You never said anything to me about not liking Christopher.'

'I'm not saying I don't like him. I'm just saying he wasn't right for you.'

'Well, I wish I felt the same. I was sure he was the one. I really thought I'd found Mr Right.'

John flicked his ash. 'There is no Mr Right,' he said, relishing the drama of it all. 'There is only Mr Right Now. The sooner you realise that, the happier you'll be.'

But Martin wasn't listening. 'I wonder what Marco's answerphone message sounds like?' he said, clutching his beer and staring intently at the table. 'Very butch I bet, with a thick Italian accent. That's what people want to hear when they ring a whore. I bet he's not nearly as butch in real life though.'

'He's probably not even Italian,' John sniffed. 'Although I did happen to come across his ad in *QX*, and I must say he certainly looks the part. I think I've still got it at home if you're interested . . .'

Martin shot him a warning look.

'No, of course not,' John said hurriedly. 'Sorry. Anyway, nobody uses Italian rent boys any more. That is just so '90s!

I read an article about it somewhere. It's all Brazilians now. Brazilians are the new Italians.'

Martin groaned and went back to his beer. John was always quoting from an article he'd read somewhere, usually in some stupid fashion magazine if his turns of phrase were anything to go by, although this latest pearl of wisdom did sound more like something he'd read in one of the gay bar rags. Most people only picked up those papers to look at the pictures – John based his entire world view on them. He never read newspapers, never watched the television news, and wasn't remotely embarrassed to say that he had no interest in current affairs, other than who was currently fucking who and whether or not they were likely to be caught out. There were times when John's behaviour led Martin to suspect that he hadn't been raised in the real world at all, but grown in a gay test tube. He viewed the world through a gay glass, sometimes darkly, sometimes with rainbow colours, but always with his eye firmly focused on the next opportunity he could exploit for either profit or pleasure. According to John, there were three ingredients necessary for achieving happiness as a gay man – plenty of money, a well-toned body, and a boyfriend (or preferably more than one if there was enough of you to go around and you could get away with it). Right now, Martin scored a resounding nil on all three counts. The more he thought about it, agreeing to meet John for drinks this evening probably wasn't the smartest decision he had ever made.

To make matters worse, Kudos had never been one of Martin's favourite gay bars. Some years before, it had been the setting for one of the biggest rows he had ever had with Christopher. It started when Christopher kept going on about how attractive all the bar staff were. Martin had responded by asking if he thought the management might consider giving him a job behind the bar – not that he wanted one, but since Christopher clearly found the bar staff here so desirable, he wanted to know where he rated in the scheme of things. Christopher had laughed and said that Martin was a little too old and a little too overweight for that kind of opportunity to ever come his way. John had heard this story several times, but that hadn't stopped him from insisting that Kudos would be the ideal place to meet.

'I think rent boys should be forced to pay back some of their earnings to the gay community,' John went on. 'I mean, they don't pay any income tax, so they should pay some sort of community tax. God knows, they make enough money out of other gay men. It wouldn't hurt them to give something back. And the pressure they put on the rest of us is so unfair. I mean, it's easy to have a perfect body when you don't have a proper job and can spend every waking hour at the gym. And the attitude of some of them! You'd swear they were pop stars or something, the way they swan around the place. There was this one holding up the queue for the loos in the Departure Lounge at Heaven the other week. We got into a right slanging match. She told me, "Prostitution is the oldest profession." I said, "Yes, dear, and you've obviously been in it since the beginning".'

'I thought you had to be some sort of VIP to get into the Departure Lounge,' Martin said. 'Isn't it supposed to be members only?'

'Oh, they'll let anyone in these days,' John replied airily, oblivious to the fact that he didn't exactly qualify as a VIP himself. 'Someone told me they saw the Pet Shop Boys in there once, but I've never seen anyone remotely famous. Just a few dried-up club promoters, a couple of "scene celebrities" and a load of old whores reeking of Kouros.' He paused to inspect his stomach, which was virtually non-existent beneath a white ribbed T-shirt. 'Do you think I need to lose a bit of weight?'

'You look fine,' Martin said, wondering when the conversation was going to get back to him and his painfully new single status.

John smiled. 'Yeah, I suppose so. It's probably just the lager. It really bloats me up. I'll tell you what I need – a weekend of serious drug abuse and plenty of sex. That should soon sort me out.' He stopped and looked disapprovingly at Martin's paunch. 'Actually, it wouldn't do you any harm either. Remember, you're single again now. And you know what they say – no pecs, no sex. By the way, what's with the baseball cap?'

'Dodgy hair cut,' Martin said, gritting his teeth. He really wasn't in the mood for fashion advice.

'Give us a look, then,' John said, whipping off the cap before Martin could stop him. 'Oh yes, very butch. Actually, it quite suits you short. It makes your eyes look bigger.'

Martin smiled half-heartedly and glanced around the bar. The early evening office crowd was beginning to thin out, the young fruits in suits making their way back to their designer flats and designer boyfriends, the older, shabbier types sneaking off to Charing Cross station for a train back to suburbia and the wife. Soon the bar would start filling up with bright young things in combat trousers and tight T-shirts, gearing up for a night of clubbing and endless sexual possibilities. God, it was unbearable!

'Time for another, I think,' John chirped suddenly, rising from the table. 'Another Red Stripe? Or shall we move onto the vodka? Yes, I think a large vodka and Red Bull is what you need. It gives you wings, you know. Not that I don't see enough of those at work. Back in a tick.'

Martin watched John disappear in the direction of the bar, and wondered whether it was worth making a quick escape. What time was it? Just gone nine. If he left now he could be back home in time for *Frasier*. This was assuming there were no delays on the Northern Line, of course. Still maybe there'd be a film on later, some old horror movie or something. Or one of those really tacky telemovies with Barbara Eden playing a woman half her age. They were usually good for a laugh. Or maybe one of those 'Ibiza Uncovered' type programmes, with lots of sex-crazed straight people on holiday, behaving the way most gay men behaved every week of the year.

'Look who I bumped into!' Martin looked up to see John swinging off some guy in a T-shirt two sizes too small. He was cute, though, there was no denying that – quite beefy, with short dark hair that showed no sign of receding and solid black eyebrows over the bluest eyes. He looked a bit like Christopher in fact. Other than that, Martin had absolutely no idea who this person was. Of course John wasted no time in introducing him. The guy's name was Matthew, and he and John had met in a chat room on the internet.

'I didn't know you came here,' John said. He was looking at Matthew, although his remark was clearly for Martin's benefit. 'Have a seat,' John went on, gesturing to Matthew to join them at the table. 'You don't mind, do you, Martin?'

'No, of course not.' Martin smiled feebly. He was frequently amazed at how little time it took for John to get his claws into someone. One night of passion, and they were joined at the hip for the next three weeks – which was about as long as any of John's relationships ever lasted. Trust him to throw himself into a new relationship just as Martin's was ending, and with someone guaranteed to remind Martin of Christopher.

Several vodka and Red Bulls later, Martin was starting to feel a lot better. Matthew was really quite nice – far nicer than the men John usually went for. He was obviously intelligent, which was always an unexpected bonus where John's sexual conquests were concerned, and considering how attractive he was, he didn't seem too full of himself. What's more, Martin had a suspicion that Matthew liked him too. He was very chatty, and even quite flirtatious at one point. John had gone to the bar and Martin was telling Matthew about Christopher and the way he had just upped and left, omitting the bit about the unfashionable Italian prostitute and the possibility that he may have given him crabs.

'If you ask me, it's his loss,' Matthew said. 'You're in pretty good shape. You seem like a decent guy. I'd say you were quite a catch.'

He smiled at Martin as he said this, and for a split second their eyes locked. There was an awkward pause while Martin considered the possibility that Matthew was going to kiss him. Part of him secretly wished he would. Matthew was far too nice for John anyway, and it hardly seemed fair that John should be with him while Martin was faced with being alone. It was probably the drink, but he was about to blurt this out to Matthew when suddenly John arrived back from the bar, clutching a round of drinks. He stopped abruptly, and gave an awkward smile, as though he were embarrassed at having interrupted the conversation. Martin had seen this routine before. John was the only person he knew who was capable of looking slightly bashful and extremely full of himself both at the same time.

'Been talking about me, then?' John said, looking first at Martin and then at Matthew.

'Of course,' Matthew replied, sliding an arm around his waist and giving him a little squeeze. 'Who else?'

Martin smiled sheepishly and wondered what on earth someone with Matthew's many attributes could possibly see in someone like John. Not that John wasn't fairly attractive – in a bland, blond sort of way. He had pale blue eyes which he sometimes darkened with the aid of coloured contact lenses, and lashes that were tinted once a month to emphasise their length. He worked out regularly and never seemed to put on weight no matter what he ate – unlike Martin who only had to look at a quarter pounder and regular fries to start piling on the pounds. But John certainly wasn't anything special. He didn't have a particularly handsome face, and unlike Martin, nobody had ever mistaken John for being a decent guy. Take his behaviour tonight, for instance. Martin doubted whether it had even crossed John's mind that seeing him together with his latest catch might be the very last thing Martin needed right now.

For the next hour, he watched with growing irritation as John draped himself around Matthew at every opportunity, laughing at everything he said and generally behaving like a love-struck teenager. He even nibbled his ear once, though Martin noticed with some satisfaction that Matthew didn't seem too pleased. By the time they called last orders, Martin was left feeling like a complete gooseberry, and wishing that he had just snogged Matthew himself when he'd had the chance. He vowed that, should the opportunity ever arise again, he would grab it by both ears.

As they left Kudos, and began walking in the direction of Leicester Square, John announced that he and Matthew were heading on to a club.

'We thought we might try G.A.Y.,' he said, looking back at Martin over his shoulder. 'Come with us, if you like.' Martin could detect from the tone of his voice that John was simply being polite – for Matthew's benefit more than his. He toyed with the idea of accepting John's half-hearted invitation, just to annoy him, but decided against it.

'It's okay,' he said. 'I'm feeling pretty tired. I think I'd rather just go home.'

They said their goodbyes outside Leicester Square tube station, and Martin watched as John and Matthew headed off up Charing Cross Road. He was feeling tired, but the mere thought of going home alone at 11 p.m. on a Friday night was too depressing to contemplate. Besides, all the vodka and beer he had knocked back in the past two hours was making him horny. Caroline had once joked that this was the one thing the entire male species had in common, whether they were gay or straight – give them a few drinks, and their body turns into a life-support machine for their penis. Martin smiled to himself as he turned and started walking in the direction of Charing Cross.

Heaven was the first gay club he had ever gone to. He was nineteen at the time, new to London, and only out to two people – his personal tutor at college, and Caroline, who was renting a room in the same house as him. Both fugitives from towns they vowed never to return to, both eager to make a new life for themselves, they hit it off immediately and quickly became friends. It was Caroline who had encouraged Martin to 'go out and paint the town pink', although that hardly described his frame of mind at the time. He had stood outside the club for over an hour, chain-smoking his way through an entire packet of cigarettes, before finally summoning up the courage to go in. Once inside he had stood frozen to the same spot for half an hour, terrified that someone might talk to him, equally terrified that they might not, before finally leaving, alone, but feeling strangely proud of himself, as though he had achieved something small but significant. The following week he was back again, a little more relaxed and high on the sheer number of sexually available men all under one roof. That was Heaven's main appeal. In those days, sooner or later every gay man in London ended up there. And while this no longer held true, it was a reputation the club was only too happy to trade on.

It was almost five years since he'd last been to Heaven. Not a lot had changed. The club was still as busy and the staff were just as surly. Trying to blag his way into the Departure Lounge, he was turned away by a bolshie lesbian with a walkie-talkie, who took great pleasure in informing him that this area was for members only. He considered asking whether she would allow him in if he said he was a hooker, but thought better of it. Wandering back towards the main dance floor, he noticed there were a few more women than he remembered. And if he wasn't very much mistaken, there were a few more drugs in circulation, too. Back in the days when he used to hang around Heaven every week, looking for love and picking up fashion tips, the only drugs you ever saw were poppers. Actually, you usually smelt them long before you saw them. Some of the older cloney types would soak their bandanas in the stuff, and then leave them hanging around their necks so they could inhale the fumes without having to constantly fiddle about with those little bottles. Now everyone was on E, and the smell came from the toilets and all those drug-induced bowel movements. Why were the toilets always so disgusting in gay clubs? There was never enough toilet paper, the doors on the cubicles never locked properly, and there was always a horrible stench coming from somewhere. How anyone could even think of having sex in a place like that was beyond him.

Nobody seemed to mind, though. They were all running around gurning like maniacs or dancing with their shirts off. He spotted a few faces he vaguely recognised, only they looked as if someone had surgically removed their heads and sewn them back onto different bodies. Pot bellies and skinny, sunken chests had been replaced with glistening six-packs and gleaming great slabs of muscle. Martin didn't need to be told why this sudden transformation had taken place. Ever since the arrival of AIDS, gay men had been piling into the gym in ever greater numbers, desperate to be seen to be healthy, or to build up a solid mass of muscle as security in the event of being struck down by a wasting disease. In an age of sexual anxiety, a strong body was like an insurance policy. Still, he felt intimidated by the amount of muscle on display. He remembered the first time he took Caroline to Heaven. She spent the whole night commenting on how attractive the men were – and those were the days before every gay man in London started going to the gym and having his chest waxed. Suddenly Martin found himself wishing that Caroline was here with him. Gay clubs never seemed half as scary with her by his side.

He bought a bottle of water from the sullen hunk behind the bar and wandered around for a bit, trying desperately to sober up. He hated that feeling, when you suddenly realise that you're too drunk to do anything, and nothing you do seems to make it any better. He staggered to the toilets, and stood at the urinal for a full ten minutes, silently debating whether or not he was about to throw up. Suddenly, he became aware of someone hovering next to him. He turned to find an old queen with a jet black, comb-over hairdo standing at the urinal with his penis in his hand, staring at Martin's crotch and gently playing with himself. Martin gave him a dirty look. Some people had absolutely no dignity. Here he was, practically on the verge of vomiting, and all this queen could see was the opportunity for a quick fiddle. He lurched out of the toilets and along the main corridor, knocking into a few people who were either as pissed as he was, or too high on drugs to notice. Finally, he found a space at the edge of the dance floor and stood there for a while, leaning against the wall, taking it all in.

And that was when Martin spotted him – Christopher. He was right in the middle of the dance floor, waving his arms in time to the music and grinning all over his face. It was less than forty-eight hours since Martin had last seen him, but already he looked like a different person. He'd had his hair cut, which wasn't such a surprise, and he appeared to be in the process of growing a goatee, which was. He was shirtless, which was a new development, and around his neck he wore a thick silver chain which Martin had never seen before. And he looked happy, far happier than Martin had seen him look in ages, though of course he could recognise a chemically enhanced smile when he saw one. He didn't recognise the man dancing next to him though. He couldn't see him clearly at first, but he was sure it wasn't one of Christopher's friends – at least no one that he had ever been introduced to. He was slightly shorter than Christopher, with black hair and a broad back. His vest was hanging from the back of his jeans, and as he turned around and moved into his line of vision, Martin saw that he had an amazing body – big arms, well-defined chest, washboard stomach, the works. Even in this room full of muscle Marys, he stood out. He must have been going to the gym every day for the past five years to get a body like that – not an easy thing to do when you had a job like Martin's, a job that demands that you be at your desk from nine till five, five days a week, forty-seven weeks a year . . .

Martin didn't need a copy of *QX* to know who this dream-boat was – Marco! At that precise moment he threw those big beautiful arms of his around Christopher and the two of them began snogging like it was going out of fashion. Martin turned and lurched away from the dance floor, stumbled out of the club and fell into the nearest taxi. It wasn't until he was halfway across London that he asked the driver to stop the cab, stuck his head out of the door and began throwing up.

Chapter three

On a good day, Caroline was the first to admit that she spent more time and far more money on her personal appearance than was strictly necessary. As she often joked, she was every bit her own woman – there wasn't one bit of her body she hadn't refashioned in some way, shape or form, so the only person sharing any of the credit was the surgeon who performed her boob job.

But today was not a good day, and Caroline was not in the mood for jokes. What she was in the mood for was some serious pampering. Getting an appointment at Tony's hadn't been easy. It was Saturday after all, and Tony wasn't just any old hairdresser. He was Tony of Belgravia, hair stylist to the stars. He had fingered more famous follicles than Elton John had hair plugs. People didn't just come to Tony's for a quick trim and blow dry, they came for a brush with celebrity. This was why he could get away with charging such exorbitant prices, and why his appointment book was always full months in advance. Luckily for Caroline, there had been a late cancellation, and since she was one of Tony's favoured non-celebrity clients, he had graciously agreed to squeeze her in.

She was sitting with her damp hair wrapped in a towel, enjoying the reassuringly expensive aroma of Tony's own-label hair products and flicking through a copy of *Vanity Fair* when her mobile rang. Graham, she thought. About bloody time too. She dived into her bag, flipped open the phone and pressed it to her ear.

'Hello, dear, it's your mother.'

Caroline stifled a groan. The last thing she needed today was one of her mother's little lectures about the vast amounts she squandered at the hairdressers. This was one of the reasons Caroline had always felt far closer to her grandmother than she ever had to her mother. It was her grandmother who had first encouraged her to 'make the best of herself' as she put it. And she certainly knew what she was talking about. She was in her seventies now, but she never left the house without a protective layer of make-up and a good strong coat of nail varnish. Clearly the glamour gene had skipped a generation, because her mother couldn't have been more different. Caroline had long since given up trying to justify her expenditure at the hairdressers to her mother. Try as she might, there was no point trying to explain the high cost of contemporary styling to a woman who had absolutely no concept of the vagaries of fashion, and who had worn her hair in the same casual style for the past thirty years. Besides, Caroline didn't really want her mother to know that it was the kind of hairdressers where favoured customers were treated to a line or two of cocaine with their double espresso.

'Hi, Mum. Yes, I'm fine. The thing is, I'm a bit tied up right now. Can I call you back later?'

There was a pause, and for a moment Caroline thought that she might actually have pulled it off. Then she heard that familiar wounded tone and knew that further resistance was useless. It didn't matter how busy she was. There was an unspoken rule that any telephone conversation between Caroline and her mother should last a minimum of five minutes, and should contain reference to at least four of the following subjects – the cost of things today, the neighbours, the weather, Europe, the National Health Service, and the latest developments regarding the house that Caroline's brother Kevin and his lovely wife Louise had bought just outside Coventry, and were in the process of doing up before they started planning a family. This last topic of conversation had been a particular favourite of late, ever since Caroline had made the mistake of mentioning Graham and her mother had made the mistake of thinking another family wedding might soon be on the cards.

Eight minutes and one gentle reminder about the cost of living later, Caroline said goodbye to her mother and finished off her coffee, though a part of her secretly wished it could have been the other way around. Caroline was very rarely lost for words. She had spent the best part of her adolescence locked away in her bedroom poring over the collected works of Oscar Wilde, so she usually had an answer for everything. For instance, if anyone dared to suggest that she had her priorities wrong, or that her obsession with looking good indicated that she was a little shallow, she was always quick off the mark: 'Only shallow people don't judge by appearances.' But when confronted with her mother's quiet but persistent disapproval, Caroline's usual defences simply weren't enough. Words failed her. Her mother knew her too well. She knew that behind those carefully selected phrases and that polished delivery was a girl who had grown up in a terraced house on a dead-end street in Swindon, a girl who had never been considered pretty as a child, and who still had moments, hours, even days of self-doubt. For every minute she spent on the phone to her mother, Caroline could feel the years of grooming and self-improvement slipping away. By the end of a typical conversation she was no longer a successful account executive who despite having left school with virtually no qualifications had studied hard and long to learn everything she needed to know about the world of advertising. She was a shy fifteen-year-old with a weight problem and a room full of books for comfort. And the worst part of all was knowing that her mother had a sideboard full of photographs to prove it. That was why parents never threw old school photos away. It had nothing to do with sentimentality. It was just another means of ensuring that you didn't get ideas above your station, another way of keeping you in your place.

Just then an assistant appeared, advising her that Tony would be with her shortly. Caroline nodded as he picked up her empty coffee cup. He hovered meaningfully for a moment, before asking whether madam would be requiring anything else in the way of refreshment. Recognising this as her cue to pay a quick visit to the private room at the back, Caroline smiled and confirmed that a little of the usual wouldn't go amiss. Damn her mother. Damn Graham. She was about to spend £200 of her hard-earned cash in a conscious effort to make herself more attractive, and nothing and nobody was going to spoil the experience. She stood up and followed the assistant to the back of the salon, reaching into her purse for her silver-plated cocaine straw as she went.

By the time Tony was running his expert fingers through her long blonde tresses, Caroline was feeling much happier.

John was bored. He had spent the best part of the afternoon online, checking out the various gay chat rooms, and so far he hadn't met anyone who took his fancy. Actually, that wasn't strictly true. About half an hour ago he'd had a fairly steamy conversation with someone by the name of 'HotFitGuy', who listed his hobbies as 'computers, gym and sex with HOT, FIT and GOOD-LOOKING guys'. HotFitGuy's on-screen profile contained a personal quote that suggested that, in addition to simply fancying himself, he also fancied himself as a bit of a philosopher – 'If life is a waste of time, and time is a waste of life, why don't we get together and waste ourselves? And above all, aim to be the best. Second place is the first loser.' John was quite taken by this, but unfortunately the profile omitted to mention a few important details. Only after a prolonged exchange did it finally emerge that 'HotFitGuy' wasn't quite as hot or as fit as he made out. In fact, he was pushing forty, balding and appeared to have spent the past twenty years pumping up his pectorals in order to distract attention from his expand-ing midriff.

Then there was 'HornyStud'. His profile said that he was twenty-seven years old, six feet tall with brown eyes and dark hair, a 32-inch waist, a 40-inch chest, 16-inch biceps and a seven-inch uncut cock. It listed his hobbies as 'sex, men and more sex' and his occupation as 'something manual'. It also contained a personal quote which read, 'A Hard Man Is Nice To Find'. What it neglected to mention was that he was Oriental. In fact it was only when they swapped photos that this became apparent.

To say that John was disappointed would be an under-statement. He hadn't felt so let down since the day he discovered that the smooth, firm buttocks the new, gym-fit Robbie Williams was happy to expose on the cover of *Vogue* weren't entirely his own work but had been touched up by someone in the art department. Of course John knew that on-screen profiles weren't always entirely reliable, and that people were prone to exaggerate. As he had soon discovered the first time he visited a gay chat room, there were lies, damned lies and chat-room statistics. It wasn't a coincidence that almost everyone in the chat rooms had a 32-inch waist and 40-inch chest, or that they all worked out regularly and had nice pecs and a firm arse (or 'ass' as most people preferred to call it – masquerading as an American gay porn star was another popular pastime). John's own profile was pretty close to the truth, although he did add an inch to his height and another to the length of his cock. He also claimed that he was a natural blond, rather than someone who spent a small for-tune on highlights. And of course he didn't actually tell people that he was an air steward. He'd heard enough cracks about 'trolley dollies' to know better than that. Instead he said that he worked as a security guard for an airline, which sounded far more butch without being a complete lie. There was an element of security involved in his job. He was just leaving out the bit about the trolley, that was all.

But to go to the trouble of measuring your biceps and then neglect to mention that you were Oriental wasn't just a minor oversight. It was a deliberate act of deception. John fired off a message saying 'Sorry, not my type' and wondered whether it was worth amending his profile, making it clear that he wasn't interested in Orientals, then decided against it. He was pretty certain you weren't allowed to say things like that anyhow. You could say that you were 'straight acting' and would 'like to meet similar'. You could say that you were interested in 'real men' and not 'queens'. You could specify 'no fats or fems'. You could even say that you were looking for 'bareback' sex, or that you were 'disease free and expect similar'. But you couldn't say anything that would be considered offensive to ethnic minorities. Who invented these stupid rules anyway? One of Shane's lot, probably. Well, it was easy to appear politically correct when you had exotic tastes. That was no justification for making everyone else feel guilty about theirs. Before long they'd be telling you not to specify that you liked blonds, on the grounds that it made you a Nazi.

There had been very little activity on John's computer screen since then. Someone called 'TryWaterSports' had sent him a couple of messages, accompanied by a photo of their erect cock, which left him in little doubt that 'TryWaterSports' had the kind of face guaranteed to scare people off. A couple called 'UsTwo4Fun' had tried to talk him into joining them for a threesome somewhere in Leytonstone, which might have been worth considering had the photo they sent been a bit clearer. As it was, John couldn't tell if they were both as fit and beefy as they said, or simply fat and holding their stomachs in. Shortly afterwards, he received several increasingly annoying messages from someone looking for a sex slave and offering a monthly salary of £500 for the successful applicant. John sent a message back to 'MasterTom' informing him that he had a perfectly good job already, and that he wasn't remotely interested in playing silly games with some sad old leather queen.

He was about to shut down the computer and dig out a porn video when a message flashed up. 'Hi', it said. 'How r u?'

John looked at the screen name – 'CuriousCute28'. Interesting. He clicked open the profile. The guy described himself as straight and in a relationship, but looking for 'discreet fun with other straight-acting lads'. John had met this type before. More often than not, they turned out to be the sort of screaming queens who thought a bit of sportswear was all it took to transform them from the bitchy window dressers they were into the butch manual labourers they fantasised about being fucked by. But there was something about this one that seemed genuine. Maybe it was the wording of the profile, or rather the lack of it. There was no name given for a start, which made the emphasis on discretion sound authentic. There were no detailed statistics either, just a line which read 'Tall, dark and told handsome'. A queen would have given himself away with a detailed description of his gym routine. And while most people in the chat rooms had spent hours pondering over a personal quote which summed up their attitude to life and made them sound like a really interesting person, this guy had left the quote box blank. This was a refreshing change. There were far too many people on the internet claiming to 'Live Life To The Max' – not an easy thing to do when you clearly spent half your life in front of a computer screen.

Yes, this was definitely one worth pursuing. John typed in a message reading 'Nice profile', added the word 'mate' for good measure, and clicked on the reply box.

'You poor thing!' Caroline said, clutching Martin's hand across the kitchen table. She cleared a space in front of her, reached into her handbag for her compact and the little Tiffany pouch containing a wrap of coke and her silver-plated cocaine straw, and proceeded to chop two fat lines. 'Come on, this will soon perk you up.'

'Isn't it a bit early for that?' Martin replied, pulling his hand away and pouring himself another cup of tea. It was barely an hour since Caroline had arrived, coked to the eyeballs and playing havoc with his entry phone. Somebody must have taken pity on her and let her into the building, because the next thing he knew she was hammering at his front door. He had stumbled out of bed in a daze, half thinking that the building must be on fire, but too hungover to even care. He'd had a terrible night – dreaming that Christopher had given him some dreadful venereal disease, and waking up at regular intervals to throw up. He still had that stale sickly taste in his mouth. And since when did Caroline start doing coke at five o'clock in the afternoon? He couldn't remember the last time he had seen her so wired.

'He hasn't even called,' he said. 'Though after seeing him and his hooker looking so cosy together last night, I don't care if I never hear from him again.'

'But you have to tell him exactly what you think of him,' Caroline said, pressing a finger to her nostril and hoovering up a line in one swift, smooth action. 'The best thing that could happen now would be if he called. At least then you could tell him to crawl off and die somewhere. Unless you still want him back. Oh, Martin, you don't still want him back, do you?'

'Of course not!' he snapped, sounding far more defensive than he'd intended. 'Sorry. It's just that this has all happened so quickly. Three days ago I wasn't even aware that there was anything wrong. Now I'm left with a flat I can barely afford and an ex-boyfriend who's off playing happy families with someone who gets his cock sucked for a living and probably earns more in a week than I make in a month. It's like a bad dream. I still haven't got used to the idea of him not being here. I keep expecting him to walk through the door at any moment.' He could feel himself welling up as he spoke, and fell silent, embarrassed that he might start snivelling.

'Have a line,' Caroline said gently, sliding the compact across the table and handing Martin the straw. 'I know it's not really your thing, but nobody died from a little line of coke. Believe me, you'll feel a lot better than you do now.'

Martin hesitated for a moment. Snorting cocaine in the afternoon definitely wasn't his thing. In fact, he'd only ever taken coke once before, at a party with Christopher one New Year's Eve. He couldn't really remember what the effects were, except that he drank an awful lot more than usual that night and talked non-stop about things he normally had very little interest in. Still, coke on its own was probably no worse than alcohol. It certainly didn't appear to have done Caroline any harm. And God knows he had just cause for getting out of his head if that was what he wanted. He took the straw from her fingers.

'You'll be okay,' Caroline continued, watching as he struggled to get the crumbly white powder up his nose with short, clumsy sniffs. 'And don't worry about the rent. I can always help out if you're stuck, you know that. The important thing is for you to concentrate on getting over him. Deciding you don't want him back, that's the first step. The next step is to make sure that he knows you don't want him back. That's why it's best if he phones you. It's all about power. He dumps you, so you feel powerless. You have to find a way of taking control of the situation, then you won't feel so bad. Well, that's the theory anyway. I think it probably works for men better than for women. It's a macho thing. Men are so much more competitive. It's pathetic really.'

Martin snorted, scattering the remains of his line across the table. For all her feminine ways, Caroline was one of the most competitive, macho people he had ever met. 'So how are things with you and Graham?' he asked, sensing that Christopher wasn't the only specimen of manhood Caroline was thinking of. 'Are you seeing him tonight?'

Caroline shrugged and lit up a Dunhill International. 'I don't know. We had a bit of a row yesterday, and I haven't heard from him since. To tell you the truth, I've been expecting something like this to happen for a while. There's something going on, something he isn't telling me.'

'What do you mean?' Martin asked, sniffing hard until he felt the coke hit the back of his throat and the tip of his tongue go numb. 'You don't think he's cheating on you, do you? No, not Graham. He's crazy about you. Anyway, he's not the type.'

'I'm not sure what type he is,' Caroline said, dabbing her finger on the few remaining crumbs and rubbing it against her gums. 'I feel funny just talking about it. The thing is, I've got a feeling that he might actually be gay.'

Martin laughed. 'Caroline, you have always had a feeling that Graham might actually be gay. Besides, I thought that was what attracted you to him in the first place. Isn't that what you said, that you had always fantasised about having a gay man for a boyfriend and that now you finally had one?'

Caroline scowled. 'Yeah, well obviously I didn't mean it literally. I just meant that he had the qualities I look for in a man, and which most of the straight men I meet lack in abundance. You know. He's gentle. He's sensitive. He isn't afraid to show his feelings. He knows how to dress properly. He loves shopping. And he can dance. He's like a gay man, only straight. Or at least I thought he was. Oh, you know what I mean.'

Martin knew exactly what she meant. Graham was one of the gentlest, most sensitive, most 'gay-acting' men he had ever come across. In fact, Graham presented a far softer front than a lot of the men you saw on the gay scene these days, who to all intents and purposes were just like a straight man, only gay. The irony of this wasn't lost on Martin. He wondered if a straight woman fancying gay men was the same thing as gay men fantasising about sex with straight men. Did it involve a certain element of self-loathing? Was there even such a thing as 'internalised heterophobia'? He did find the whole thing rather confusing. Most of the women he knew seemed to spend half their waking hours complaining that men were insensitive, selfish animals who didn't know the first thing about personal hygiene. And then when they finally met one who wasn't like that at all, they invariably found something else to complain about. He was too fussy, or too vain, or just not manly enough. It did make you wonder if straight men these days weren't getting a bit of a raw deal. No wonder some of them were envious of the gay lifestyle. You rarely heard a gay man complain that somebody was 'too macho'. On the contrary, most of them would give their eye teeth for a man who acted the way straight men were supposed to behave. And thinking of teeth, he had heard it said that gay men generally gave far better blow jobs than women. All things considered, there were quite a few advantages to a straight man choosing to have sex with other men. Even a straight man with a girlfriend as gorgeous as Caroline.

'People are always assuming that Graham is gay,' he said eventually. 'It doesn't mean anything. You know that.'

Caroline reached for the compact and began chopping another line. 'I don't know what I know any more. I told you how he never talks about his family.'

'So? How often do you talk about yours?'

'Come on, Martin! You've met my mother. You know what an embarrassment she can be. It's different with Graham. I get this feeling that his family know something about him that I don't. And he's been acting very strangely lately. I told you he joined a gym recently. And he went for a sun bed the other day. He's even started reading *Men's Health*.'

Martin laughed. 'Oh well, in that case he must be gay. No question!' He paused, and quietly scolded himself for being so insensitive. 'I think you're being just a little bit paranoid,' he continued in a softer voice. 'Reading *Men's Health* does not prove that a man is turning homosexual. Not conclusively anyway.'

Suddenly the phone rang. 'If that's Christopher . . .' Caroline shouted as Martin bolted into the bedroom. She heard the door click shut behind him, and turned her attention back to the little fold of paper in front of her. Not for the first time, it struck her how much she loved the rituals involved with taking coke – the positioning of the mirror, the careful unfolding of the wrapper, the precise arrangement of the lines of pure white powder on the glass. There was something so satisfyingly methodical about it, so neat and orderly, like a well-planned shopping list, or a two-page presentation complete with bullet points. It wasn't a drug she associated with people whose lives were spiralling out of control. There was nothing remotely messy about it, nothing that fitted with the popular image of a drug addict. It was all so clean, so tidy. It was, she decided, a very minimalist chic kind of drug, and one which suited her lifestyle perfectly. Once she had finished chopping two of the neatest lines she had ever seen, she poured herself another cup of tea, lit another cigarette and sat tapping out the seconds with her coke straw.

She was on her third cigarette by the time Martin reappeared, looking decidedly flustered. 'Sorry about that,' he said, reaching for his mug and gulping down the lukewarm tea.

'Well?' said Caroline impatiently. 'Was it him?'

'No,' Martin replied. 'It was my dad. He's coming to London next weekend, and he wants to stay here. Says he'd like to spend some quality time with his favourite gay son, or words to that effect.'

'How many gay sons has he got?'

Martin smiled. 'Just the one. My brother is so straight, it hurts. That's just Dad's way of letting me know I'm not a disappointment to him.'

This was typical of his father. While most of the gay men Martin knew complained of fathers who flew into a homophobic rage at the mere mention of their offspring's sexual leanings, his own father had always been fine about him being gay. In fact, he had handled the news far better than his wife. Martin's mother meant well, but she spent far too much time worrying about what the neighbours might think. This wasn't something ever likely to concern his father, who never stayed in one place long enough to develop more than a passing acquaintance with the neighbours. This pattern had been set years ago, when Martin's mother filed for divorce on the grounds of irreconcilable differences and his father moved out of the family home and into the first of a string of temporary abodes. Much as this had upset him at the time, the only thought Martin gave to his parents' failed marriage now was trying to work out how they ever got together in the first place. These days, the differences in their outlook on life were more pronounced than ever. His father saw himself as a free spirit. His ex-wife saw him as just another victim of the male menopause.

Caroline had met Martin's father once before and found him rather sweet – a bit of an old hippie perhaps, but a damn sight more fun than her mother. She was certain he didn't keep old photos of Martin around the house, just to embarrass him. Plus he had probably experimented with more drugs than his son. She could think of worse people to have as a house guest. 'Well, I think it'll be nice for you to spend time with him,' she said, hoovering up her line.

'Are you *mad*?' Martin said. 'Next weekend is Gay Pride. I tried telling him that, but it only made him more determined. He said it would be the ideal opportunity for him to get to know my people, whoever they are. The biggest gay party of the year, and I'm going to have my father in tow. What am I going to do?'

Caroline laughed. 'Finish your dinner,' she said, pointing to the one remaining line of coke. 'Then get dressed. I'm taking you out.'

Chapter four

'No, not there,' Caroline said, grabbing Martin's arm and steering him towards an empty table at the opposite end of the bar. On a video screen above their heads, Ricky Martin was shaking his bon-bon for what was probably the third time that evening. In the middle of the room, a man with terrible skin was dancing with a fat girl in a fuchsia-pink party frock. Brightly coloured drinks in hand, they sashayed between the tables, doing their best to imitate Ricky's moves and failing miserably.

'The lighting is terrible over there,' Caroline explained as she and Martin sat down. 'Look at that girl at the far end, the one in the yellow top. She's probably fairly attractive, but she looks awful in that light. I just can't understand girls like that. You'd think someone would have told them by now. What's the point of going to all that trouble with your hair and make-up and then ruining the effect by sitting under a bad light? She might as well go home. There isn't a man here who'll chat her up while she's sitting there.'

Martin smiled politely. He had heard Caroline's theory about good lighting many times before, and he was still no closer to understanding it. To him, the girl in question looked perfectly presentable. And if the men weren't exactly queueing up to talk to her, that was probably because most of them here happened to be gay. They were in Soho after all, albeit a short walk from the gay stronghold of Old Compton Street. Martin preferred slightly more mixed venues like the Escape Bar – places where straight women and even some straight men came to hang out with gay friends, and everyone appeared to have a good time, even if they were sitting under the wrong kind of light. It was so much more relaxing than standing around in a bar full of gay men where nobody really talked to each other and you were left feeling like a piece of meat. He could still remember the first time he took Caroline to a gay bar – the Brief Encounter on St Martin's Lane. Some old queen in a tuxedo who had stopped off for a swift drink on his way to The Coliseum announced very loudly that he could smell fish in the room and that it was making him feel sick. Martin had felt sick too, not to mention angry that another gay man could even think like that, let alone talk like it. Of course that was in the days when he still believed that the gay world was one big happy family, rather than a vipers' nest full of people waiting to ruin your one chance of happiness by stealing your boyfriend.

'You okay?' Caroline said. 'I thought I'd order a bottle of champagne to get us in the party mood. My treat. What do you say?'

Martin looked up. 'Sorry? I was miles away. What are we celebrating?'

'I'm sure we'll think of something. That's the great thing with champagne. A few glasses and you feel like you've got something to celebrate even if you haven't. Anyway, it's the only thing to drink with coke. I've got another gram somewhere. I was going to save it for later. Sex on coke is just the best, but I don't think I'll be seeing Graham this weekend. And you know me. I can't sleep if there's a gram of coke in the house.'

Martin forced a smile and wondered if he was the only person in London who hadn't experienced sex on cocaine. He wished Caroline wouldn't insist on ordering champagne every time they went out together. He always felt so conspicuous drinking champagne in a gay bar. It made him feel like one of those ageing queens you saw hanging around the clubs, flashing their money about in a desperate attempt to impress the younger pretty boys. Still there was no point arguing with Caroline when she was in this mood, and it was kind of her to offer to pay. 'Right,' he said brightly. 'Champagne it is.'

They polished off the first bottle in less than an hour, punctuated by frequent trips to the toilets for what Caroline liked to describe as 'cheeky little bumps' of coke. By the time the second bottle arrived, Martin didn't care how flash he looked. He was feeling more confident than he had felt in a long time. He was also beginning to understand how Caroline managed to stay so slim, despite her aversion to exercise and a job that seemed to revolve around boozy business lunches. He hadn't eaten anything except a slice of toast all day, and he had no appetite whatsoever. A few more nights like this, and he could soon stop worrying about the love handles. What's more, he couldn't remember the last time he had felt so horny. So this was what Caroline meant about coke being the best social and sexual lubricant there was. Not only did it keep you slim and give you the confidence to chat people up, it also turned you into some kind of sexual athlete. He felt like he could fuck for hours. The only problem was, at this precise moment in time he didn't have anyone to fuck with. Images of Christopher engaged in a variety of sexual positions with Marco flashed before his eyes like the trailer for a particularly bad porn movie, and he felt his confidence begin to drain away.

'That guy over there keeps looking at you,' Caroline said, nudging him under the table. 'The one standing by the cigarette machine. Sexy, don't you think?'

Martin looked. It wasn't often that he agreed with Caroline's assessment of what made a sexy man – Graham was a rare exception – but there was no denying that the hunk standing next to the cigarette machine with the curly black hair, the tight red T-shirt and the bulging biceps was indeed sexy. As a matter of fact, he was one of the sexiest men Martin thought he had seen in his entire life. And to top it all, he was smiling – not in a cocky 'Yes I know I'm gorgeous' sort of way, but in a friendly 'Yes I'd like to meet you' sort of way. Martin's mouth went dry. A sheepish grin spread across his face. He blushed and quickly turned to Caroline.

'I think you're in there,' Caroline said. 'Quick, go and talk to him before he decides you're not interested.'

'But I'm not really used to this sort of thing,' Martin protested. 'What shall I say?'

'Well, you could always start by saying hello,' a voice said. Martin looked up. His admirer was standing over him, still smiling and looking even sexier at close range. 'I'm Rob,' he said, offering Martin his hand. Then, glancing at the half-empty champagne bottle: 'So, what are you two celebrating?'

Martin shook Rob's hand and blushed even more intensely. 'Nothing really,' he mumbled.

'Actually, that's not true,' Caroline said firmly. 'We're celebrating the fact that my friend Martin here has finally seen the light and ditched the boyfriend from hell. He is now young, free and single again. If you'd like to join in the celebrations, you're more than welcome. Isn't that right, Martin?'

Martin nodded bashfully. 'Yeah. Of course. The more the merrier.'

Rob, who hadn't taken his eyes off Martin for one second, pulled up a chair and sat down. 'Thanks,' he said, looking directly at Caroline for the first time. Then, turning back to Martin, 'That's the best offer I've had in a while.'

Martin didn't believe this for a moment, but he wasn't about to argue. 'Great,' he said, suddenly aware that his nose was about to drip and sniffing sharply. 'Sorry. I've just got to nip to the toilet. Don't go away.'

Rob grinned mischievously. 'Don't worry,' he said, checking out Martin's groin as he stood up. 'I'm not going anywhere.'

John was sitting in front of his computer, wearing nothing but his Calvin Klein briefs. Next to the keyboard, the ashtray was overflowing with cigarette butts. Apart from a brief break for something to eat and a quick trip to the newsagents for another packet of cigarettes, John had been on line for almost six hours. The phone bill would be enormous, but he didn't care. It wasn't every day that he met someone in a chat room who was as stimulating as 'CuriousCute28'. Their initial conversation had lasted a little over an hour. By the time it drew to a close, John was convinced that this guy really was the genuine article. It was a shame that he didn't have a photo to swap, but from the way the conversation had gone, John had already formed a pretty clear mental picture of him. He was six feet tall, clean shaven, with dark hair, brown eyes and the kind of naturally muscular physique that came from years of playing contact sports and lifting building materials, rather than months of intensive weight training at the gym. He had a girlfriend, lived a completely straight life, and had only recently begun to explore the possibility that he might be bisexual. He had never stepped foot inside a gay bar, never bought a Madonna record, never shaved his chest and never worn an item of clothing that was a size too small. He was the ultimate gay fantasy figure, the 'Great Dark Man' that old queen Quentin Crisp had dreamed about, and John was about to have mad passionate sex with him – sort of.

Their earlier conversation had only been a warm up, a kind of first date, a means of discovering if they were really compatible. Clearly 'CuriousCute28' had decided that they were, because he had asked John to meet him again, online at 9 p.m. The plan was that they would both be naked, and would indulge in a spot of cyber sex, exchanging sexually explicit instant messages whilst simultaneously masturbating. John had heard of people doing this, and had even read somewhere that cyber sex was the new phone sex, but he had always considered this sort of behaviour beneath him. Tonight he felt rather differently. He had drunk the best part of a bottle of wine to get himself in the mood, and had a bottle of poppers waiting. He had spent the last half-hour checking out some of the gay porn websites, and was feeling extremely horny, if a little ridiculous.

What if the whole thing had been a wind up? It was already 9.10 p.m. and there was still no sign of 'CuriousCute28'. What if he didn't show up? It would be so humiliating. That was the funny thing about the internet. Unless you had a web cam, you knew that nobody could actually see you, that nobody need ever know that you had spent the past half hour sitting there in your underwear, waiting in vain for a man who probably didn't even exist, or at least not in quite the same way, shape or form that you imagined. Still, the lure of the chat rooms was so strong, and the fantasy so seductive, that just as you could picture the man of your dreams at the other end of the line, so you could convince yourself that a thousand prying eyes were watching you through your computer screen and laughing quietly at your misfortune. It gave a whole new meaning to the phrase 'mind fuck'.

John flicked in and out of the various gay chat rooms, and felt his erection dwindling. He took another slug of wine and lit another cigarette. Five more minutes, then it would have to be that porn video.

A message flashed up. It was him. 'Hi', it said. 'Feeling horny?'

John stubbed out his cigarette and typed furiously. 'Very. How about you?'

'Yeah. Sorry I'm a bit late. Playing squash with a mate. Worked up quite a sweat.'

John felt his cock harden. This was even better than he had anticipated. He stabbed at the keyboard. 'So what are you wearing?'

'Just a jock strap. You?'

John typed in 'Calvin Kleins' then decided it sounded too gay. He quickly deleted the words, replacing them with 'Same here'.

'Cool', came the reply. 'You like to get fucked from behind, or on your back?'

John reached for the poppers and inhaled deeply. For someone who claimed never to have had gay sex before, 'CuriousCute28' certainly knew all the right things to say.

Martin couldn't remember the last time he had enjoyed himself quite this much. It felt odd to be feeling so happy after the events of the past few days, but then admirers with Rob's many attributes didn't come along very often. He was so attentive, such good company, so good looking, and such a good listener. This last quality was especially welcome. Caroline, bless her, had made her excuses and left shortly after Rob appeared, slipping Martin the remains of the coke as she hugged him goodbye. Since then, Martin hadn't stopped talking. It was partly nerves, he was certain, but he just couldn't seem to stop. He talked about his job, how he hated it, and how nobody respected him at the office. He talked about Caroline, how he loved her, and how she was the best friend a gay man could wish for. He talked about his father, how he meant well, and how his arrival in London next weekend was certain to end in social embarrassment if not complete disaster. And he talked about Christopher, how he had lied and cheated, and how his sudden departure had left Martin feeling foolish and miserable and barely able to carry on – until tonight that is, tonight when he had met Rob and was feeling on top of the world.

Rob smiled and nodded. Martin thought he resembled one of those agony uncles they trotted out on daytime television shows, only a far better listener and far better looking. He really was extremely handsome, so handsome in fact that Martin wouldn't have minded at all if Christopher and that Italian hooker with the beautiful arms had strutted into the bar at that precise moment and spotted him sitting here feeling fabulous with this gorgeous man lending a sympathetic ear. Besides, Rob's arms were every bit as beautiful as Marco's, and Martin was certain that Rob didn't spend every day in the gym or make his living sleeping with ugly old men in exchange for vast amounts of money which he never paid any tax on. He was sure that Rob had a proper job, one that involved a certain degree of responsibility. He just didn't know what it was.

Had Rob told him this already? Or had they not got around to the subject of what Rob did for a living yet? Did he know anything about Rob at all, aside from the fact that he smiled a lot and was clearly a match for Marco any day of the week? Had he really been talking about himself all this time? Oh God, was he being boring? Maybe he should make a joke about it, say something like, 'Well, that's enough about me. So what do you think of me?' Would that work? Would it sound funny? Did lines like that ever sound funny? Or was it already too late? Did Rob have him down as an alcoholic, egotistical bore? Or worse, had he written Martin off as some kind of drug addict? Maybe the constant sniffing had given him away. He could always say that he had a bit of a cold. Then again, it was late June. Allergies, then. He could claim that he had hay fever, and that his doctor has prescribed antihistamine tablets and that they had made him speedy.

Just then Rob cut in. Martin was pleased to see that he was still smiling, though not quite as broadly as before. 'Listen, Martin,' Rob said. 'You seem like a nice guy, but I think I should probably be going now. Maybe we'll bump into each other again some time, when you're feeling less . . . preoccupied.' He stood up and hesitated for a moment. 'It really was nice meeting you,' he said finally. 'And your friend of course.'

'Don't go just yet,' Martin said, trying hard not to sound desperate and failing miserably. 'I've been talking too much. I know. I'm sorry. I'm not normally like this, really. It must be the drink. I've hardly eaten anything all day, and champagne always goes straight to my head. It's still early. We could go and get something to eat, some pasta or something. I know a few places near here, all fairly cheap. I'm sure we could find a table. We could order some food, and you could tell me about yourself.'

Rob frowned slightly and shook his head. 'Maybe some other time,' he said, and flashed a half-smile. 'Bye.'

Martin watched him leave. Then he rushed into the toilet, tore off some toilet paper, and blew his nose until it bled.

Caroline was heading home in a taxi when her mobile rang. It was Graham. 'Hi, baby,' he said. 'What's up?'

Caroline felt her heart leap at the sound of his voice, but she was determined to play it cool. 'I'm fine,' she said briskly. 'Just on my way to a party as a matter of fact.'

'Really? Whose party?'

'Nobody you know. Just one of the girls from work.'

'That's a pity. I was hoping I could see you tonight.'

Caroline, still giddy from all the champagne, felt her resolve melting. 'Well, you've left it a bit late, Graham,' she said, secretly wishing she had hung on to that remaining half gram of coke. 'People are expecting me.'

'Well, how about if we go together? You could drop by on your way and pick me up. Where is this party anyway?'

Caroline racked her brains for a suitable location. It had to be close enough to Graham's flat in Belsize Park to make it seem as though she wouldn't be putting herself out too much, but not so close as to arouse suspicion. 'Finchley Road,' she said eventually. 'Though to be honest I'm not sure if it'll be much good.'

'Well, why don't you stop by anyway?' Graham said gently. 'We can have a drink and then see how we feel. I've really missed you, y'know. And I know it was stupid of me storming off like that the other day. Say you'll come over, and at least give me a chance to try and make it up to you.'

He could be very persuasive, there was no denying that. And it did sound as though he was genuinely sorry about the way he had acted before. Caroline knew that she was caving in, but she put up one last valiant struggle. 'Okay,' she said. 'But this doesn't mean that I've forgiven you. You've still got a lot of making up to do.'

Twenty minutes later, the taxi pulled up outside the three-storey Edwardian house where Graham had lived for the past year, and where Caroline was forced to admit that she had spent some of the happiest times of her life. She paid the driver, checked her make-up, and walked up to the front door. She pressed the buzzer to the basement flat and waited for Graham to answer. There was a short pause before she was buzzed in. She walked down the hallway to Graham's door and knocked gently. 'Just a minute,' Graham's voice shouted. Then the door swung open.

Caroline almost keeled over. Graham was standing in the doorway, completely naked except for the cowboy hat tilted on the back of his head, and the cigar dangling from his mouth. In one hand he held a bottle of champagne. In the other, two glasses. He grinned. 'Glad you could make it. I thought we could have our own party right here. What do you say? Wanna come?'

Caroline smiled and stepped inside.

Chapter five

Martin hated Monday mornings at the best of times, but this particular Monday morning he was convinced that the whole world was conspiring against him. It was bad enough that his colleagues in the design department regarded him with the kind of wide-eyed curiosity normally reserved for visits to the reptile house at London Zoo. There were times when he regretted his decision to be so open about his sexuality at work. Barely a day went by without someone asking him why gay men were so promiscuous, or whether he thought he was born gay, or what he made of the latest homo-sexual subplot used to liven up whichever soap opera happened to be losing ratings that month. The questions weren't deliberately offensive. On the contrary, some were clearly intended as compliments. Michelle on frozen foods had got it into her head that gay men were all expert dancers with fabulous wardrobes and impeccable taste in home fur-nishings, which was one stereotype Martin was prepared to live with. Let's face it – it would be better than living alone, and he could use a little help with the decorating. Still, the constant enquiries about his lifestyle did get on his nerves. And this was from people who worked and socialised in central London. God knows what it would have been like if he had stayed in Cardiff.

To make matters worse, it seemed that the past year had been declared mating season in the design studio, with the entire female workforce disappearing on maternity leave and returning with albums full of baby photos which their colleagues were expected to coo over. Today was the turn of Karen, whose ability to reproduce was being treated as some kind of minor miracle by the other girls, though Martin felt it barely made up for her complete lack of creativity in every other department. She was supposed to be a qualified graphic designer, not that you'd know it from the quality of work she produced. During her pregnancy, whenever Karen had complained about the extra weight she was carrying, he felt like telling her he knew exactly how she felt – he'd been carrying her for months. There were no prizes for guessing who was expected to pick up the shortfall when one of the team was incapacitated. After all, gay men were naturally creative, weren't they?

'Come and see these photos, Martin,' someone shouted. He looked up from his desk. It was Melanie, one of the few people at work he actually liked. But today even she was beginning to grate on him.

'Just got to dash to the loo,' he called back, and slipped out of the door before she could argue. He hurried towards the gents, praying that he wouldn't bump into one of the lads from the accounts department downstairs. The last thing he needed today was some number-crunching moron getting all jumpy at the urinal, paranoid that the queer was looking at his cock. It never ceased to amaze him, the way straight men assumed that because you were gay you were automatically guaranteed to find them sexually desirable, regardless of what they looked like. More often than not, it was the least attractive ones who made the greatest fuss. Perhaps it was just wishful thinking on their part. Or maybe they genuinely believed that gay men were so obsessed with sex that they would happily do it with any man who happened to be in the right place at the right time. Which was a ridiculous idea, obviously.

The toilets were empty. Relieved, he dashed into one of the cubicles, locked the door and sat on the toilet seat. What was wrong with him today? He was never normally this crabby, even on a Monday morning. Maybe it was lack of sleep. Saturday night he'd hardly slept at all. The cocaine had kept him awake for hours. When he did finally lose consciousness he was tormented by nightmares in which his nose kept bleeding until the whole room was awash with blood and he watched helplessly as his furniture floated out of the door on a crimson tide. Last night he'd gone to bed early, and lain awake until one, torturing himself with fantasies of what Christopher was up to. Come to think of it, it was hardly surprising if he felt out of sorts, considering everything that Christopher had put him through these past five days. He'd been stood up, lied to, cheated on, dumped in favour of someone who advertised their services in the pages of the gay press every week, and left the sole occupier of a flat he could ill afford. As break-ups went, it was pretty spectacular.

And to top it all there was his father's imminent descent on London to contend with. The thought of his father hanging out with the gay folk at Gay Pride filled Martin with dread. Pride was supposed to be about having fun, watching crap pop acts and feeling, well, proud. It wasn't meant to be about chaperoning relatives. He had often wondered about the mums and dads who tagged along to Pride with their gay off-spring, marching under a banner that read 'Parents of Lesbians, Gays, Bisexuals and Transgendered Individuals' or whatever the politically correct, all-inclusive term was these days. What exactly were they doing there? Were they simply showing their support, or was there some other hidden agenda? Were they overcompensating for the fact that, deep down, they would be far happier if their kids weren't queer? And what did they really think of the drag queens in their eight-inch spike heels and the SM dykes marching along with their tits out? There were plenty of gay men out there who felt embarrassed by some of the people who turned out for Gay Pride, so God knows what some middle-aged mum from sub-urbia would make of it all. And as for his father, he might be an old hippie who supported every radical cause under the sun, but that didn't necessarily mean that he would take Pride in his stride. No amount of liberal soul-searching would have prepared him for the sight of men in full leather, many of whom were certain to have their backsides exposed. How he would react to that was anyone's guess. Knowing his father, he probably found leather deeply objectionable to begin with.

Martin slumped forward and cradled his head in his hands. This really was shaping up to be the worst week in his entire life. He'd already been shat on from a great height. The last thing he needed now was an opportunity for further humili-ation. He needed time to get his life back in order, to take control of things the way Caroline had said. Changes would have to be made, that much was certain. He probably ought to think about joining a gym, although he had no idea how much it would cost, or whether he could really afford it.

Maybe he should consider getting a flatmate. That would go some way to alleviating his money worries. It would be company for him too, someone to help fill the space vacated by Christopher. Yes, a flatmate was definitely a good idea. He would make some phone calls and place an ad in one of the gay papers as soon as he returned to his desk. He would just wait here for a few more minutes, give everyone time to pore over Karen's baby photos and rest his eyes.

Half an hour later he was awoken by the sound of someone flushing the toilet next door. He glanced at his watch, leapt to his feet and stumbled out of the cubicle. Standing at the wash basin was one of the lads from the accounts department. He caught Martin's reflection in the mirror and sneered. 'What have you been doing in there?' he said, eyeing Martin's crotch and laughing. Martin looked down and felt the blood drain from his face. He could see straight away where all those red blood cells were headed. His erection was clearly visible through his trousers, straining against the fabric. It was a nightmare made flesh, a flashback to the school showers and the constant fear of being revealed as a 'poof'. He stood rooted to the spot as his accuser walked away, laughing to himself. By lunchtime, the news would be all around the office.

Caroline had taken the day off work, claiming that she was suffering from 'female problems'. This was the one excuse she knew her boss would never dare question. He was just relieved to get off the phone before she mentioned the dreaded word 'period'.

She spent the morning pottering around Graham's flat, watching daytime TV and flicking through a couple of magazines she found spread on the floor next to the sofa. She loved men's magazines, especially the so-called 'new lad' mags with their constant diet of busty babes, cool cars and articles on 'How To Cheat On Your Girlfriend And Get Away With It'. It was a pity more women didn't read them. They gave such an insight into the way men behaved. It didn't take a degree in psychology to work out that all that macho bravado was simply a cover for a deep-seated insecurity about what it meant to be a man in these days of high unemployment and low sperm counts. Her own father had never been in any doubt about his role in life. He was the man, the breadwinner, the wage earner, the head of the family. He wouldn't have been caught dead reading a magazine. Magazines were for women, and besides he was always too busy laying patios or building extensions to read up on 'The 100 Best Mountain Bikes', or 'The 30 Essential Items Every Bachelor Needs'. Men today didn't have that same sense of purpose, so they looked to men's magazines to give them an idea of who they were. It was kind of sweet in a way. And the grooming pages were always a bit of a giggle. It was comforting to know that men were just as insecure, just as neurotic, just as obsessed with their appearance as women.

It had been a nice weekend, all things considered. The sex on Saturday night was better than ever, and when she woke up on Sunday morning Graham was there with breakfast on a tray and a single red rose in last night's champagne bottle. It was corny as hell of course, but after his stunt with the cowboy hat and the cigar she could hardly accuse him of lacking imagination. They spent most of the day cuddled up on the sofa, catching up on the week's catalogue of misery in *EastEnders* and sipping red wine through an old Bette Davis movie about a woman who goes on a cruise and discovers that she is beautiful and lovable after all. Graham had never seen *Now Voyager* and showed very little interest in Bette

Davis's transformation from ugly duckling to belle of the ball, all of which helped alleviate Caroline's niggling doubts about her boyfriend's sexual orientation. They ordered a takeaway from the local Chinese, and by the time it got dark they were back in bed and Graham was burying his face between her legs, offering further evidence of his heterosexuality while she held onto his curly brown locks and moaned appreciatively. She slept better than she had slept in weeks.

She hadn't showered today, preferring to savour the smell of his body on her skin as she sat wrapped in his bathrobe. She loved the smell of his sweat mingled with anti-perspirant, and was glad that he rarely wore aftershave, or anything which would overpower his natural odour. She could sit like this all day, reading his magazines, dressed in his bathrobe, smelling of him. But just because she had taken the day off work it didn't mean she didn't have things to do. Her own flat was a tip, and if she didn't sort out the laundry she'd be going to work tomorrow minus her knickers. Besides, she didn't want Graham to return home after work and find her still there, not so soon after her suggestion that they move in together and the row that had led to. He'd apologised for that little outburst, of course, and reassured her that cohabitation was something he was willing to consider, just not yet. Still, there was no point in tempting fate.

She showered quickly and phoned for a cab. She spent the next ten minutes looking for her knickers, and was just putting the final touches to her make-up when the phone rang. She heard the answerphone click on and Graham's business-like voice announce that he couldn't come to the phone. The next voice she heard stopped her in her tracks. It was a male voice. A slightly nervous male voice. A slightly nervous, vaguely effeminate male voice. 'Hi, Graham', it said. 'It's me,

Darren. We met on Friday, at the group? I was just calling to say it was great to meet you. See you next time maybe, or perhaps we could get together for a drink or something if you're not too busy. Anyway, call me if you fancy meeting up. You've got my number. OK. Bye.'

A million thoughts raced through Caroline's head. Who the hell was Darren? Why was he phoning her boyfriend and inviting him out for a drink? What was this group he was talking about? Is that where Graham was on Friday night? What kind of group was it exactly? And if there was nothing remotely funny going on, why did Graham clam up when she asked him about Friday night? She had to find the answers somehow, and since he obviously wasn't willing to cooperate, the only other option was for her to do a bit of detective work. She knew that Graham kept a diary next to the phone, in which he kept a record of any pressing engagements – doctor's appointments, birthdays, that sort of thing. She picked it up and began flicking through the pages. The sudden toot of a car horn told her that her taxi was waiting. Just a minute, she thought, turning the pages faster and faster until finally the diary fell open on last week. Written in the space for Friday were just four letters: C.L.A.G.

It was John who suggested that they go to an underwear party. Martin only agreed because he was desperate for an excuse to get out of the flat. He had spent the best part of the evening staring blankly at the television set, running over the day's shameful events in his head. So far as he was aware, the news of his unruly erection hadn't got back to the design department, but it was bad enough knowing that the lads in accounts were all having a good laugh at his expense. John wasn't exactly brimming over with sympathy. 'It sounds to me as if you're in need of a good de-spunking,' he said, before neatly segueing into the suggestion of an underwear night. 'If you must go around popping out of your trousers, you'd be better off doing it somewhere where it will be appreciated. When was the last time you and Christopher had sex?'

'For Christ's sake, John, he only walked out a few days ago!'

'I know that. What I asked was, when did you last have sex?'

Martin hesitated. 'About two months ago,' he said glumly. 'Maybe three, I can't remember.'

'Exactly!' John said triumphantly. 'I'll meet you outside Brixton tube at 11 p.m. And make sure you wear clean knickers.'

Martin had never been to an underwear night before, and right now he seriously doubted whether he would ever go to one again. It was all so embarrassing. The first shock came when he was forced to undress in full view of the cloakroom attendant, who could have passed for a serial killer if only he'd possessed a little more charm. The club's policy of storing customers' belongings in black binbags only served to reinforce the image. Watching as the bag stuffed with his clothes was tossed onto the pile of shiny black parcels behind the counter, Martin couldn't help but wonder where the bodies were buried. Half an hour later, he had managed to banish such morbid thoughts from his mind, but even with two drinks inside him he was finding it difficult to relax. Clinging to the bar, dressed in his pristine Calvin Klein briefs and Caterpillar boots, he didn't feel sexy at all, just silly.

'I'm really not sure about this, John,' he said, downing the last of his Red Stripe and reaching into his sock for his cigarettes. 'I think I might just go home.'

John, who had his eye fixed on a visibly well-endowed skinhead leaning provocatively against the cigarette machine, spoke without turning his head. 'But we've only just got here. Have another drink. You'll soon get into the swing of it. You can't tell me there isn't a single person here you don't fancy.'

Martin surveyed the room. John did have a point. There were quite a few sexy-looking men dotted about, more than he had expected to see in fact. He had always imagined places like this to be full of old men with beer bellies exposed and dim-witted wives tucked away somewhere. While it was true that there were some men here who fitted this description, the majority were reasonably good looking, and there were even a select few who were not only strikingly handsome but had the kinds of bodies that wouldn't have looked out of place in an ad for a telephone sex line – all bulging biceps, pert pecs and washboard stomachs. He suddenly became very conscious of his own stomach, protruding over the elasticated waistband of his Calvin Kleins. He definitely had to join a gym, regardless of the cost. He breathed in deeply and lit a cigarette.

'Oh, look who it is!' John said, nodding in the direction of a beefy blond standing at the far end of the bar. 'I see she's back on the steroids.'

'I think he looks sort of sexy,' Martin replied, smiling shyly at the blond, who held his gaze for a second or two before turning away.

'Don't be taken in by that butch exterior,' said John. 'She's a typical muscle Mary that one, a proper legs-up Lucy.'

'Muscle Mary' and 'legs-up Lucy' were two of John's favourite put-downs. If the Mary in question happened to be on the small side, or had legs that were not only free-floating but somewhat shorter than normal, then he was referred to as a 'muscle midget'. Like a lot of gym-obsessed gay men at the more effeminate end of the scale, John didn't regard himself as a muscle Mary, or even remotely camp, and was generally scornful of anyone he thought deserving of either description. Martin had noticed over the years that the more muscular John became, the more inclined he was to camp it up, as if the exaggerated masculinity of his body gave permission for a degree of effeminacy he would never have dared reveal otherwise. Martin had never discussed this with John. Once, he had made the mistake of asking him what it was that distinguished him from the muscle Marys he was always so quick to criticise. John's answer had been short, and delivered with a slightly incredulous tone, as though he were stating the obvious: 'Muscle Marys have tattoos!'

'I knew a couple who picked that one up once,' John went on. 'Cock the size of a button mushroom, apparently. Not that it mattered. They were barely through the door before she was begging to be spit roasted. Squealed like a pig, or so I was told.'

'Spit roasted?' Martin looked puzzled.

'A cock in either end,' John said impatiently. 'Don't tell me you and Christopher never tried that with someone.'

'No, we didn't.' Martin frowned as the memory of his one disastrous attempt at a threesome came flooding back.

'Well, there's no need to look so miserable about it,' John said, misinterpreting the look on Martin's face as one of regret for what he hadn't done, rather than remorse for what he had. 'I'm sure there'll be plenty of other opportunities. Anyway, you're better off single. In my experience threesomes work best when you're the fresh meat in someone else's sandwich. That way you're sure to get most of the attention. I remember my first threesome, with a couple in Kilburn.

They'd been together for years and were obviously bored to death with each other. I didn't mind, though. I got a great fuck out of it, and they wanked each other off afterwards. Anyway, that's enough talk. I think it's time for some action. What about that guy over there? He looks like he could show you a good time.'

Martin looked and spotted an enormous muscle queen with a shaved head and tattoos. 'Not really my type,' he said. 'He looks a bit rough.'

'We all need a bit of rough in our diet,' John replied, rolling his eyes. 'I see what you mean, though. He looks like he'd fuck you over the sofa then wipe his cock on your curtains.'

Martin shuddered. The thought of anyone fucking John over a sofa was not one he cared to entertain. Besides, he was pretty certain there weren't any curtains in John's flat. It was all micro blinds.

'Good job I shaved my balls this morning,' John said, leering at the tattooed guy, who scowled back in what passed for an alluring manner. 'I had a feeling I might get lucky tonight.' Readjusting his crotch, he headed off towards the main area of the club where groups of men were already huddled together under camouflage netting. 'See you back here in an hour,' he called over his shoulder. And with that he disappeared into the darkness.

Martin sucked furiously on his cigarette, and felt his stomach twisting itself up in knots. He wished he could just throw himself into things, the way John did. He still felt self-conscious, still felt silly, only now he was vaguely aware that he was beginning to feel horny too. He ordered a large vodka and knocked it back in one gulp. He had never been in a situation quite like this before. Sure, he'd had casual sex with people he didn't know, but always in bed, and always one at a time. Now here he was, practically naked in a room full of strangers, poised to throw himself into a writhing mass of bodies where any number of people could touch him, taste him, possibly even tear huge chunks out of him if they wanted to. It was terrifying, and exciting at the same time. God knows what the girls at work would think if they could see him now. Still, he'd come this far. There was no point in backing out now.

He edged his way through the bar and into the dim recess of the club. Pausing until his eyes grew accustomed to the dark, he gradually became aware of a couple of men to his right, one kneeling in front of the other. The man on his knees grabbed Martin's leg as he pushed by, and ran a hand up his thigh. He flinched, and moved on. Directly ahead of him was a pool table. As he drew closer he could make out the shape of a man lying spread-eagled, face down on the table, while a second man fucked him from behind. A small group of men had gathered around. Some were muttering words of encouragement – 'Fuck him harder!' 'Give it to him!' 'Yeah, fuck him!' Others watched silently as they masturbated. The air was heavy with the stench of poppers.

Martin felt a hand on his crotch, and his cock stiffen. As far as he could make out in this light, the two men fucking seemed fairly attractive. If he could just concentrate on them, then it didn't really matter what the others looked like. He kept telling himself this as he felt a hand tugging at his Calvins, and a mouth closing around his cock. Someone pressed themselves against his back. A hand reached over his shoulder and held a bottle of poppers under his nose. He inhaled deeply and felt his head spin and the world disappear. It all slipped away – Christopher, his job, his father. The only thing he was conscious of now was the intense tingling sensation in his groin. That and the hands reaching under his armpits, playing with his nipples. He thrust his hips forward, faster and faster, until the tingling sensation ran all the way up from his balls to the tip of his cock, and he came in short, violent bursts.

Martin stooped to pull up his Calvins, and felt a hand on his arse. As he struggled to push it away, the figure kneeling in front of him rose up and the light from the bar spilled onto his face. Martin couldn't place him at first. Then it hit him. It was Matthew, John's date from Friday night.

'Hello again,' he said with a gloopy grin. 'Fancy meeting you here.'

Martin turned and fled.

Chapter six

'What do you mean, where was I last Friday night?' Graham was pacing the room in that determined, precise way he always did when he was really angry. Three days had passed since the mysterious Darren had left a message on Graham's answerphone. For three whole days Caroline had been biting her tongue, until finally, tonight, she just couldn't take it any more.

Watching Graham stalking up and down her living room, still clutching the bottle of red wine he had been about to uncork, she wondered how long it would be before he wore the varnish off the wood veneer flooring, but didn't dare say anything. There was no point talking to him when he was in this mood. It was best just to leave him until he calmed down, as he invariably did. His temper was like a petrol fire – ferocious while it lasted, but short lived. Caroline had a sneaking suspicion that these little outbursts were really just his way of playing for time, a delay tactic designed to ward her off while he struggled to come up with a credible excuse. If she was right, then he was bloody good at it, there was no denying that. Still, she resented him for stealing her thunder. She had every right to question him about his whereabouts on Friday night. There was something funny going on, and she was entitled to know what it was.

His pace was beginning to slow now, which usually meant that he was cooling down. Another minute or two and it would be safe to prod him a little further.

'Well?' she said eventually, trying hard to disguise the impatience in her voice. She didn't want it to sound like an interrogation. That would only fuel his temper even more.

'Well what?' Graham wasn't giving an inch.

'Where were you?'

'Why do you keep asking me that?' He certainly had her there. The problem was, she hadn't actually mentioned to Graham that she had overheard the answerphone message. She had gone over it in her head dozens of times, torturing herself with visions of who this Darren character was, and what her boyfriend was doing at a group called C.L.A.G. She was no closer to knowing what this mysterious group was all about, but she was certain of one thing: the 'G' stood for 'Gay'. It was some kind of gay support group, and her boyfriend had been to one of their meetings, which could only mean one thing. She had been right all along. Graham was secretly gay, and his relationship with her was a total sham. This would explain why he was so set against the idea of them moving in together. He needed the security of his own flat to help conceal his deception.

She should have confronted him with it straight away, she knew that. It was silly to let it go for days like this. She should have simply told him that she had overheard the message and asked him to explain what it was all about. But she hadn't. She told herself this was because she didn't want Graham thinking that she was spying on him, but deep down she knew that, had it been a woman's voice she'd heard, she would have confronted him about it immediately. It was okay to fly off the handle if a strange woman called up and left a message for the man you'd been dating for the past year. In fact, it was expected. But to interrogate your boyfriend over a phone call from a strange man? Well, that was a bit different. Life wasn't like the *Jerry Springer Show*. People didn't just change sex at the drop of a hat, or turn gay overnight. Those weren't the sorts of things that happened in West Hampstead, certainly not to people like her. What was she supposed to say exactly? That she suspected Graham of harbouring homosexual tendencies? Somehow, she didn't think that would go down too well.

'I only asked,' she said finally. 'There's no need to get so uptight about it. Honestly, anybody would think you had something to hide.'

If this struck a nerve, he didn't let it show. 'If I'm upset it's probably because I don't like being cross-examined about my whereabouts all the time,' he said, disappearing into the kitchen and returning with a corkscrew. 'Now can we just leave it, please?' He opened the bottle and poured two glasses. 'C'mon, babes,' he said softly, handing her a glass and gently squeezing her shoulder. 'Don't you think you're being just a little bit silly about this? I don't demand to know where you are every minute of the day.'

That's because I'm not the one receiving messages from strange men, Caroline thought, but she knew there was no point in pursuing this any further – not unless she wanted Graham to storm off again, which she didn't. Heated arguments always left her feeling horny, and he had just opened a bottle of wine. It would be a shame to waste it.

'You're right,' she said, raising her glass and smiling sweetly. 'Just forget I said anything.' She genuinely hoped that he would forget. At least then she might stand a better chance of catching him out.

It was Thursday evening when John finally phoned. Martin didn't know whether he was relieved to hear his voice or not. John had every right to be angry with him. His behaviour at the underwear night had been pretty bad. He'd left the club without even telling John that he was going, which was a terrible thing to do to a friend in those circumstances. He could picture John hanging around at the end of the night, anxiously waiting for him to reappear and cursing his name as the lights came up and the taxi queue grew and grew. Of course Martin had no choice but to leave after what had happened, but John probably wouldn't see it that way. Matthew was John's latest catch after all. There was no telling how he would react to the news that his new boyfriend had given his best friend a blow job while he was in the room, but it seemed reasonable to assume that he might not be too chuffed about it. The chances were John had bumped into Matthew himself after Martin had left, heard all about their little encounter, and had spent the past few days plotting his revenge.

'So what happened to you the other night?' John said. He didn't sound like someone hell bent on revenge. In fact he sounded strangely cheery.

'Nothing,' Martin lied. 'I just went home, that's all. I looked around for you before I left, but I couldn't really see very much in there. And I didn't want to just wade in and find that you were in the middle of something.'

'Good job you didn't,' John laughed. 'I met this really

amazing guy. Fabulous body. Great sex. Of course everyone else tried to join in. You know what some of those older queens are like – hands everywhere. And don't tell me I'm being ageist. I don't see them chasing after men their own age, so they're just as bad. There was this one old git, a proper scary Mary, she was. It was like being groped by a wax work. And it isn't easy fending them off in your underwear. I ended up stubbing a cigarette out on her arm . . .'

'So what about this guy?' Martin interrupted.

'What?' John said. 'Oh, right. Well, he's called Fernando and guess what? He's Brazilian! He works in a bar in Soho, but that's just pocket money. He's really a drug dealer. Coke, Ecstasy, K – you name it! I couldn't believe my luck. And to top it all he's a great fuck too. I can almost picture myself settling down.'

'But what about the guy you were with on Friday?' Martin couldn't help asking. 'Matthew, wasn't it?'

John groaned. 'That was last week! You don't have to move in with every man you have sex with, you know. God, you're such a lesbian sometimes.'

Martin bristled. Given John's attitude to women in general, and to lesbians in particular, this clearly wasn't intended as a compliment. Personally, Martin couldn't see anything wrong with lesbians. So what if they were known for falling in love and setting up home together quicker than you could say 'cat flap'? Was that really so bad? At least they weren't afraid of commitment, which was more than could be said for certain gay men. It was just like that joke that did the rounds a few years ago – 'What do lesbians take on a second date? A removal van. What do gay men take on a second date? What second date?' There were far worse things to be compared to than lesbians. All things considered, he would rather be mistaken for a lesbian than for a gay man like John.

'Anyway, listen,' John said. 'The reason I'm calling is about Saturday. Gay Pride. You are still planning on going?'

An image of his father squeezed between two drag queens flashed before Martin's eyes. 'I suppose so,' he said, half-heartedly. 'Well, actually I'm not sure. The thing is, it's a bit awkward. I don't know if I mentioned it, but my dad is coming to stay this weekend and, well, he says he wants to come along.'

'Oh, I see,' John faltered for a moment. 'Christ, he isn't about to announce that he's queer or something is he?'

'Of course not!'

'Well, I hope you're right, 'cos that would be too gross. Can you imagine? Your own dad, a queen! And at his age too! It would be so embarrassing! Not as bad as finding out that he likes to dress up in women's clothes and call himself Brenda I suppose, but even so . . .'

'Okay, John,' Martin snapped. 'Can we change the subject now please?'

'What? Oh, right. Well, I suppose we'll just have to work around him. We could always pair him off with some sad git from one of those gay parents' groups. He'll be fine. They can compare notes and we can get on with the serious business of having a good time. Talking of which, Fernando says he can sort us out with whatever we want. I just have to call him tomorrow with a shopping list and he'll have it all ready on the day. I thought we could get a couple of Es for the march, maybe some coke to tide us over the afternoon, then a few more Es for later, and maybe a bit of K for the club later. Oh, and guess what? We were talking about which club to go to, and Fernando said he can put our names on the guest list wherever we fancy. He knows all the club promoters, DJs, everyone. We won't even have to queue.'

Martin's heart sank at the prospect of a whole day playing gooseberry with John and his latest catch. He wasn't sure which was going to be worse – having his father tag along at Gay Pride, or watching John falling in love again for the second time in a week.

'Yeah, great,' he said. 'I'm not sure about taking E though. Isn't it a bit dangerous?'

John laughed. 'I can't believe you've never had an E. Where have you been? You'll be telling me you haven't tried Viagra next.'

'I haven't,' Martin said crossly. 'I may not be twenty-one any more, but I'm hardly at the age where I'm having trouble getting it up.'

'Try telling me that after your first E,' John sniggered. 'Anyway, you shouldn't believe everything you read in the papers. More people die every year from alcohol than from E. And alcohol makes you fat, as I'm sure you know. All those horror stories you hear about E, that's just the crap they sell to kids in the clubs. This is the good stuff. I popped one with Fernando the other night and it was fabulous. We were as high as kites and as horny as hell. And that was just at the club. By the time we got back to his place we were tearing each other's clothes off. So, I'll order you two, okay? Trust me, you'll have the time of your life.'

Martin doubted this very much, but he couldn't see any point in putting up a fight. 'Okay,' he said. 'See you Saturday.'

The first thing Caroline did when she got home from work on Friday evening was call Graham. His answerphone came on after the second ring. She hesitated before hanging up, and then debated whether or not to try him on his mobile. She didn't want him to think that she was checking up on him, though of course this was precisely what she was doing. After all, Graham had told her that he was going out with some of the lads from the office tonight. He probably wouldn't be too pleased to have her calling up to confirm his whereabouts in front of his work colleagues. Come to think of it, she didn't really want them jumping to the conclusion that she was some mad, possessive bunny boiler. Then again, this was assuming that he was actually out with his work colleagues, and not simply using them as an alibi. For all she knew, he could just as easily be in bed with some ex-girlfriend he'd bumped into on the tube, or even worse, some man called Darren he'd met at a gay support group a week ago. That was the trouble with mobile phones. They were so bloody mobile. Great if you were stuck in traffic and needed to let an important client know that you were going to be late for a meeting. Even better for tracking down a coke dealer on a Saturday night. But when it came to confirming whether the man you were dating really was where he said he was, with the people he said he was with, they were no use at all. Which, presumably, was part of the reason men liked them so much.

She could always pretend that she was calling to confirm details of the dinner party they had been invited to tomorrow night, though she knew perfectly well that Graham's old school-friend Jeremy and his wife Pip were expecting them at 7.30 p.m. sharp. Caroline felt nauseous at the mere thought of it. Jeremy and Pip were two of the most irritating, smug, middle-class twits she had ever met. The prospect of spending an entire evening facing them over the dinner table made her stomach churn. No doubt they'd be sampling some exotic new recipe Pip had picked up at one of her evening classes. What was it last time? Braised pheasant with pancetta? Followed by grilled peaches with a raspberry and red wine sorbet? Designer food, her mother would have called it. For once Caroline was forced to concede that she had a point.

What was Pip doing learning all these fancy new recipes anyway? It wasn't as if she actually ate anything. Caroline could picture her now – moving her food around her plate, rearranging it in a series of ever more decorative displays, before finally whisking the plate away and tipping the whole lot into the bin. Pip was one of those annoying stick insect women who took absolutely no pleasure in food. Cooking was just another means of drawing attention to her superior breeding and impeccable good taste.

Caroline resented women like Pip, and berated herself for feeling so intimidated by them. She wondered if it was worth skipping dinner tonight, and maybe having a few lines of coke instead. It wasn't as if she made a habit of it. How much harm could come from missing the odd meal here and there? And how much weight could she expect to lose in a day? Half a pound perhaps? Not a lot, but just enough to give herself that extra boost of confidence. And maybe she should wear that slinky black dress, the one that drew attention to her cleavage. Pip may have been blessed with narrow hips and the appetite of a bird, but she was obviously at the back of the queue when other assets were given out. As for Jeremy, Caroline had yet to meet a married man whose eyes didn't wander when there was a decent pair of breasts on show.

It probably wasn't a good idea to call Graham now, she thought, wandering into the bedroom and opening her wardrobe. Better to concentrate on making a big impression tomorrow night. One thing was certain – if she wore that dress, nobody would be admiring Pip's cooking for very long. It would be worth it just to see the look on her face.

Martin was lying on his back with his legs in the air. Inches above his face, Carl was issuing instructions. 'Okay, Martin. Take it nice and slowly. Tighten those tummy muscles for me. That's good. Now, three more . . .'

The gym was far busier than Martin had expected. In fact, he wasn't quite sure what he had expected, but it certainly wasn't this. The YMCA didn't advertise itself as a gay gym, but it might just as well have been a queer-only zone for all the straight men in evidence. Everywhere he looked there were gay men working out in pairs, or chatting together by the water cooler. The scene reminded him of his first ever visit to a gay bar. Everyone looked so at ease with one another, and so comfortable with their surroundings, that he was left feeling strangely out of place. It was just as well he'd decided to hire a personal trainer for his first few sessions.

'Is this a gay gym?' he asked, looking up at Carl with a slightly pained expression.

Carl grinned. 'All gyms are gay,' he said with a wink.

Martin smiled back, silently noting that while Carl may have been prematurely balding, he compensated for his lack of hair by having a perfectly proportioned physique. And a perfectly proportioned boyfriend tucked away at home too, no doubt.

Carl's services didn't come cheap, but aside from ensuring that Martin didn't do himself an injury or expend vast amounts of energy on exercises that wouldn't make much difference, his solid, friendly presence meant that Martin wasn't the only person working out alone. For the first time in his life, Martin had a sense of what it must be like to hire an escort for the evening.

The programme Carl had devised for him wasn't quite as demanding as he had anticipated. It helped that he knew his way around some of the equipment. Those few occasions when he'd tagged along to the gym with Christopher hadn't been a complete waste of time. Still, it wasn't exactly painless either. Straining to control the barbell as Carl showed him the correct method of performing bicep curls, Martin had felt as if the veins in his forearms were about to pop. But that was nothing compared with the agony he was in now. Stomach crunches were definitely the worst, he thought, as he raised his knees and curled his head and shoulders up for the last time.

'That was great,' Carl said as Martin collapsed, red faced and breathless, onto the rubber mat. 'Now just five minutes on the Stairmaster to cool down, then a good stretch and you're done.'

Standing under the shower afterwards, gazing down as the water bounced off his naked body, Martin decided that John was right. He was definitely looking a bit flabby. He could do with losing a few inches around the middle, and adding a few inches to his chest and arms. It would take a great deal of discipline and a lot more pain before he started to look anything like some of the bodies on display out there. And there was still the question of where the extra money was going to come from. The gym membership alone came to almost £600. Plus there were Carl's fees, and some new trainers wouldn't go amiss. In fact, a whole new gym kit would probably help keep him motivated. He would have to advertise for a flatmate soon.

Still, at least he'd made a start. He was taking control of things. Inside this slightly overweight, thirty-two-year-old body, there was a whole new person just waiting to emerge. He felt better already.

Chapter seven

Martin's relationship with his father had been through many different phases over the years. As a small boy, he had been painfully conscious of the fact that his father didn't look or act like dads were supposed to. Other kids' dads went to work in a suit and washed the car on Sundays. His dad rode around on a motorbike and spent Sundays leafleting the neighbours about the dangers of nuclear power and the benefits of smoking pot, or protesting about fascist dictators in far-off places. By the time Martin entered his teens and began staging his own form of protest with the aid of silly clothes and hair dye, his father's casual dress sense and firm beliefs had become a source of pride. When his parents' marriage fell apart, it was his dad he sided with. For a time he blamed his mother for driving his father away, before finally waking up to the fact that his father never did anything he didn't want to, least of all compromise his principles for the sake of practical considerations like putting food on the table. His father had many fine qualities, but being a responsible husband wasn't one of them.

These days, his father was something of a distant figure –
partly because he moved around so much, and partly because,
like many gay men, Martin had chosen to keep both his parents at arm's length. This wasn't because he felt embarrassed
about the fact that he was gay, or even because he feared
rejection. Both his mother and father had reacted pretty well
to the news. His mother did spend the first few weeks blaming herself for the way her son had turned out, but she soon
hit on the far happier notion of pinning it all on his absent
father who, being absent in a very physical sense, wasn't there
to argue. But Martin felt that he had outgrown his relationship with the people who had raised him, and who now
occupied a very different world from his. Maintaining a slight
distance from his parents was a way of acknowledging the
true nature of their relationship. Caroline pointed out that
this wasn't a situation peculiar to gay people. The difference
was, their parents were much less likely to poke their noses
into their lives for fear of what they might discover. Caroline
only wished her own mother could know something of that
fear.

The last time Martin had seen his father was over a year
ago, at a family christening. They tended to keep in touch by
phone, though the phone calls had become less frequent.
Every now and then a postcard would arrive from whichever
part of the country his father happened to call home at the
time. The most recent communication had come from
Brighton, and revealed very little except to say that the business was doing fine – the business being a small shop that
sold wind chimes, aromatherapy oils, yak-hair sweaters and
the like. The postcards tended to be the sort you could pick
up free in bars and restaurants, advertising mobile phone net-
works or forthcoming films, though occasionally there would

be one bearing the campaign slogan of some little-known pressure group. Martin often wondered why his father didn't just send letters, given that he seemed to have missed the point of postcards entirely. Maybe the postcards were just his way of maintaining contact, whilst acknowledging that there was really very little to say.

Despite all of this, and the fact that his timing couldn't have been worse, Martin found himself feeling oddly excited as he awaited his father's arrival. It was approaching 10.30 a.m. and he had been up for almost three hours, tidying the flat, trying on various outfits and generally working himself up into a state of eager anticipation bordering on high anxiety. John would be on his second champagne cocktail by now, as he entertained Fernando and whoever else he had managed to round up for his regular pre-Pride brunch. If nothing else, his father's visit had given Martin the perfect excuse to wriggle out of this annual gathering, which tended to be less of a social occasion and more of a floor show, with John not so much the host as the star attraction. He could just picture it now – a room full of gay men who shared little in common except that they were having sex with John, had once had sex with John, were planning on having sex with John at some point in the future, or had been his closest friend for the past nine years and were too polite to refuse an invitation. It was an invitation Martin could happily do without – although a champagne cocktail would go down very well right now.

Maybe there was time to nip to the off licence, he thought, peering out of the kitchen window at the overcast sky. It was always threatening to rain on the morning of Gay Pride – every year, for as long as he could remember. Perhaps it was God's way of urging gay men to drag up as Barbra Streisand

and march down Park Lane singing 'Don't Rain On My Parade'. Mind you, it wasn't as if Streisand was a major gay icon any more. Half the people at Pride probably didn't even know who she was, despite her having a gay son and a reputation for egomania which even John couldn't match. He grabbed his keys, slipped a denim jacket on over his freshly pressed Diesel T-shirt, and headed for the door. In the hallway, he stooped to flick through the morning's post, spotted a couple of official-looking envelopes with his name on, and stuffed them in his jacket pocket. Today was not the day to face up to his mounting debts. After all, Pride was supposed to be a day of celebration.

He stepped out of the building and stopped in his tracks. Walking up the path towards him was his father, dressed in his usual attire of loose, collarless shirt, pale blue jeans and motorcycle boots. His hair was long and ruffled, his beard short and fading to grey, his face tanned and smiling. For years, Martin had been told how much he resembled his father – more often than not by his mother, who seemed to regard physical likeness as a measure of personal loyalty and sounded slightly resentful that her son hadn't inherited more of her own genes. Martin recognised that he and his father shared the same soft green eyes, firm brow and strong, slightly upturned nose. But he had always felt that these features somehow suited his father, whereas he hadn't yet grown into them. Perhaps this would be one of the compensations of getting older, he thought – that he would gradually grow into his face, the way his father had. On the other hand, he couldn't recall a time when his father didn't look completely at ease with his features.

Gazing at him now, he looked exactly as Martin remembered. Except for one small but important detail. Pinned to his father's shirt was a badge the size of a beer mat. Emblazoned across it in bright pink letters were the words 'Proud To Be An Embarrassing Parent'.

John's brunch was going well – swimmingly well in fact, he thought, as he marched into the kitchen and cracked open another bottle of champagne. Fernando was certainly making a big impression, and not just because of the quality of his cocaine. John's remaining guests, in order of appearance, were as follows. First to arrive was Neil, who John knew from the gym and with whom he had once had a disastrous one-night stand, the problem being that neither of them had shown particular interest in playing the part of the top. Despite this, or perhaps because of it, they had remained friends. The theory was that so long as they remained friends they were less likely to dish the dirt on one another, which was fine in theory but didn't always work out in practice, as many of John's past friends had learned to their cost.

Next through the door was David, sometimes known as Camp David, who had a thing about men in uniform. In itself, this wasn't so unusual. Scattered all across London there were clubs devoted to the pursuit of such pleasures. However, David's choice of uniforms was rather specific. What did it for him wasn't the usual army gear or even the Nazi regalia favoured by more hardened sadomasochists. He preferred the kinds of uniforms worn by those in less commanding professions – kitchen staff, council workers, even (and this is where John came in) cabin crew. They met when David attempted to chat John up during a flight to South Africa. His attempt hadn't been very successful, but the fact that he was travelling first class prompted John to think that he might be someone worth knowing. Only later did he discover that David's ticket had been paid for by an elderly aunt, who had amassed a small fortune during the days of apartheid and who David visited once a year in the hope that he might be rewarded in the event of her death. So far, this event hadn't developed beyond the planning stages.

Finally, there were the two Steves. Steve One was a shy young student with an impressively large chest who John had met a year ago through the internet, and had been grooming as potential boyfriend material until the sudden arrival of Steve Two threw his scheme off kilter. John's admiration for Steve One's chest had since given way to resentment and the indignant belief that disco tits were somehow wasted on the young. The way John saw it, a decent body was one of the few compensations of hitting thirty. Queens who had barely learned how to shave had enough going for them already, and should show some respect for their elders by staying away from the gym, at least until their skin started crying out for liposomes. The only excuse for developing muscles before the age of thirty was if you earned them through manual labour, the way John was certain 'CuriousCute28' had done long before he began questioning his sexuality and discovered the pleasures of internet chat rooms and cyber sex. Maybe this was something they could discuss the next time they met online, assuming they ever did. In the virtual world of the internet, men came and went even more quickly than they did in real life. All it took was a change of screen name. For all John knew, 'CuriousCute28' might have already dropped out of the world wide web, never to be seen again.

Not that any of this really mattered now. What mattered was that his living room was full of living, breathing people assembled to bear witness to his gorgeous new boyfriend, and to demonstrate their approval, which so far they were doing rather enthusiastically. Neil had practically choked on his Bucks Fizz the moment Fernando arrived. David hadn't taken his eyes off him all morning. Even the two Steves, who had been together for almost six months now and who always made such a nauseating public display of their mutual affection and deep desire for one another – even they were sizing him up at every opportunity. And who could really blame them? Fernando was looking exceptionally horny today, dressed in a pair of baggy combats and a black sleeveless T-shirt which accentuated his biceps. Fernando did have incredible arms, the kind of arms a muscle Mary like Neil would go green with envy for. After all, pecs were two a penny these days. There wasn't a queen in London between the ages of twenty-nine and forty who hadn't joined a gym and developed a pair of disco tits. And now that young upstarts like Steve One were muscling in on the action, it was only a matter of time before the more discerning gay men moved their sights onto a different prize. Yes, pecs were definitely old news, John decided as he chopped himself a quick line of coke on the stainless-steel work surface. Biceps were the new pecs. He rolled a twenty-pound note and hoovered up the line.

'Aha! Caught you!'

John didn't have to look round to know who it was. David was a notorious coke whore, the kind of queen who never had enough money to buy any drugs of his own, but who was always more than willing to share yours. What made it worse was that he had an uncanny knack of knowing when somebody, somewhere was chopping a discreet line with no intention of offering him one. John wondered if maybe David had been a sniffer dog in a previous life. He turned to find him standing in the doorway, champagne glass in hand, nostrils flared in anticipation.

'I was just looking for a little top up,' David said, waving his empty glass. 'But if you're offering . . .'

'I wasn't,' John said. 'But I suppose I can spare you a line. I mean, it's not as if I have to go looking very far if I fancy a bit more.'

'I know,' David said, reaching for the champagne bottle and refilling his glass as John opened the paper wrap and began chopping a line. 'That Fernando's quite a catch. I don't know where you find them, dear. Your poor sister here hasn't had a bite in months. So spare a thought for us poor single girls, and don't be mean with the charlie.'

David had the kind of face that had never been particularly attractive to begin with, and which years of rejection by men better looking than himself had done little to improve. For all his oily charm, he was the picture of petty jealousy and seething resentment. Smiling mischievously to himself, John tipped out a little more of the powder, carefully arranging it into the longest, fattest, most generous line he had ever made. Then, just as David's eyes were about to pop, he chopped it in two and quickly snorted the bigger half before handing David the note.

'Thanks,' David said, the smile wiped from his face. 'You're too kind.' He hoovered up the remaining half and ran the tip of his finger over the work surface before popping it into his mouth, like a small child licking the bowl clean after his mother has prepared a chocolate cake. 'So, where's Martin?'

John made a point of carefully folding the wrap of coke and sliding it back into his wallet. 'We're meeting later. He's got his father staying with him.'

'How is he?' David's eyes grew wide with concern, though it could just as easily have been the effects of the coke. 'I heard about Christopher running off with that hooker. He must be in a terrible state.'

'He's okay,' John said. 'I keep telling him he needs to get out more. But he's going to have a good time tonight. I'm going to see to that.'

'He's lucky he's got friends who care for him,' David cooed, eagerly eyeing the wallet in John's hand. 'Especially ones who know how to make a girl happy.'

'I suppose so,' John snapped, tucking the wallet into his pocket and picking up the champagne bottle. 'Shall we join the others?'

They returned to the living room in time to find Neil engaging Fernando in a conversation about the best protein shakes for building up muscle.

'I'm surprised you need any advice on that subject,' John snapped, glaring menacingly at Neil and placing a possessive hand on Fernando's shoulder. 'Neil's a bit of an expert when it comes to protein shakes. He's got quite a reputation at the gym. Never happier than when he's got a mouthful of protein. Isn't that right, Neil?'

Neil smiled icily and retreated to the far corner of the room where the two Steves were busy sampling the cocaine they'd purchased from Fernando at a special introductory price. David, of course, was already seated with them.

John glanced at his watch. 11.25 a.m. Shane still hadn't shown up, and they would have to leave soon if they were to meet up with Martin as planned. This was typical of Shane. Punctuality had never been his strong point. God knows how he managed to hold down a career as a flight attendant. It was a wonder he ever made it to the airport in time for take-off. John wouldn't have minded him being late today, only Shane had ordered enough Es to keep him gurning for the next forty-eight hours, and John wasn't exactly keen on the idea of carrying them around on the off-chance that they might bump into one another on the march. Then again, he could just locate the banner for the Long Yang Club Oriental gay group and wait for Shane to make an appearance, as he invariably would. And if they didn't meet up, there were bound to be plenty of people around who would be more than happy to take any surplus pills off John's hands. It wasn't even as if the police were a particularly heavy presence at Pride these days. They were too concerned with community relations to be seen searching people for drugs, today of all days.

John slipped into the bathroom and took the bag of small white pills from out of his toilet bag. Then, pausing to check his hair in the mirror, he popped a pill into his mouth, drained his glass of champagne, stuffed the bag down his sock and returned to his guests.

'Right, everybody,' he said, checking his watch. 'Half an hour till take off. Time to go.'

Caroline was draped across the sofa, half watching the television with the sound off, and flicking through the latest copy of *Vogue*. She was feeling marginally slimmer and just a little light-headed from lack of food and sleep. That was the problem with coke. One line was never enough, and before you knew it you were lying awake for hours staring at the ceiling. She must have finally drifted off around 3.30 a.m. which would account for the dark circles under her eyes. Still, that was what make-up was for. If there was one thing Caroline knew about, it was make-up. She had spent years researching the subject, seeking out the best products, and learning how to apply them with an expert touch. It amazed her, the number of women her age who clearly didn't have a clue where beauty products were concerned. It wasn't as if there weren't enough magazine articles on the subject, or sales girls eager to lend a helping hand in the hope of picking up a decent-sized commission. Yet you still saw women walking into fancy bars, or sitting down in posh restaurants, looking for all the world as if they had climbed into the tumble dryer with the contents of their handbag and simply hoped for the best.

Her own handbag was packed with what she considered the essentials for a night out – lipstick, mascara, blusher, compact. Not forgetting the little Tiffany pouch she used to carry her coke. She liked to tell people that she was just popping into the loo to powder her nose – inside and out. If one of the girls accepted the invitation to pop in with her, then more often than not they would emerge quite some time later with dilated pupils and a whole new face. Caroline could never resist the opportunity to give a girl in need a quick makeover, least of all when they were locked in a cubicle and already beholden to her. Luckily for her, most people were so familiar with the various makeover shows that dominated the TV schedules, and so used to the idea of a complete stranger stepping into their life and telling them how to make their house/garden/self more beautiful, they accepted her advice in the spirit in which it was given. Somehow, she doubted whether Pip would be quite so keen on the idea of letting another woman loose on her face. In fact, she would be almost certain to take offence. Well, that would liven things up a bit after dinner . . .

An image on the television caught her eye. A man dressed as a nun was walking hand-in-hand with another man in leather shorts. Behind them, two women dressed in rainbow tie-dyed dungarees with matching purple spikey hair were holding up a banner that read 'Survivors of Lesbian Abuse'. Maybe, but they were still victims of lesbian fashion, Caroline thought as she reached for the remote control and turned up the volume. A man's deadpan voice announced that it was 'a big day for Britain's homosexual community' (he didn't really pronounce the second 'o' in 'homosexual', so the word actually came out as 'homasexual'). Of course, Caroline thought, it was Gay Pride. Suddenly, she was transported back to the Pride festival she had attended five years ago. She had gone along with Martin to show moral support. It wasn't the best day out she ever had. She couldn't understand why anyone should be expected to stand around in a muddy field watching Dannii Minogue and eating veggie burgers, simply because they happened to be gay. And for someone whose previous exposure to the gay scene had led her to believe that gay men were either naturally better looking than straight men or at least knew how to make the best of themselves, some of the sights Caroline witnessed that day had come as rather a shock. For every well-groomed, handsome man who caught her eye there were a dozen more who wouldn't have looked out of place at a stag night in Swindon, not to mention a few who appeared to derive some perverse satisfaction from making themselves as unattractive as possible. The odd facial piercing she could just about cope with, but there were people walking around looking as if they were held together with staples.

The combination of bad pop acts, bad weather and a perfectly reasonable aversion to self-mutilation meant that Caroline's first Gay Pride was also her last. Martin did try to coax her along the following year, but once he picked up on her lack of enthusiasm the invitations soon dried up. Of course for the past few years he'd had Christopher for company. Given that this was no longer the case, Caroline did feel a tiny bit guilty that she hadn't suggested to Martin that she tag along this year, if only on the pretext of helping him cope with his father. Still, if she couldn't be there in person, she could at least be with him in spirit. Perhaps she would even spot him on the television. Leaning forward on the sofa, she stared intently at the screen as a steady stream of colourfully dressed people paraded past, many of them waving into the camera or blowing whistles as they went by.

Then she spotted him. It wasn't Martin, but it was someone she knew. Or at least she thought it was. She couldn't see his face, not properly, but she recognised the hat instantly. It was a cowboy hat, the exact same cowboy hat Graham had worn the night she went around to his flat and they had the best sex they'd had in weeks. And now here it was again, bobbing along at a Gay Pride parade. Right, she thought. Damn Graham and his temper. Damn his feeble excuses and his mysterious telephone calls. Damn his fancy friends and their posh dinner party. And damn his bloody cowboy hat. Tonight there was going to be a showdown.

Chapter eight

Martin and his father arrived at Hyde Park just in time to see the tail end of the march disappear down Park Lane. The sky had finally cleared, and the sun was glinting off the polished heads of the gay skinheads and the drag queens in their sequinned costumes as they snaked their way into the distance. Even from this vantage point, the cacophony of cheers, screams and catcalls was enough to drown out the sound of the traffic, edging its way slowly around Marble Arch. Martin spotted a man selling whistles, the kind that came on a fluorescent string you hung around your neck, and were moulded out of cheap plastic – pink of course. These days no gay event was complete without them, which was fine for those gay people who liked nothing better than to produce high-pitched noises at regular intervals, but a complete pain for everyone else. John always referred to them as the kind of whistles that were so shrill, they could only be heard by dogs and homosexuals. Martin usually found this funny, but thinking about it now he wondered if it perhaps contained an element of self loathing, and was therefore an inappropriate thought to have running through one's head on Gay Pride day.

'C'mon, son,' his dad urged, snapping him out of his dilemma. 'We'd better hurry up or we'll miss all the fun.'

'Are you sure about this?' Martin replied. He cringed as he caught sight of a drag queen hobbling towards them, dressed as Ginger Spice in a tiny Union Jack dress and enormous platform boots, swinging a bottle of champagne and blowing kisses at the tourists gawping down from the upper deck of an open-topped bus. 'We could just go back to the flat if you like. Or I could show you around the museums or something. Or how about one of the art galleries? We could go and have a look around the Tate Modern. Or there's the Eye of course. Maybe we could get tickets if we're quick. I can always meet up with the others later.'

'Nonsense,' said his dad. 'I can take in the sights anytime. And I didn't come all this way just to go poking around some museum. I'm not as old as you seem to think. I told you I wanted to come on this march of yours and I meant it. And there's no need to feel embarrassed on my account. I know you don't all want to dress up as women. This isn't the first Gay Pride I've been to, you know.'

'It isn't?' Martin felt his stomach churn. What if John was right? What if his father had come to visit him with the express purpose of revealing that he too was gay? What if he had been leading a double life all these years? What if that was the reason his parents had split up? It was all too awful to contemplate.

'Hell, no,' his dad went on. 'A mate of mine took me to the Mardi Gras in Sydney a couple of years back. We had a great time. I'll say one thing about your lot, you sure know how to throw a party. Some fella we met there gave me one of those

Ecstasy pills. It was just like old times. I haven't been so high since Woodstock.'

Martin struggled to take all this in. His father had been to Mardi Gras? Who was the 'mate' he referred to? And what exactly was the nature of their relationship? And he had taken Ecstasy? What happened then? Did it turn him into a sex-crazed monster? Did he wake up in the morning lying next to some strange man, with no idea of how he had got there, or what he had done the night before? These were the questions that raced through Martin's mind as he ran to keep pace with his father and they took their place with stragglers at the back of the march. What he actually said was: 'You were at Woodstock?'

'Not exactly,' his dad said, smiling. 'Your mother wasn't very keen. I did see the film though.'

'And you went to Mardi Gras in Sydney?'

'Yep. And I had a stall at our local Gay Pride down in Brighton last year. Where do you think I bought this badge?' He pointed at the badge with its 'Proud To Be An Embarrassing Parent' lettering. Martin wondered if his father had any idea of just how embarrassing this reunion was turning out to be.

'Anyway, enough about me,' his dad said, reaching into his shirt pocket and pulling out what looked suspiciously like a joint. 'When am I going to meet these friends of yours? And what about that fella you were with at our Emily's christening? Nice-looking chap. Christopher, wasn't it?'

Martin forced a smile. 'It's a long story, Dad. I'll tell you all about it later, okay?'

His father lit the joint, took a long drag and sighed contentedly. 'In your own time, son. In your own time. Now, which banner shall we march under?'

*

John was coming up on his second E of the day. It was several hours later and he was suspended in some strange underwater world, surrounded by shoals of shiny, saucer-eyed fish. This was very odd, since only moments ago he could have sworn he was in the Trade tent at the Pride festival in Finsbury Park. The march itself had been a blur. He hadn't seen Martin or his father, nor had he spotted Shane, and somewhere along the way he'd lost track of the two Steves. He still had his bag full of pills though, and he was pretty certain that Neil and David were in here somewhere, but he couldn't remember when he had last seen them. Was it ten minutes ago? Or an hour? He really couldn't tell. Everything seemed to have gone into slow motion, and yet time passed so quickly. He felt weightless, as if his entire body had gone to sleep, and at the same time every nerve was tingling to the beat of the music. It echoed inside him like a pulse, pounding out the distance between his last clear memory and his present sense of where he was and how he was feeling. Nothing else mattered. Time and pleasure were measured in beats per minute.

Someone brushed against him, and shivers of sweaty excitement shot through his naked torso. He opened his eyes, expecting to see Fernando. A strange face grinned back at him. 'I wish I had some of whatever you're on, mate.' John replied by lifting his arms high above his head, closing his eyes and smiling happily. There didn't seem much point in actually saying anything. What could he say? What words could possibly describe how he was feeling right now? How did that Madonna song go again? 'Words are useless, especially sentences.' It sounded so stupid at the time, as if she'd written it when she was sitting on the toilet or something, but suddenly it all made complete sense. It was easy to mock

Madonna, but that woman knew what she was talking about, even if nobody else did. Apart from him, of course. He knew exactly what she meant. In fact, he had always known, right from the very beginning. He just hadn't realised it until today. 'Only when I'm dancing can I feel this free.' That was what this was all about! The lights, the music, the energy generated by all these people dancing together, all these men with their shirts off! It was all about freedom! It was all about being yourself! It was all about the freedom to be yourself by dancing in a room full of people who all looked exactly like you! It was all about . . . Pride! Of course! He understood it all now! He just had to get it all straight in his head, then he would find Fernando and tell him, and then he would understand it all too!

He opened his eyes. God, it was strong, this E. He couldn't remember the last time he'd felt so mashed. Or so thirsty. He reached into his back pocket for his bottle of water. That was funny. He was sure he'd had it a minute ago. Maybe it had dropped onto the floor. Or maybe someone had stolen it. He looked around at the heaving mass of muscle, of glistening chests and waving arms. Biceps were the new pecs. He had to try to remember that. Dancing on E was all about Pride, and biceps were the new pecs. It was amazing how clear everything had become. And there were still hours to go, and plenty of pills left. If only Martin would show up soon, then he could share this with him. And his father, if he wanted. There were enough pills for everyone. Except David. He could buy his own drugs for once. Fernando would probably still have some left for sale, and if he didn't he would know someone who did. Maybe he should go and look for him. Hang on a minute, though. What was this song? Some screaming diva singing about how life was a bitch and how men needed to be kept on a firm leash? He loved this one! He would just dance to this song, then he would go and look for Fernando.

Suddenly a bottle of water appeared in front of John's face. He grabbed it and drank the entire contents in one gulp. 'Where have you been?' said a familiar voice. It was David. John could tell that he was agitated. His eyes were enormous, and he was grinding his teeth, causing untold damage to hundreds of pounds worth of dentistry. 'I've been looking for you everywhere,' David said. 'We're sitting outside with Martin and his dad. You have to come and meet him. He's a real scream. Oh, and Fernando said to tell you he'll be back shortly. He's gone to get more supplies. And, well, I hate to ask, but I don't suppose you've got any coke left, have you?'

John thought for a moment. David really was the biggest drug whore ever. On the other hand, he had just given John a bottle of water. In gay clubland, people fell head over heels in love on the strength of such gestures. Or should that be 'heels over head'? John smiled to himself and dug his hand into his pocket. 'I haven't got coke,' he said. 'But I have got something better.' And with that he handed David a pill.

Caroline took a stab at her crab salad with sweet chilli dressing and smiled across the dinner table at her hosts – Pip in her annoyingly girly Laura Ashley frock, Jeremy in his ridiculous embroidered waistcoat. 'This is really lovely, Pip,' Caroline said, in the same honeyed tone of voice she normally reserved for balding male business associates and very young children. 'I don't know how you do it. You must be so proud of her, Jeremy.'

Jeremy, who was in the process of topping up everyone's wine glasses with a 'simply marvellous' Australian chardonnay he had ordered from the *Sunday Times* wine club, hesitated for a moment before casting his wife a slightly nervous look. 'I am,' he said. Then, with a little more conviction: 'Very proud.' Pip smiled bashfully and began moving her food around her plate.

Graham was beginning to sense that something was seriously wrong. He knew that Pip and Jeremy weren't exactly Caroline's favourite people in the world. In fact, for some time now he had suspected that she only ever agreed to spend time with them in order to keep him happy. She was never rude, or outwardly hostile. And she was an extremely good conversationalist. In fact, it was one of the things that first attracted him to her. She could talk to practically anyone, about virtually anything, and you were never really able to tell whether she was enjoying herself as much as she appeared to be. Caroline could turn on the charm better than anyone he had ever met. Far from seeing this as a sign of shallowness, he regarded it as a measure of her eagerness to always make the best of a situation, both for her own sake and for other people's. It wasn't just good manners. It was the advertising executive in her, and at times like these it was a quality he appreciated more than he could say.

Still, there was something about her behaviour tonight which didn't seem quite right. There was that dress, for a start. He knew Caroline was never one to just throw something together at the last minute. She always spent time over her wardrobe, and was always immaculately groomed. Even so, a backless, black sequinned sheath with a plunging neckline did seem a little over the top for an intimate dinner party with friends. And why she had felt the need to dress it up even further with a chiffon and black feather wrap was quite beyond him. It looked like the kind of dress Diana Ross would refuse to wear, on the grounds that it was too vulgar. And was he just imagining it, or did Caroline's breasts seem even more voluptuous than usual? She couldn't have a Wonderbra on under that dress, could she? Whatever it was, it was clearly having the desired effect. Jeremy had barely taken his eyes off her cleavage all night.

Then there was all that talk about his and Jeremy's university days. Caroline had never expressed much interest in his time at university before, yet tonight she had steered the conversation back to it over and over again, first asking Jeremy about the time he and Graham had first met, and then making some very strange observations about the sorts of things young men might get up to and the kinds of emotional attachments they might make when they first find themselves living away from home. What exactly was all that about? He knew Caroline hated hearing about his ex-girlfriends as much as he hated hearing about her ex-boyfriends. Why would she want to drag up the past now? It wasn't even as if he'd had that many girlfriends at university. In fact, there had only been the one, and she hadn't lasted very long. He was far too shy around women in those days. Normally, he preferred to skip over the details of this chapter in his life. It was embarrassing, admitting that he had gone through university with barely a single shag under his belt. But under the circumstances he was glad that Jeremy had responded to Caroline's prying by pointing out that Graham's university days were not quite the orgy of womanising she imagined. Hopefully that had satisfied her curiosity and assuaged any nagging doubts she might have. Maybe now they could continue with their dinner in peace.

Graham's hopes were dashed the very next instant, as Caroline put down her fork and gazed across her crab salad into Jeremy's eyes. 'So tell me, Jeremy,' she said, cocking her head to one side in the style of a concerned daytime television talk show host. 'When did you first realise that Graham was gay?'

Martin was beginning to think that going to Gay Pride with your father wasn't such a bad idea after all. True, the day hadn't started off too promisingly. His father's enquiry after Christopher had sent him into a gloomy mood for much of the march, and try as he might, he couldn't get used to the idea of marching alongside a member of his own family, least of all one who made his relationship to you known to all and sundry with the aid of a frankly tacky badge. But by the time they had got to the park, Martin's mood had lifted considerably. This was mainly due to the vast quantities of dope his father encouraged him to smoke as the day went on. It was years since he had been this stoned, and he had forgotten just how relaxed it made him feel. He wasn't even embarrassed when, just after Steps had finished performing on the main stage, his father turned to him and launched into a long, rambling speech about how proud he was, knowing that he had a son with the courage to be true to himself in the face of so much adversity. The truth was, Martin didn't feel courageous at all, although it did strike him that there was a certain amount of courage involved in sitting through the kind of acts Gay Pride threw at you every year. But just having somebody say it made him feel good about himself in a way he hadn't felt for a long time.

He was still feeling chilled out when they ran into John's friends David and Neil outside the Trade tent, though he did think it was a pity that Matthew wasn't with them. That was until he remembered that the last time he had seen Matthew was at the underwear party. His father might have been proud to have a gay son, but he didn't think he would be quite so proud if he discovered what his gay son had been doing last Monday night. There were some things you really shouldn't share with your parents, however understanding and supportive they might be, and casual sex in gloomy basement clubs was one of them. Come to think of it, he wasn't sure if he was ready to see Matthew again, especially not when John was around.

'John's off dancing in there,' David said suddenly. 'In case you're wondering. I wouldn't mind, but I'm supposed to stay here until Fernando gets back, and I'd rather be watching the fireworks. Who's that you're with?'

'It's my dad,' Martin said, watching anxiously as his father wandered up to the entrance to the tent and stood peering inside. Please don't let there be somebody having sex in there, he thought. Not when things are going so well.

'John said you were bringing your dad,' Neil chipped in. 'I thought he was having us on.'

'Is that really your dad?' David practically shrieked. 'He's very good looking. For an older guy, I mean. I can see where you got those lovely green eyes of yours from. Actually, he looks a bit like Kris Kristofferson. Y'know, from *A Star Is Born*? I'll just go up and say hello, shall I?'

'Well he's a bit shy, actually,' Martin said, suddenly noticing the coke crumbs falling out of David's right nostril. 'Why don't we just sit down here and wait for him to come over? Then I'll introduce you.'

'I wouldn't mind a drink actually,' David said. 'I'll tell you what. You wander off to that beer tent over there and get us a couple of cans. I'll go and find John, and Neil can wait here for Fernando. Then we can all have a nice drink together. How about that?'

'Well, I'm not sure about leaving my dad on his own,' Martin protested.

'He's fine,' David replied. 'I'm sure he can look after himself for a few minutes. Now, off you go.'

As he trudged off reluctantly in the direction of the beer tent, Martin felt the soothing effect of the dope evaporate from his body. In its place came the uneasy feeling that things were about to take a turn for the worse. This feeling intensified as he stood queueing for the best part of half an hour. By the time he returned, clutching four cans of warm Red Stripe, a full forty minutes had passed, and his stress levels were the highest they'd been since he first stepped foot out of the door that morning. Where was his father? There was no sign of him anywhere. And what about the others, David and Neil? They had disappeared too. And John? Where was John? Surely they hadn't all just gone off and left him here on his own? He dropped the cans on the ground, stepped over a group of drug-fucked muscle boys sprawled on the grass giving one another head massages, and entered the Trade tent.

He spotted his father immediately. He was dancing with his arms high in the air, stripped to the waist, drenched in sweat. Around his neck he wore a pink plastic whistle. Dancing around him were John, David, Neil and a handsome Latin-looking guy Martin had never seen before, but who he presumed must be Fernando. And judging by the look on all their faces, Fernando's Ecstasy pills really were as good as John had said. His father's eyes were practically out on stalks as he turned and caught sight of Martin standing in the entrance.

'C'mon, son!' he shouted joyfully, popping the whistle into his mouth and blowing furiously. 'Get yourself over here, and let the old man show you how it's done!'

Martin stared in disbelief. It was one thing seeing his father stoned. After all, it was hardly the first time. But seeing him on E? That was a different story. What would it be next? Dressing up in drag? Fist fucking? He already knew that David found his father attractive. What if the E turned his father into a sex maniac? Would he be able to resist David's advances? Would he want to?

'C'mon, Martin,' his father shouted again. 'You don't know what you're missing.'

Martin paused. His father was right. He didn't know what he was missing. But whatever it was, he had been missing out on it for a long time. He couldn't remember the last time he had really let go, really lived for the moment. It was about time he had some fun. And what choice did he have, really? He could hardly abandon his father here with John and his friends. Anything could happen. And they did look extremely happy, all these people with their wide eyes and their waving arms. And it was Gay Pride after all. And he had just been through a painful break-up. And he was among friends, of sorts . . .

Suddenly John was standing in front of him. His pupils were so enormous, Martin could barely tell what colour his eyes were today. 'Here you go,' he said, pressing a pill into Martin's hand and grinning madly. 'This is a present from me. Because I'm completely off my face. And because you're my best friend. And even though I am off my face and I'm probably talking crap, I do love you. C'mon, take it. I want you to know what it feels like. It's like the music is inside you. It's like you're part of something. And it's like nothing else matters. Honestly, it's the best feeling ever.'

For a moment, Martin looked back at John, trying to remember the last time he had been so affectionate, or talked like such a complete idiot. He looked across at his father, who was still blowing his pink whistle and gesturing at him to come over and join in. Then he popped the pill into his mouth and followed John to the spot where his father and the others were huddled in a sweaty embrace. For the next half hour he felt nothing. He began to suspect that John may have given him an aspirin for a joke. Then he felt a strange tingle in the pit of his stomach, followed by a rise in his body temperature and a sudden, inexplicable urge to tell everyone within arm's reach just how much he loved them. For the next few hours Martin felt happier than he had ever felt in his life.

part two

Muscle

Chapter nine

It was incredible, Martin thought, how your life could turn around in just three months. Now that he had upped his gym routine to four visits a week, and his aerobic workouts to 30 minutes a session, he found that he had plenty of time for philosophising. Sweating away on the Stairmaster this particular Saturday afternoon, glancing appreciatively at his trim, Nike-clad reflection in the mirror opposite, he let his mind wander, happily taking stock of all the positive changes that had taken place since Gay Pride.

For one thing, he had a new flatmate. John's friend Neil wouldn't have been the obvious choice, but Neil had been pretty desperate for somewhere to live when the reputedly 'vile opera queen' who owned the flat he had called home for the past two years suddenly decided to sell up and move to San Francisco.

'It's bad enough that she only gave me a month's notice,' Neil had complained at the time. 'But San Francisco? Some queens have no imagination. Someone should have told her it's not the seventies any more and San Fran is nothing like "Tales of the City". More like "Tales from the Crypt".'

So Martin relented and invited Neil to move into the spare room. To begin with, he wasn't convinced that this had been such a good idea. Neil's habit of using female pronouns when referring to other gay men was even more irritating than John's. At least with John, Martin didn't have to listen to it morning, noon and night. And ideally he would have preferred to share with someone who kept similar hours to himself. Neil worked as a waiter at one of the gay cafés in Soho, but seemed to spend most of his time in the flat, talking on the telephone, watching daytime soap operas or playing music so loudly that the straight couple in the flat above were constantly banging on the ceiling to complain. On the Saturday when Neil moved in, he managed to annoy every other resident in the building by blocking the entrance hall with his belongings for the best part of the day. He then made matters worse by knocking on every door and accusing people of stealing a CD rack he swore he had left in the hall that morning, but which he later remembered belonged to the vile opera queen and was more than likely being used to store opera CDs in San Francisco.

On the other hand, Neil did have an impressive CD collection, large enough to fill a dozen CD racks, and mainly comprised of dance compilations with cover shots of half-naked hunks, the soundtracks to every film and television series featuring a gay storyline, and the complete back-catalogues of every remotely 'gay' artist. His video collection was equally large, covering everything from classic Victoria Wood to the latest hardcore American porn. He was also the proud owner of a handsome three-seater leather sofa, a wide-screen digital television with built-in video player, a state-of-the-art hi-fi, a laptop computer, juice-extractor, water-filter, humidifier, ioniser, exercise bike and enough skin care and grooming products to open a small beauty salon.

Neil also had a Ford Escort (purchased second-hand from a pre-operative transsexual who needed a quick sale to pay for her boob job), and an ex-boyfriend called Brian for whom he seemed to do an inordinate amount of fetching and carrying, whether it involved collecting relatives from airports or driving over late at night to help diffuse a situation with a casual pick-up who refused to leave or administer advice on which service to call when a pipe burst or the washing machine stopped working. Earlier this afternoon, Neil had driven Brian to Ikea to pick out some new kitchen cabinets. Martin suspected that Neil was still deeply in love with Brian, despite the fact that they had broken up almost three years ago when he came home early from work one evening and found Brian in bed with the gay couple from across the road. Whether it was the trauma of the break-up that first drove Neil to act out his sadomasochistic fantasies at some of London's heavier SM clubs, Martin couldn't say for certain. But he couldn't help noticing that, like a lot of gay men who spent much of their spare time suspended in a sling or lying in a bath tub full of urine, Neil tended to wear the wounded expression of a homosexual twice his age. John's take on all of this was typically acerbic. 'I don't know what the problem is with SM queens,' he sniffed when Martin raised the subject. 'If they want to know what pain is, why can't they just listen to Barbra Streisand's *Guilty* album like everybody else?' Neil's sexual practices aside, the real wonder was that his leisure pursuits hadn't led to any real physical harm, given his insistence on driving to and from the various fleshpots he frequented on a weekly basis, never once allowing the fact that he was driving to curb the amount of drink and drugs he consumed.

How Neil managed to finance this kind of lifestyle on his meagre salary, and could still afford to see a therapist once a week, Martin couldn't quite work out. But the fact that he always paid his rent on time, and was more than happy to share the benefits of his various appliances with his new flat-mate soon persuaded Martin that living with him might not be such a bad idea after all. Besides, Neil was really quite nice once you got to know him. True, he could be a bit moody at times. Tuesdays tended to be the worst, when he was coming down from the excesses of the weekend. And yes, he did have a habit of bringing pieces of trade back at all hours of the night and having noisy sex. On a couple of occasions he had even given out his address to people he'd met at some club or other and told them to call round if they fancied a shag later, resulting in Martin being rudely awoken at 5 a.m. and answering the door to some drug-fucked queen looking for a bed for the night, or what was left of it. On the other hand, Neil did have many fine qualities. Once a fortnight he dragged himself out of bed early on a Sunday morning and drove to the offices of a charity in Kentish Town where he helped deliver meals on wheels to people with HIV and AIDS. What's more, he was clean and tidy, and he did his share of the wash-ing up, which was more than could be said for Christopher. In all the time that they had lived together, Martin couldn't recall a single occasion when Christopher had lifted so much as a finger to help with the housework. And as John said, at least with Neil you knew exactly what you were getting. Try find-ing a flatmate through Gay Switchboard or one of the accommodation agencies and for all you knew you could be sharing a bathroom with the next Dennis Nilsen.

It was partly thanks to Neil, as well as John's ongoing relationship with Fernando, that Martin's social life had changed so dramatically. With Neil's financial contribution to the flat, and Fernando's enviable connections in gay clubland, weekends that were once spent holed up at home worrying over bills were now an endless social whirl of guest lists, VIP areas, free-drinks tickets and chance encounters with new and interesting people. Thanks to Fernando, he had even made it through the hallowed doors to Heaven's Departure Lounge, although on balance he was forced to agree with John's assessment that the bar attracted the kind of people he would happily cross a crowded dance floor in order to avoid. Not that this bothered Martin in the slightest. For years he'd felt as if he was on the outside looking in. Now finally he was in the midst of the action and on nodding terms with some of the gay scene's key players.

Martin had lost count of the number of minor celebrities he had rubbed shoulders with over the past few months – the DJ who once shared a squat with Boy George; the drag queen from Detroit who fronted every cross-dressing talent contest on Channel 5; the club promoter with the public-school education who careered around in head to foot Vivienne Westwood, feeding coke to anyone willing to tell him how wonderful he was; the door whore who once modelled for a famous fashion designer and whose face was never missing from the pages of the gay freesheets; the French photographer who fancied himself as the next Herb Ritts and took moody black-and-white photographs of moody black, white and Brazilian men in their underwear; the porn star who spent two months a year on the film sets of LA where he punished eager young pups with his famously large appendage, and the rest of his time working the arty circles of London where he presented a more sensitive front by reciting his poetry; the camp comedian who seldom smiled and could usually be found slumped in a corner at whichever club happened to be fashionable or wherever there was a steady supply of keta-mine. It was all a far cry from the life Martin used to know – so much so that, some Monday mornings, he could hardly wait to get into work and tell the girls in the design depart-ment all about his latest adventure. Their weekends were so dull in comparison, they never failed to be impressed.

They were beginning to comment, too, on the changes in his body. All those weeks of careful dieting and hours of painful effort at the gym were finally beginning to pay off. He had a flat stomach, a firm chest, and biceps that showed even when he was wearing long sleeves.

'You'd best watch out, Martin,' Melanie had said teasingly one morning during a coffee break. 'You're starting to look like that bloke from the Diet Coke ad. You know what us lib-erated women are like. Flash a bit more muscle and before you know it we'll be tearing your clothes off.'

Martin had feigned shock at the time, but secretly he was thrilled. This wasn't the sort of compliment he was likely to get from other gay men, at least none that he knew. Neither John nor Neil had been moved to comment on his new, improved physique. This was hardly surprising. They were generally too busy bickering with one another or comparing their own chest sizes to be remotely interested in his. Still, it was nice that somebody had noticed. In fact, it was the Saturday after Melanie complimented him on his muscles that Martin found the confidence to take his shirt off in a club for the first time.

Despite this, there was one aspect of his busy social life which he didn't share with the girls from work, and that was the number of men he had slept with over the past couple of months. There were enough gay stereotypes floating around the office as it was, without him fuelling further speculation about the sex life of the promiscuous homosexual. The truth was, he had dragged quite a few people back to his flat recently, each time hoping to fill the void left by Christopher, but somehow never quite succeeding. There was the tattooed, muscle-bound make-up artist he met one night at Crash, who once did Margaret Thatcher's make-up and who carried a note in his back pocket stating that, in the event of his sudden death from a drugs overdose, he wanted the world to know that he had died happy and didn't want to be turned into another Leah Betts. There was the tax inspector he picked up at Coco Latté, who had the softest skin Martin had ever felt but who turned out to have a boyfriend and some rather extreme views concerning under-age sex and capital punishment. There was the Canadian he met during a rare visit to a gay sauna, who later revealed that he was an escort and claimed to have slept with all the prettiest boys in Hollywood. There was the shop assistant he met one Friday night at G.A.Y., who came back and stayed for the entire weekend before suddenly announcing on Sunday evening that, much as he liked Martin, he was really holding out for a boyfriend with a place in the country.

The strange thing was, considering how often he went clubbing these days, he hadn't once seen Christopher. Of course that was one of the great things about living in London – the gay scene was so big, you weren't always encountering ex-boyfriends. It wasn't like Cardiff, where the gay scene amounted to a handful of bars and clubs and you were condemned to bump into the same people every night. On the other hand, bumping into Christopher now might not be such a bad idea. At least that way he would be able to see what he was missing.

Caroline hadn't had sex for three months. Three months! Any longer, and she would qualify for invalidity benefit. There had to be a law against this kind of thing, or at the very least compensation for all those smart, attractive, career women out there who, against all odds, simply weren't getting any. It was past lunch time and she was still wrapped in her dressing gown, nibbling half-heartedly at a cheese and tomato sandwich and flicking through an old copy of *Cosmopolitan*. She couldn't remember the last time she had gone so long without a good fuck. And to make matters worse, there was no promise of a good fuck in the immediate future. A bad fuck she could get anytime, anywhere. She only had to walk into a bar and men started undressing her with their eyes. She didn't mind this at all. It was just that, nine times out of ten, such men promised far more than they ever delivered. Their eyes were invariably bigger than what lay beneath their bellies. It was at times like this that she really missed Graham.

Their relationship was well and truly over. She knew that. It was hardly surprising really, bearing in mind that she had effectively outed him in front of two of his closest friends. As Martin said at the time, publicly accusing your boyfriend of being a closeted homosexual wasn't in quite the same league as falling out over who washed the dishes, or whose turn it was to sleep on the damp patch. The memory of that night at Jeremy and Pip's still haunted her. What possessed her to say those things? She would have blamed it on the coke, but she hadn't seen so much as a crumb that evening. It was one of the promises she regularly made to Graham whenever they socialised together as a couple – no drugs before dinner.

Claiming to have broken that promise would only have added to his sense of betrayal. The truth was, she wasn't even that drunk when the accusation sprang from her lips. It just sort of came out, if that wasn't too literal a phrase. She still couldn't say exactly why. A mixture of things, probably – frustration, anger, his secretiveness, her insecurity. She knew it wasn't the best way to tackle a problem. Getting back at someone you loved by using other people as an audience was cheap and cowardly, not to mention embarrassing for all concerned. How could she have stooped so low?

And why choose that particular audience? She could still see the look of thinly disguised glee on Pip's face as Graham stood up from the table, apologised for his girlfriend's behaviour and calmly announced that they were leaving. Once they were safely inside the car, he turned on her with a ferocity she had never seen before.

'What the hell was all that about?' he demanded.

Slightly shaken, she fought back as best she could. 'Why don't you tell me about Darren?'

'Darren? Darren who? I don't know anyone called Darren.'

'Darren who left a message on your answerphone. Darren who you met at that group you went to on Friday night.'

'What do you know about Friday night?'

'Just that you went to some group or other, and that you met some guy called Darren who sounds as if he's pretty keen on you. What does C.L.A.G. stand for anyway? Closeted lesbians and gays? What is it? Some kind of coming-out group?'

Graham's tone was one of forced calm, heavy with the threat of an explosion at any moment. 'Have you been going through my personal stuff? Listening to my phone calls? Reading my diary?'

'You didn't leave me much choice. You were so cagey, I had to try and piece it together for myself!'

'Piece it together? Piece what together? Who do you think you are? Nancy Drew?'

Caroline smiled triumphantly. 'Nancy Drew? That's a very camp reference!'

The expression on Graham's face hovered somewhere between pity and contempt. 'Well, let me tell you something, Nancy. You drew the wrong conclusion this time.'

And those were the very last words he had said to her. For the duration of the journey, he stared straight ahead, not catching her eye even once. She tried to break the ice by suggesting they could always find a man they both fancied, set up home together and then sell their story to the *Daily Mail*. He didn't laugh. By the time the car pulled up outside her flat the atmosphere inside was cold enough to freeze the elderflower sorbet Pip had allowed to thaw slightly in preparation for dessert and which was at that very moment returning to the icebox. Graham sat in silence, waited for Caroline to step out of the car, and then drove off. In the days that followed she tried calling several times, left messages, and waited for him to call her back and say he was ready to talk. He never did.

So here she was, a woman in her prime who hadn't had sex in three months, alone in her flat on a Saturday afternoon, and without even the vaguest hint of a date lined up for a Saturday night. It was pathetic really. There was only one thing for it, she thought, reaching for her address book, picking up the phone and dialling a number she hadn't dialled in almost two years.

A man's voice answered at the third ring. 'Hello?'

'Hi, Dylan. It's me, Caroline.'

'Caroline! Wow! Great to hear from you. How's things?'

'Oh, you know. Busy as always. You?'

'Can't complain. Well I suppose I could, but it wouldn't change anything.'

'No, I suppose not. Anyway, Dylan, I was wondering – what are you up to tonight?'

Martin was just leaving the gym when his mobile phone rang. The mobile had been a present to himself, a reward for all the misery and heartache he had been put through, and for the strength and determination he had shown in putting all that negativity behind him in such a short space of time. Besides, practically everyone he knew owned a mobile. Gone were the days when any gay man seen carrying a mobile phone was presumed to be either a drug dealer or a prostitute.

The call was from John. 'Hello, Daughter!' he said, sounding surprisingly bushy-tailed for a Saturday afternoon. Martin was finding it increasingly difficult to understand what John was talking about. Greater exposure to the club scene, coupled with the excessive amounts of drugs he took these days, seemed to have heightened his natural aptitude for finding ever more baffling ways of expressing himself. The fashion-speak which had formed the basis of his conversation for years had gradually given way to a strange hybrid of club-talk, old-fashioned double entendre and contemporary American street slang as evidenced on talk shows such as *Ricki Lake* and *Jerry Springer*. These days John no longer danced – he 'hookered it up' on the dance floor. He didn't take drugs – he 'larged it'. If he didn't like what somebody was saying to him he would invariably tell them to 'speak to the hand'. And when he signed off at the end of a telephone conversation, the chances were his parting words would be something along the lines of 'see you in the chill-out area'. 'Daughter' was his latest term of endearment, picked up from a conversation with a journalist from QX, the gay scene magazine, who was as famous for his flippant writing style as for the serious amounts of drugs he consumed. They'd met the previous weekend at a club in Green Park, squeezed into a tiny room adjacent to the DJ booth where the resident drug dealers and other assorted gay glitterati congregated to do lines of coke and bumps of ketamine. The journalist referred to the room as 'the broom cupboard of shame', which Martin personally found funny but John seemed to have a problem with, possibly because he refused to entertain the idea that anything he regarded as a source of pleasure might be in any way shameful. Instead he latched onto the term 'Daughter', which would have been funny and possibly even rather endearing, had he not taken to using it at every opportunity, and applying it to just about everyone he came into contact with. Still, it was marginally better than 'Girl', which was the term he'd insisted on using until recently.

'So what's new?' John went on. 'Anything to report?'

'Not really,' Martin answered, not exactly enthused by the conversation but still relishing the novelty of a mobile phone. 'I've just been to the gym.'

'Anything to see?'

'What?'

'No cute boys soaping up in the showers?'

'I wouldn't know. I wasn't looking.'

'Still playing hard to get, eh? Anyway, from what I hear there's nothing to see at the Y these days. I told you, you should have joined the Soho Athletic Club. Believe me, there's always plenty to see there.'

'So, what's the plan for tonight?' Martin asked, changing the subject before John could start regaling him with tales of all the gorgeous men who had eyed him up during the past week.

'Fernando thinks we should try Love Muscle,' John replied.

'I thought Love Muscle was finished,' Martin said.

'If you ask me, it is. But Fernando thought he might be able to drum up a bit of extra trade there. We can always go on to Crash later. So what'll it be for you tonight? Still just the one E? Or are you ready to experiment a bit?'

'What do you mean exactly?'

'Well, nobody sticks to one drug for the whole night these days. It's all about mix and match.'

Martin hesitated. 'But isn't that dangerous?'

John laughed. 'Haven't you heard of combination therapy? Leave it with me. Let's just say we might be in for a bumpy night.'

Dylan Morris was the man everyone assumed Caroline would end up marrying. That is, everyone except Caroline. Sure, she'd had a bit of a crush on him for a while. But that was way back when she was fifteen. She'd had crushes on practically everyone when she was fifteen, including Simon Le Bon and several members of Spandau Ballet, so that hardly meant anything – to her, at least. To Dylan, it had meant a lot more. They started off as friends. Both bookish, both outsiders at school – Caroline on account of her weight, Dylan on account of the fact that he was named Dylan – it was inevitable that they would team up at some point. Their friendship was forged at Mr Archer's reading group, where Caroline would indulge her love of Oscar Wilde and Dylan would brood quietly and strike poetic poses with the aid of his heavily gelled quiff. She made a point of ignoring him at first, thinking him arrogant and pretentious. But as the months went by she found herself drawn to this strange boy with his troubled eyes and his Morrissey fixation. He was the nearest thing to a boyfriend she had ever had, or would ever expect to find in a place like Swindon. During Caroline's last year at school they were practically inseparable, and when Dylan suddenly confessed that he was in love with her, that Friday afternoon behind the bike shed, she felt it only fair to say that she loved him too, regardless of whether she actually meant it or not.

She had loved him to a degree. Not in the way that he loved her perhaps, but enough to derive some pleasure from their fumbled attempts at sex, enough to make him the person she turned to when her dad died, and enough to carry on seeing him after she left school and he went on to study for his A-levels. But things weren't the same after that. He had a whole new world of higher education opening up in front of him, while she had a sudden urge to get as far away from her home town as possible. Gradually they drifted apart. When Caroline was offered a job in London and Dylan was offered a place at Leeds University, they swore that they would stay in touch. But in reality the letters and phone calls became less and less frequent, and the distance between them grew and grew, until finally it seemed pointless pretending that they were still a significant part of one another's lives.

So when they suddenly bumped into one another again, two years ago at a party in the Docklands, it was practically as strangers. She hardly recognised him at first. The Morrissey quiff had gone, together with his trademark black shirts and tortured look. He was dressed in a crumpled linen suit and a bright blue shirt and seemed remarkably at ease with himself, as if this colourful new ensemble reflected a happier outlook on life. He complimented her on her weight loss. She asked him about his job in publishing. They shared a joke about what ridiculous teenagers they used to be, and how silly it was that they had never kept in touch. They swapped phone numbers and promised to make more of an effort in the future. Then, just when Caroline's friends decided it was time to call for a taxi, Dylan offered to drive her home. She knew immediately that if she accepted his offer they would end up in bed together. Part of her worried that it would all turn out to be hideously embarrassing. Part of her worried that it would turn out to be perfect, and that she would regret never having made a go of it with Dylan all those years ago, the way her mother had always said she should. But she was a little drunk and more than a little curious, and she hadn't had sex in quite a while, so she accepted.

The sex was good. Not mind-blowingly, earth-shatteringly good, but pretty pleasurable and fairly satisfying, which was exactly what she'd hoped it would be. Dylan was gentle and considerate, and had obviously learned a few things since they were both teenagers. But he didn't drive her wild with lust. He didn't turn her world upside down. He didn't make her feel as if she had missed out on something, the likes of which she would never find with another man ever again. So when Dylan suggested that they meet up again, maybe for dinner or possibly to see a film, Caroline could see no obvious harm in it and agreed. It was only on their third date that it became clear that Dylan was expecting rather more out of this relationship than she was. They'd been for dinner at Joe Allen's and were in a taxi heading back to Dylan's flat in London Bridge when suddenly he turned to her and confessed that he was falling in love with her all over again. She stopped the taxi there and then, jumped out and, apologising for not having made herself clearer at the outset, told him that it was probably best if they didn't see each other any more.

The next day she sent him a letter, explaining at great length why she felt the way she did, how she didn't want to hurt him, and how she wasn't ready for a relationship. What she didn't say was that she would never be ready for a relationship with someone like him, someone who reminded her too much of her past, someone who would have been perfect for an uncomplicated fuck but who always had to complicate things, someone who asked more of her than she was willing or able to give.

And that was the last time Caroline had any contact with Dylan Morris, until this afternoon when, on a sudden impulse she was already beginning to regret, she had picked up the phone and dialled his number. And now here she was, sitting in the back of a taxi dressed in one of the sexy black numbers she kept for Saturday nights, on her way to meet a man whose heart she had broken once, possibly even twice, but who she kept telling herself was just an old school friend.

Chapter ten

It was Dylan who suggested they meet in the bar at the Sanderson Hotel. Walking through the entrance hall with its chic minimalist decor and fashionably underweight receptionists, Caroline paused for a moment to consider her options. Dylan was perched at the bar with his back turned, chatting to one of the barmen. It wasn't too late for her to back out. She could just turn around now, and slip away into the mild October night before he even realised she was there. It wasn't the most mature way of handling the situation, but considering the way things had turned out in the past, it might be the kindest option. Dylan was a nice guy – he deserved better than to be treated as her play thing.

On the other hand, who was to say that he didn't derive some strange satisfaction from being toyed with in this way? There were plenty of men out there who liked nothing better than to have a woman walk all over them. And it wasn't just the spike heels and nipple clamps brigade she was thinking of either. You didn't have to dress up in fetish gear to be a complete and utter masochist. You only had to look at the way some women cut themselves up over men to know that. In a sense, toying with Dylan's emotions was simply a way of redressing the balance of power between the sexes. And if he happened to get off on it, then ultimately there was no real harm being done, was there? Satisfied that her decision to come here tonight was the right one, Caroline strode casually over to the bar and tapped Dylan lightly on the shoulder.

He spun around so quickly, she barely had time to register that he was drunk. 'Hi, Caz,' he slurred, leaning in to kiss her cheek. As he did so, the glass he was clutching in his right hand tipped forward and roughly half an alcoholic unit of chilled export lager splashed down the front of Caroline's little black dress. She let out a gasp and took a step backwards, stumbling over a handbag which somebody had thoughtfully placed on the floor behind her and only just managing to maintain her balance. Realising what he'd done, Dylan grabbed a white paper napkin from the bar, leapt forward and proceeded to attack the soggy patch at the front of her dress, rubbing so hard that the napkin quickly began to disintegrate, leaving a smudge of soggy white paper particles. 'Sorry about that, Caz,' he said, still rubbing away. 'You took me by surprise there.'

Caroline bristled. 'It's fine,' she said icily, snatching the napkin from his hand before he could inflict any more damage. She wasn't sure which was worse – hearing someone call her 'Caz' for the first time in fifteen years, feeling every eye in the room on her as the lager seeped down her stomach and into her knickers, or seeing the mess Dylan had made of her dress. 'Just leave it, Dylan,' she snapped, as he reached for another napkin. 'I'm going to the ladies' room. Wait here. I won't be long.'

It took her five minutes to find the ladies' room, and a further twenty minutes to fix herself up and regain her composure. She removed her soggy knickers and placed them in her handbag, sponged the stain from her dress and dried the damp patch under the hand drier. Then, just to give herself the confidence she needed to go back into the room, she touched up her make-up before nipping into a cubicle, taking out her Tiffany pouch and snorting a quick line of coke. By the time she returned to the bar, Dylan was in drunken remorseful mode and Caroline was no longer in any mood to spare so much as a thought for his feelings.

'I really am sorry about that, Caz,' he said as she arranged herself as elegantly as she could on her bar stool and accepted his offer of a champagne cocktail. Considering the embarrassment he had caused her, it was the least he could do.

'It's okay,' she said. 'But do me a favour, Dylan. Stop calling me Caz, okay? Nobody calls me that any more.'

'What? Oh, yeah. Right. Well, Caroline, like I said, I really am sorry. And just to show how sorry I am, I'd like to buy you a new dress. If you'd allow me to, that is.'

Despite herself, Caroline felt her mood lightening. 'There's no need for that,' she said, smiling at him. He really was a sweet guy, for all his faults. It was hardly surprising that he'd had a few drinks before meeting her here tonight. He was probably as nervous as hell.

'But I'd like to,' he insisted. 'I don't know how much these things cost. Would a hundred quid cover it?'

The smile vanished from Caroline's face. 'Hardly,' she snapped, insulted by the suggestion that she would turn up for a date on a Saturday night wearing anything less than a designer dress. Then, remembering that Dylan was a straight man after all, and that straight men generally had little grasp of fashion, least of all those who worked in publishing, she softened. 'I can't take your money, Dylan,' she said. 'It wouldn't be fair.'

There was a long pause before he spoke again. When he did finally speak, he looked at her strangely, with a crooked smile and a glint in his eye. 'But what if you weren't taking it exactly?' he said. 'What if you were to give me something in return?'

'I don't understand. What do you mean?'

'Well, say for instance that I take out my wallet now, and I give you a hundred pounds. And say that I was to suggest something you could do for me in exchange for that hundred pounds. What would you think of that?'

Caroline took a sip of her champagne cocktail. 'I really don't know what you're getting at, Dylan,' she said, though in reality she was beginning to get a pretty good idea. He couldn't really be propositioning her for sex, could he? He didn't really think that she was the kind of woman who would have sex with him in return for money? It was such a disgusting thought, such an insult. On the other hand, she had called him up today with the express purpose of getting laid tonight. She had been planning on having sex with him anyway. And if paying her for sex gave him some sort of kick, or made him feel that he was in control in some way, then at least it removed any fears she might have about hurting his feelings.

Dylan must have been reading her mind, because at that precise moment he took out his wallet and discreetly removed five twenty-pound notes. 'Here's the money for your dress,' he said, pressing the notes into her hand. 'Now, provided you're willing and you think it's a fair deal, I'd like you to finish your drink and follow me into the toilets, where I propose to go down on you. What do you think?'

Caroline felt the hairs on her neck stand on end. She could-n't believe she was hearing this. She couldn't believe that this man she had known since she was fifteen years old, this man she had long regarded as sweet and kind and just a little too soft for his own good, this man she would have been perfectly willing to sleep with tonight if it weren't for the fear of break-ing his heart again, that this man was actually offering to pay her to have sex with him. And more importantly, she couldn't believe that the mere thought of this excited her as much as it did. It wasn't even as if a hundred pounds amounted to a lot of money, not for someone in her position. But somehow the thought of it turned what promised to be an otherwise dull fuck into something rather dangerous and thrilling.

'Well?' Dylan said. 'What do you think?'

Caroline casually slipped the money into her handbag, stood up and drained her glass. 'Well, Dylan,' she said. 'I hope I don't live to regret this. But I think you've got yourself a deal.'

John was busy baking. As a rule, cooking wasn't an activity he found enjoyable. In fact, he hated it. John was the kind of person who tuned in to Delia Smith's *How To Cook* and mar-velled at her ability to boil an egg. Tea and toast was about as far as his culinary skills went. When he wasn't faced with the promise of a tray of airline food, he tended to dine out or order takeaways from the local Chinese.

But then this wasn't cooking in the usual sense. The oven was set at 250 degrees centigrade, which was the temperature Fernando had specified before going out to make his regular early evening drop-offs in the West End. He had been gone for just over an hour. Soon it would be time to remove the Pyrex bowl from the oven and allow its contents to cool, before scraping the white residue onto a cool plate, grinding it into a fine powder, and then weighing it into little plastic bags with the scales Fernando kept for such occasions. But not just yet. Peering through the oven door, John could still see a trace of liquid in the bottom of the bowl. How much longer it would take for the remaining liquid to crystallise was anyone's guess. One thing John had learned over the past few months was that there were no hard and fast rules about these things. Fernando was right. Cooking ketamine was a complicated business, more an art than a science. Smiling to himself, John wondered what Delia would make of it.

This was the first time Fernando had entrusted him with cooking the K, so naturally he was feeling a little apprehensive. He'd watched Fernando doing it dozens of times, and had helped with the weighing and the bagging up. But to be left in charge of the cooking felt like a real honour. It was a sign that their relationship had progressed to a different level. A new bond of trust had been established. And despite the slightly worrying overtones implicit in the fact that Fernando was currently out striking deals while he was at home slaving over a hot oven like a dutiful wife, John couldn't help but feel a warm glow of contentment, the likes of which he had never experienced before. After years of sleeping around, and insisting that relationships were only for fools and lesbians, he was finally forced to admit that he was in love.

Of course it helped that the object of his affection was a drug-dealing Brazilian with a body to die for, whose arrival in John's life had made him the envy of all his friends. But there was more to it than that. The sex was the best he'd ever had, and after three months showed no sign of letting up, either in its intensity or its frequency. Fernando had a voracious sexual appetite, and not only when he was coked up to the eyeballs.

Some nights they barely touched the stuff and still they were at it hammer and tongs. And on those rare occasions when the coke did its worst and it was difficult to maintain an erection, help was always at hand in the form of Viagra, the illegal sale of which Fernando had recently added to his drug-dealing activities and which was proving every bit as popular at home as it was in the clubs. It was a wonder they hadn't exhausted their curiosity in one another, the number of times they'd done it and the variety of positions they'd tried. Their sex life was like a porn movie – so much so that these days John rarely felt the need to watch porn at all.

He had also cut down dramatically on the number of hours he spent online, cruising the gay chat rooms. True, he had enjoyed the odd encounter with 'CuriousCute28'. In fact, over the past few months their little cyber-sex sessions had become a welcome distraction from the boredom of long afternoons, and one that John enjoyed with increasing regularity. But masturbating over your computer keyboard while some hunky straight fantasy figure sent you dirty messages didn't really count as sex. And given that Fernando was the classic strong, silent type in every respect, John could hardly be blamed for getting off over an anonymous stranger whose way with words wasn't so much a threat to his relationship as a complement to it. No, all things considered, John was satisfied that what he got up to in the privacy of an internet chat room was nobody's business but his own. And unless you counted one very minor indiscretion with a Cuban go-go boy during a stopover in Miami, he hadn't had actual sexual contact with anyone other than Fernando in three whole months. Really, it was amazing what love could do.

Not that he had mentioned the 'L' word. Fernando was rarely given to outbursts of emotion. The exception was when he was at the point of orgasm, and would sometimes mutter unintelligible things in Portuguese. But declarations of affection weren't in his nature, and John knew better than to spoil things by coming on too strong. Besides, he didn't need soppy talk to know that he was in a solid, loving relationship. It was enough that he was here right now, carefully grinding up the K, while the man he loved was out making money in preparation for tonight's dance and drugs marathon.

Smiling to himself, John put the latest dance compilation on the CD player and turned the volume up to full. Then he helped himself to a bump of K and waited for the familiar syrupy sense of being suspended in time, in a place quite like the one he had left, but at the same time strangely different. He was living the life he had always dreamed of, and loving every interminable second of it.

Caroline left the Sanderson Hotel with a spring in her step and a warm glow in her groin. Hailing a black cab in Berners Street, she climbed in the back and instructed the driver to take her to Hampstead.

'Off home already, love?' the driver asked. He was the kind of cab driver she usually went out of her way to avoid – aged around the fifty mark, with greasy, nicotine-stained hair and one eye in the rear-view mirror constantly scanning the back seat for the slightest glimpse of flesh. Paranoid that he could tell she wasn't wearing any knickers, or worse, that he knew exactly what she'd been doing for the past twenty minutes, Caroline squeezed her knees tighter together and stared purposefully out of the window, hoping he'd get the message.

He didn't. 'You off to a party or something then, love? Only it seems a bit early to call it a night, a pretty girl like you.'

'I'm going to my boyfriend's house, actually,' Caroline replied, thinking off the top of her head. 'Now if you don't mind, I'm really not in the mood to chat.'

This caused the eye in the mirror to narrow slightly, but the voice remained irrepressibly chirpy. 'I don't mind at all, love. I was just making conversation. If you'd rather I didn't, that's fine by me. After all, you're paying.'

Relieved at the prospect of a few minutes' silence, Caroline sank back in the seat and cast her mind over this evening's events. She still couldn't believe that she had let Dylan go down on her – in the toilet of all places. She had never had sex in a public place before. Of course she'd thought about it, many times in fact, but whenever she did she tended to picture herself lying next to a stream or rolling around on the beach with some hunk as the waves crashed around them – not squatting on the cistern in a hotel lavatory with Dylan's face buried up her skirt, his penis poised to enter her and his hand ready to pull the flush and drown out the sound of her moans.

Supposing they'd been caught, what would have happened then? There was a law against this sort of thing, surely? Would the police have been called? What would they have charged her with? And what would her mother say? She could just picture her face, hearing that her only daughter had been arrested for having sex in a hotel toilet. She could still recall the time her mother came to collect her from the police station when she was sixteen, and had been caught shoplifting a bottle of body lotion from Woolworth's. 'We've got shares in Woolworth's,' she'd said, her eyes brimming with shameful tears. 'Stealing from them is like stealing from your own family!'

Maybe the police would have discovered that money changed hands, and mistaken her for a prostitute. Then what would she have done? She'd have been given the sack, that much was certain. And without a job she wouldn't be able to pay the mortgage, so she would inevitably lose her home too. She'd be unemployed, homeless and forced to choose between going back to Swindon to live with her mother, or staying in London and making enough money to feed herself by selling her body on the streets. It was a terrible thought, but given the choice she'd choose a life of prostitution over a slow death in Swindon any day.

Anyway, enough of this mental torture. She hadn't been caught, she wasn't a prostitute, and nobody was going to sack her and send her back to Swindon. She had simply indulged in a little sexual adventure with an old friend, and she had emerged from the experience emotionally unscathed, physically satiated, and a hundred pounds better off. Of course she didn't need the money. But the fact that Dylan had insisted on giving it to her did help alleviate any guilt she might have felt about reopening old wounds. In a strange way, she would have been more ashamed of her behaviour tonight had she not taken the money. And whatever else those five twenty-pound notes had come to represent, in Caroline's mind they stood only for what she was going to buy with them – two grams of coke. That way, the evidence of tonight's little escapade went straight up her nose, and there were no physical reminders.

Just then the cab came to a sudden halt at a set of traffic lights, and she looked up. As the lights turned to green and the cab slowly pulled away, her eyes were drawn to a couple walking arm-in-arm about thirty yards ahead. She wasn't sure why they caught her eye at first. Although they were facing her, it was too dark and they were too far away for her to distinguish their features. Even in silhouette the woman didn't look remotely like anyone Caroline knew. Then, as they drew closer, the light from a street lamp spilled over them, illuminating the woman's pretty, elfin face and sending a sudden chill down Caroline's spine. The man was Graham. And judging by the way he stopped to pull the woman to him and hugged her so tightly it looked as if her skinny body might break, he was very much heterosexual and very much in love.

Martin was beginning to feel anxious. Almost an hour had passed since he'd dropped his E, and nothing was happening. They were squeezed around a table in the café-bar at Love Muscle, John, Neil and himself, waiting for their drugs to come up and for Fernando to return from the toilets, where he usually found it safest to sell a few pills without attracting the attention of the club's security staff.

Just to add to the strain of the situation, John had spent the past twenty minutes angling for compliments about his new 'Twister' jeans which, fashionable as they might have been, did little to flatter his scrawny backside. Neil, whose own backside was looking rather pert in a pair of buttock-hugging blue combat trousers, had made no secret of the fact that he found John's jeans unappealing. 'It looks like your bum's dropped,' he said when John offered his rear view for inspection. 'And you know what they say. Men don't make passes at boys with flat arses.'

And so it had been left to Martin to massage John's ego and keep the peace as best he could. As the minutes ticked by and the tension mounted, he was coming to the conclusion that his best wasn't quite good enough.

'I can't feel anything,' Martin said suddenly, hoping to change the subject and perhaps gain some reassurance that he wasn't the only one whose drugs weren't working.

'Calm down,' said John. 'Sometimes it takes a bit longer to work, that's all. Don't worry. Fernando wouldn't sell you any crap.'

'He's right, Martin,' Neil chipped in. 'Fernando's drugs are good. I've always said that, haven't I, John? I've never bought any bad drugs from Fernando. Not once. She's very reliable.'

'Er, hello?' John snapped, sounding for all the world like a guest on *Ricki Lake*. 'That's my boyfriend you're talking about. So we'll have less of the "she" if you don't mind.'

'Sorry, I'm sure,' Neil said, nudging Martin to indicate that he really wasn't sorry at all. 'I didn't mean anything by it, dear. We can all see that you've landed yourself a real man there.'

'Yes, well, you're right about that,' John said sniffily. 'I wish he'd hurry up though. I saw one of those meat-head bouncers go by a minute ago.'

Neil rolled his eyes. 'He'll be fine. Like I said, he's a real man, your boyfriend. He can handle himself – and you, I'll bet.'

John bristled. 'What's that supposed to mean?'

'Easy, dear.' Neil smiled. 'Everyone knows there's only room for one man in every relationship. And you've already told us who wears the trousers in your house. It doesn't take a genius to work out that you're the one with your legs in the air. I don't know why you're getting so steamed up about it. Being a bottom is nothing to be ashamed of, provided your bottom is up to the job.'

John spoke through gritted teeth. 'Not everyone conforms to your pathetic view of gay relationships, Neil. Not everyone chooses to be either a top or a bottom. Some of us pride ourselves on being versatile.'

Neil laughed. 'You mean you're a bossy bottom who holds her own legs in the air! Oh, hang on a minute. I think I can feel the E coming up now. I've got that butterfly feeling in my stomach. Oh, yes. I can definitely feel it working.'

'Are you sure it's not just your time of the month?' John asked, grinning menacingly.

'Very funny. No, I can definitely feel it. How about you, Martin?'

Martin frowned and shook his head. 'I still can't feel anything.'

'Right, well I'm going to the toilet,' John said, jumping to his feet. 'Why don't you come with me, Martin? Neil can wait here in case Fernando comes back. You don't mind, do you, Neil?' And with that he turned and quickly walked away before Neil had time to raise any objections.

'It's okay,' Neil said in reply to Martin's quizzical look. 'I'm happy to wait here. I could do with a break from that one anyway.'

Martin stood up from the table and hurried after John, finally catching up with him as they crossed the dance floor and entered the men's toilets. It was still fairly early, but already a crowd had gathered. Topless men with pumped-up bodies and drugged-up eyes were standing at the urinals, frowning intently as they tried to pee or blatantly checking out each other's equipment under the bright, unforgiving lights. Others had formed a queue for the cubicles which, judging by the amount of water on the floor, were already feeling the strain of such heavy usage. A large group were congregated around the wash basins, pushing and shoving as they fought to refill their water bottles.

'I can't see Fernando,' Martin said, looking around and feeling the first warm tingle of the E. 'Do you think he's okay?'

'I'm sure he's fine,' John replied, grabbing Martin's arm and steering him into a quiet corner. 'He's probably on his way back to the bar. So, how are you feeling now?'

'Okay, I think.' Martin smiled, feeling the sudden rush of the E coursing through his veins.

'Well, I think we can do better than just okay,' John said. He took a tiny bottle of white powder from out of his trouser pocket and jammed it under Martin's left nostril, pressing the right nostril shut with his other hand. 'Now, sniff hard.'

Martin sniffed and felt a burning sensation shoot up inside his nose. 'Christ, that stings,' he said. 'What is it, coke?'

'It's a lot more fun than coke,' John grinned, fiddling with the top of the bottle before taking a quick sniff himself. 'Just give it a few minutes and you'll see. Welcome to the wonderful world of K.'

Chapter eleven

'The wonderful world of K.'

The words were imprinted in Martin's mind like the opening credits to a film as he trudged along behind John, back in the direction of the café-bar and the familiarity of Neil and the table where they had been sitting only minutes ago, but which now seemed like a distant memory. He had lost all concept of time from the moment the powder shot up his nose, so he wasn't sure exactly when it had started, but something very peculiar was happening. The film was about to begin, and it felt as if a part of his brain was literally opening up to receive the picture. He could even visualise it, could actually see the process by which layers and layers of half-realised thoughts and disconnected ideas were physically unfolding and changing shape, before regrouping into a new and unfamiliar pattern which, however strange it seemed at first, nevertheless made complete sense. It was a bit like watching someone skilled in the art of origami take a flat piece of paper and quickly fold it in ten different directions at once, until finally it wasn't a flat piece of paper any more but a paper swan. Only this particular origami demonstration was taking place inside his head, and it was happening in reverse. Folds were being lifted and edges smoothed out until suddenly the world was no longer three dimensional, but flat.

He giggled at the thought – the world was flat after all. Maybe if he wandered over to the edge he would fall off. But where was the edge? He had no sense of distance, no way of gauging the physical space between himself and his immediate surroundings. He was like a partially sighted man feeling his way in the dark, vaguely aware of obstacles in his path but unable to determine their exact size or position. He walked into a pillar and held onto it with both hands. He stood there for a moment, trying to get his bearings. How far away was John? A few feet? A mile? He couldn't tell. And the dance floor he was walking on – how far down was it? He had no idea. He was still standing upright, so presumably his feet must be on the floor. But there was none of the familiar feeling of walking, no sense of his feet making contact with anything solid. It was how he had always imagined it must feel to walk on the moon. He felt weightless, as if every muscle in his body was being pulled upwards by some strange force of gravity. Maybe if he let go of the pillar he would just float up into the air, past the lighting rig and through the roof of the club and high into the sky above. Houston, we have a problem.

It was weird, this drug. It was like seeing everything from a completely different angle. The hands held out in front of him were attached to his arms, so presumably they must be his. But they didn't feel like his hands. And the pillar they were clinging to – was it the same pillar or a different one? He wasn't even sure which club he was in any more. Was it the

Fridge? Or had they left there already and gone to Crash? He couldn't remember leaving, but then he couldn't remember arriving either, so who could say for sure? Maybe they had been beamed up by aliens, or had climbed into some kind of teleporter and been transported to another club, in another dimension. Anything was possible. Perhaps they were at Trade. At least that would explain why everything looked so unfamiliar. He took a good look around, and eventually spotted a few faces in the crowd he recognised – not friends exactly, but faces you saw regularly enough when you were all part of the same gay-clubbing fraternity, faces that reassured you of your whereabouts, faces that told you where you belonged. He heaved a sigh of relief. It didn't matter which club he was at so long as there were a few familiar faces, and something to hold on to.

And then everything shifted. Was it just a trick of the lights, or had the world suddenly changed colour? Everything was tinged with a haze of red and green, just like in one of those 3D movies from the fifties, only flattened out, the way the film looked when you took your 3D glasses off. Even the people were flat, like paper cut-outs, or that moment in *Tom and Jerry* where Tom is crushed by a steam roller or an anvil lands on Jerry's head. And those muscle boys dancing in front of him with their shirts hanging from the backs of their trousers – was it just his imagination, or had they mutated into giant peacocks? He stared at them and gradually the image sharpened, like a film coming into focus. Sure enough, there they were – giant peacocks puffing out their chests, resplendent with red and green feathers, shimmering under the disco lights. So this wasn't *Tom and Jerry* after all – it was Disney's *Alice in Wonderland*. And suddenly they weren't peacocks any more – they were flamingoes. Any minute now the

Queen of Hearts would appear and they would all play a game of croquet.

Oh, but hang on. It was all changing again, blending back into some semblance of what it had been before. The muscle boys were boys again, only now they were dancing in slow motion. They looked almost as if they were suspended in treacle. And the music had stopped. All he could hear now was the sound of his heart beating, and the laughter of the boys as they danced in time to his heart beat. And the slower they danced, the slower his heart beat became, until finally he was convinced that his heart was about to stop. Shit! It was getting scary now. His vision was reduced to a tiny circle, like the beginning of a Bond film or the view through one of those peep holes people put in their front doors for security. He could just make out the shape of John, disappearing into the distance. He tried to walk, but it was like walking waist deep in water, or running from the monster in a nightmare – two steps forward, one step back. He wanted to shout out, to tell John to wait for him, but he seemed to have lost the power of speech. His whole body felt numb. He turned around, searching frantically for a familiar face. He tried telling himself to stay calm, but it was no use. He panicked.

Suddenly he felt a hand on his shoulder. John's disembodied voice bubbled into his ear. 'There you are, daughter!' it said. 'You had me worried for a minute. Come on, I think we'd better get you some sugar.'

It was 1 a.m. and Caroline was lying in bed, studying the cracks in the ceiling. Since arriving home just over two hours ago she had drunk the best part of a bottle of red wine and taken two herbal sleeping tablets and half a dozen Melatonin in an attempt to knock herself out. But it was no use. Her body may have been ready for sleep but her mind certainly wasn't and stubbornly refused to be tricked into a state of stupor by any amount of chemical inducements she pushed its way. Of course not all of the chemicals she had pumped into her body this evening were conducive to a good night's sleep. The minute she walked through the door, she had hoovered up the remains of her coke in one enormous, fat line. But needs must, and after the night she'd had tonight, Caroline's need for an invigorating, confidence-boosting line of charlie was greater than it had been since . . . well, since she walked into the Sanderson and Dylan spilled his drink down her dress. The reminder of that little mishap was now safely hanging in the wardrobe, awaiting a visit to the dry cleaners. The money was still in her handbag, awaiting a phone call to her coke dealer. As for the other physical reminders, they had been soothed away by a long soak in the bath. It was just a pity she couldn't get Graham out of her system quite as easily.

How could she have got it so wrong? How could she have jumped to the conclusion that Graham was gay, and driven him into the arms of another woman? It was like a bad joke, too pathetic for words. Having gone over it in her head a dozen times in the last half hour, she was convinced that she would have felt better had she spotted him snogging another man. At least then she would have had the consolation of knowing that she'd been right all along, and that their relationship had no real future. Seeing him with that woman only reminded her of what she was missing, what she had been missing for the past three months, and what she needn't have been missing at all if she had only known when to keep her big mouth shut. It was like being shown a glimpse of the future she and Graham could have had together, then seeing it snatched away. This was her punishment for being so stupid, and for ignoring the advice of her friends. Martin had told her she was jumping to conclusions when she let it slip that she suspected Graham was leading a double life. If only she had listened to him.

She looked at the bedside clock. 1.20 a.m. Martin would be at Love Muscle at the Fridge now – at least that was where he had said he was going when they spoke earlier this evening. He had invited her to join him, only she had made up some story about meeting up with an old girlfriend, fearing that he might have disapproved of her date with Dylan. Martin may be gay, and gay men may be reputed to have more sex with more people under a wider variety of circumstances than any other species on the planet, but there were still some things a girl didn't even share with her best gay male friend, and calling up an old flame because she was dying for a fuck was one of them. Aside from anything else, it looked desperate and desperate women generally didn't go down too well with gay men, who preferred their female companions to have balls – in the figurative sense if not the literal (although judging by some of the drag acts Caroline had witnessed over the years, a pair of balls was all that was required for a talentless twat in a dress to inspire a level of devotion few biological women could hope to achieve if they spent the rest of their lives surrounded by gay men). She realised of course that there were probably a lot of gay men out there who felt just as desperate as she had felt today. But the difference was, when they were desperate for sex, they didn't call up an ex-lover and reopen a can of worms that ought to have been sealed and properly disposed of years ago. They took the far more sensible option and went and found someone new and exciting to have sex with.

Caroline threw back the covers, hauled herself out of bed and padded into the darkened living room, stubbing her toe on her handbag as she fumbled for the light switch. She yelped with pain and hopped over to the sofa, gripping her toe and cursing the fact that every handbag she came into contact with tonight seemed intent on causing her injury. The little Tiffany pouch was where she had left it, lying flat on the glass coffee table. Empty, it reminded her of a man's scrotum after sex – no longer plump and full of promise, but limp and sagging, a shadow of its former self. The only difference was, in her experience men's scrotums had a habit of refilling themselves, sometimes in as little as twenty minutes. It was a pity Tiffany hadn't come up with a pouch that could do the same. Still, maybe there was a bit of coke she had missed, an old wrap from another night, a line or two she had put aside in case of an emergency. She picked up her handbag and emptied its contents onto the table. There were no old wraps, no emergency lines, no coke crumbs mysteriously concealed in a fold in the lining. Instead there were the usual items of make-up, plus the evidence of this evening's transaction – a damp pair of knickers and five crisp twenty-pound notes.

It was too late to call her dealer now. Even coke dealers had to sleep some time, though how they ever managed it with so much coke in the house was something she would never understand, just as she would never understand people who did one line of coke in an evening and insisted that it was enough. Still, all was not lost. It wasn't that late, and she obviously wasn't about to fall asleep anytime soon, so she might as well go out and have a good time, preferably where there was a chance that she might bump into a few friends and maybe even a dealer or two. Nobody need know what she had been up to this evening. Desperate she may have been, but with a bit of make-up and the right bra, Caroline knew she could impress those gay boys as much as any drag queen.

She picked up the phone and dialled the number for Martin's mobile. A woman's automated voice told her that the phone she was calling was switched off. She hesitated for a moment. Then she replaced the handset before lifting it up again and ordering a cab to take her to the Fridge.

With the help of a large glass of Coca Cola, a large line of cocaine and a few well-chosen words from John, Martin had emerged from his K hole and was now dancing happily in the middle of a group of muscle boys, stripped to the waist and high on his second E of the night and the remnants of whatever other substances were still coursing through his veins. He hadn't seen John and the others for quite some time, and had no idea where they were, but that hardly seemed to matter. One of the boys smiled at him, and he smiled back in what he hoped was a friendly yet casual manner, fearing that looking too eager would scare his admirer off. It must have worked, because the next thing he knew the boy was dancing right up close to him, and whispering in his ear.

'What was that?' Martin asked. 'I couldn't quite hear you.'

'I said, do you like my body?'

Martin looked down at the boy's smooth, muscular torso and nodded his head. 'Yes,' he said. 'It's very nice.'

The boy grinned and leaned in even closer, till his groin was barely an inch away from Martin's own. For a moment it looked as if a snog might be on the cards. Then the boy turned and pointed towards another muscle boy with an equally smooth, equally muscular torso dancing a few feet away. 'What about him?' he said. 'Is my body better than his?'

Martin wondered if he had heard correctly. 'It's very nice,' he said again, hoping that this would satisfy his new friend and avoid any embarrassment.

It didn't. The boy scowled. 'But you think his is better.'

'I didn't say that.'

'Yeah, well, it was nice meeting you.' And with that the boy stomped off and disappeared into the crowd.

Martin considered running after him, then thought better of it. Someone that vain and that fiercely competitive could only mean trouble, and he was having a perfectly nice time where he was. He was surrounded by beautiful boys, more beautiful boys than he had ever seen before. He was in the ideal spot. What possible reason could he have for moving away? Still, there was always the possibility that the other boys had witnessed what had just happened and had decided that he wasn't someone worth knowing. Things like that went on all the time in gay clubs. If people in a gay bar or a gay club saw you being rejected, they didn't feel sorry for you. At best, they felt that there must be some good reason for it. At worst, they derived some perverse pleasure from your public humiliation and couldn't wait for an opportunity to reject you too. All things considered, it was probably time for a change of scenery.

He left the dance floor and headed back to the café-bar, half expecting to find John and the others sitting at their table. There was no sign of them, so he turned and walked the length of the club, past the main bar and the groups of late-comers frantically searching for a dealer until he reached the stairs that led up to the chill-out room and the upper bar. That was where he needed to be. If he went to the upstairs bar, he'd be able to look out over the dance floor and hope-fully spot the others. But first he had to climb the stairs. Could it still be the effects of the K, or were the stairs carved out of marshmallows? They didn't look much like marshmallows, but every time he placed a foot on the stairs it seemed to sink into the polished surface. Still, at least he could now feel his feet, which was a vast improvement. Finally struggling to the top of the stairs, he pushed his way through the double set of fire doors and stumbled into the bar, immediately colliding with two girls in matching shiny bra tops and tiny backpacks shaped like koala bears. The Fridge had always attracted its fair share of straight girls, and for some reason the majority of them seemed to hail from Australia.

Apologising to the giggling girls, he made his way over to the balcony, and was suddenly overcome by the urge to pee. Spotting a sign in the far corner, he turned and headed straight for the toilet. Clearly he wasn't the only one desperate for the loo because there was already a queue of men so long it stretched right back out of the door. He waited patiently for five minutes or so, until two men emerged from the toilet dripping with sweat and proceeded to squeeze their way through the waiting hordes. As they slid past, Martin felt a sudden surge of movement, not dissimilar to a rugby scrum, and a tide of tightly packed bodies lifted him off his feet and carried him through the dimly lit doorway ahead. The first thing that struck him was how dark it was. The next thing he noticed was just how many men were squashed into such a small space. There must have been thirty of them at least, all crammed up against one another in a shadowy mass. Surely they couldn't all be waiting for a cubicle? Pushing through the crowd, he felt his way to the urinal, unbuttoned his fly and began to pee. The sense of relief was so great, he rested his head against the wall and heaved a sigh of satisfaction.

Someone's hand slid down the back of Martin's trousers. His first instinct was to pull away, only he had his nose pressed to the wall and was flanked on both sides, making any sudden movement impossible. Looking down out of the corner of his eye he noticed that the men on either side of him were holding their penises in their hands, and that neither one of them seemed particularly intent on peeing. Frantically buttoning up his fly, he reached behind him to remove the hand that was now busy massaging his buttocks, only instead of finding an arm to latch onto, his fingers closed around someone's penis. Someone's very large penis. Someone's very large, very erect penis. In spite of himself, he felt his own cock stiffen, and slowly turned around to face his seducer.

He had a great face – dark hair and eyes, a strong nose, full lips, swarthy-looking, possibly Brazilian. He had a great body too – a broad chest, damp with sweat and a scattering of curly black hair, tapering down to a six pack stomach. And below it, poking out through what felt like leather biker's trousers, there was that enormous cock. It must have been eight inches at least, possibly even nine. Even allowing for the poor light and the distorting effects of the drugs, that was a pretty impressive package by anyone's standards.

Martin couldn't believe his luck. 'I can't do this in here,' he whispered. 'Do you want to come home with me?'

Much to his surprise, Mr Big Cock Brazilian smiled and nodded. 'Sure,' he said. 'Why not?'

Chapter twelve

Caroline's taxi pulled up outside the Fridge just as the unlicensed minicab containing Martin and Mr Big Cock Brazilian sped off down Brixton High Street. Oblivious to the fact that her one link to the world behind those doors had just left the building, Caroline paid the driver, stepped out of the taxi and joined the dwindling queue of men in skimpy T-shirts, shivering stoically in the early morning fog. She couldn't help but be impressed by the way gay men stubbornly refused to acknowledge the passing of time. It wasn't just the years they chose to ignore – it was the seasons too. It didn't matter what time of year it was – if you were gay it was always summer, and you dressed accordingly. It was a very un-British attitude to have, and she admired it immensely. She smiled to herself, thinking what her mother would make of it all. 'Just look at them', she would say if she were here now. 'They'll catch their death of cold dressed like that. Still, I've always said it wasn't natural, two men together. Flying in the face of nature, that's what they are.' Her mother, bless her, had never fully recovered from the news that Rock Hudson was homosexual. To this day, she refused to accept that any of the fey young men who presented her favourite television shows might be anything less than one hundred per cent straight. She was probably the only viewer in the country who still thought that Dale Winton was a red-blooded heterosexual and that Lily Savage was a woman.

The two surly black bouncers at the door greeted Caroline's arrival with fierce stares and sharp sucking of teeth. Unfamiliar with life south of the river and completely non-plussed, she smiled sweetly and flicked her hair back over her shoulder, allowing her coat to fall open and treating the bouncers to an eyeful of her impossibly pert cleavage. This was a technique she had perfected over many years spent queueing outside exclusive West End nightclubs, and she saw no reason why it shouldn't stand her in equally good stead in Brixton. Bouncers were the same the world over, and since very few gay clubs employed gay security staff, feminine wiles were no less effective there than anywhere else. Sure enough, the bouncers quickly ushered her in with a chorus of slapping hands and a flash of gold fillings. Unfortunately, the sour-faced queen in the ticket office wasn't so easily impressed.

'You do know this is a gay club?' he said, scanning his beady eyes up and down her outfit with a look of barely concealed contempt.

'Of course,' she replied quickly.

'Well, judging by the way you're dressed I assume you're not gay yourself. And I don't see you here with any gay friends, so . . .'

Caroline was about to point out that she was meeting her friends inside when a voice spoke up from behind her. 'Actually, she's with me.'

She turned to find an extremely cute guy of about thirty, dressed in a pale blue T-shirt and raw denim jeans, smiling at her with a twinkle in his eye. His hair was a dirty blond, and cut into a short crop which made the most of his high cheek bones, thick neck and bright cornflower-blue eyes. Caroline thought he looked just like the man from the Tommy Hilfiger ad. She didn't care what anybody said. It was true – all the best-looking men were gay.

'That's right,' she said, turning back to her inquisitor and grinning triumphantly. 'I'm with him.'

The sour-faced queen stared at her doubtfully for a moment, then caved in. 'That'll be ten pounds each please.'

Inside the club, the man introduced himself as Phil and showed Caroline the way to the coat check before offering to buy her a drink.

'So how come you're here on your own?' he asked as they stood waiting at the bar.

'I was hoping to meet up with a friend,' Caroline explained, suddenly thinking that Phil would be the ideal man to intro-duce to Martin. 'How about you?' she asked. 'Not here with your boyfriend?'

'No, I'm single. As a matter of fact, I was supposed to be meeting some friends too, but I've got a feeling I might have missed them. Mind if I tag along with you for a bit?'

Caroline smiled. 'Of course not.'

'Great,' he said, turning to pay the barman and then handing her a vodka and tonic. 'So, shall we go and have a wander?'

Caroline nodded. 'If we could wander in the direction of a dealer, I'd be eternally grateful. I'd kill for a gram of coke.'

Phil looked doubtful. 'You'll be lucky if you find any coke in here,' he said as they headed towards the café-bar. 'The police raided the place a few months ago and all the regular dealers were busted. If you do find someone selling coke you can bet it'll be cut with cheap speed. Trust me, it's a complete waste of money. You're far better off with pills. I've got a couple on me. You're welcome to have one.'

'You mean Ecstasy?'

He grinned. 'Yes, I mean Ecstasy.'

Caroline shook her head. 'I'm not sure about that. I usually just stick with coke.'

'Are you telling me you've never tried Ecstasy?' Phil's expression couldn't have been more incredulous if she had just said that she had never tasted chocolate, or had never watched a single episode of *Coronation Street*. 'You surprise me. I had you down for a party girl!'

Caroline blushed. 'Of course I have,' she lied. 'It's been a while, that's all.'

'All the more reason for you to try one of these,' Phil said, digging into his pocket and producing two fat white pills. 'A mate of mine gets them from Amsterdam. Trust me, they're the best there is.'

'Maybe when I've found my friend,' Caroline replied, wavering slightly.

'It makes far more sense to take it now,' Phil said. 'It'll take an hour for you to come up anyway, and by then we'll have found your friend. Go on, I dare you.'

Never one to resist a dare, least of all when it involved a handsome man and the promise of a chemical high, Caroline took one of the pills and popped it into her mouth.

'Okay,' she said, washing it down with a mouthful of vodka and tonic. 'You win. Now, how about a dance?'

At the far corner of the dance floor, John was trying to get an answer out of Fernando as to whether they should go to

Crash for a couple of hours, or just head straight to Trade. He had been trying for the best part of half an hour, with no success. The situation wasn't helped by the fact that Fernando on K was even less communicative than Fernando not on K. To make matters worse, Neil had just returned from the toilets where he had shoved a combination of K and coke up his nose, and seemed hell bent on complicating matters even further.

'But what about Martin?' Neil said, gnawing at his lower lip and staring frantically around the dance floor. 'Don't you think we should look for him? I really think we should, you know. I think we should look for him.'

'We've been looking for him for over an hour,' John replied tartly. 'He's probably gone home with someone and is in bed right now, having a lot more fun than we are. I say we go to Crash. It's a lot nearer than Trade, and with the state you're in I'd feel just that little bit safer driving a few miles down the road than going all the way across town.'

Neil looked as if he was about to pop a blood vessel. 'What do you mean, the state I'm in?' he screeched. 'I'm not in any kind of state. I'm quite capable of driving us to Trade.'

Fernando opened his mouth as if he was finally about to say something, but before he could get a word out Neil was off again. 'I can't believe I'm hearing this! I didn't hear you complaining about my driving when I came to pick you up tonight! But if you'd rather pay one of those dodgy minicab drivers to take you to Trade and probably mug you on the way there, that's fine with me!'

Sensing that he wasn't about to get his way and feeling his temper rise at the injustice of it all, John looked to Fernando to back him up, only Fernando was no longer paying attention. He had turned his back and was now staring at the stage, where this evening's performance was about to begin. Announced by the familiar holler of the club's drag queen hostess, which sounded remarkably like someone herding cattle, half a dozen muscle boys in various stages of undress strutted out onto the stage and began gyrating in time to the music. Next the drag queen herself appeared, tottering on in an outfit which made her look like a cross between Diana Dors as the fairy godmother in Adam and the Ants' 'Prince Charming' video and an explosion in a textile factory – long blonde wig topped off with her trademark wonky tiara, metallic silver dress mismatched with a purple fake-fur wrap, black lycra leggings holding in her thighs and pink platform boots chunky enough to support her not inconsiderable weight. Soon the scene had degenerated into one of unadulterated debauchery as the drag shuffled around the stage on her knees, servicing each of the muscle boys in strict rotation before turning to the audience with a look of smug satisfaction plastered across her face and a drop of what could either have been sweat or semen dribbling down her chin.

Fernando, who hadn't taken his eyes off the stage for even a second, suddenly raised his arms in the air and began applauding wildly. Knowing an appreciative fan when she saw one (which clearly wasn't very often), and understandably grateful for any male attention she could muster, the drag queen gestured to him to join her on stage. Before John knew what was happening, Fernando had climbed up onto the stage, peeled off his T-shirt and was unbuttoning his trousers, cheered on by the drag queen and a fair portion of the audience, who evidently found the amateurish antics of a drug-fucked nonentity infinitely more appealing than the slightly more polished performances they had witnessed so far, from boys whose bodies may have been the best in the business, but whose over-exposure in the classified pages of the gay press had gradually diminished their erotic appeal. Furious at the way they had been upstaged, and never ones to take rejection lightly, the muscle boys stomped off into the wings, leaving Fernando and the drag queen the sole focus of the audience's attention and one man's mounting indignation.

'Right,' said John, turning to Neil with a face that said he wasn't willing to be messed with. 'I don't care where we go, just so long as we go now. Crash or Trade, I don't care. Anywhere there's decent music. Just not here, okay?'

'But what about Fernando?' Neil asked meekly.

John looked up at the stage as Fernando dropped his trousers and the drag queen licked her chops in anticipation of a glimpse of a penis she hadn't seen or sucked a dozen times before. 'Fernando can take a minicab,' John said flatly.

Mr Big Cock Brazilian was sprawled on Martin's sofa, stripped to the waist with a sizeable erection clearly visible through his black leather trousers. Martin muzzled his chest contentedly. Mr Big Cock Brazilian wasn't actually Brazilian. In the cab on the way home, he had told Martin that his name was Clive and that he actually came from Barrow-in-Furness. But so far as Martin was concerned, the fantasy of the man he had been groped by in the packed toilet at the Fridge was still very much alive and lying on his sofa, waiting to have sex with him. So what if he didn't come from Brazil? He still looked the part, and considering the amount of drugs Martin had put away tonight, he knew it wouldn't be long before any piece of information that threatened to spoil the fantasy was conveniently erased from his memory.

That was the great thing about drugs. Whether you liked it or not, they forced you to live in the moment. And Martin liked it very much. He liked the way drugs made him feel. And he liked the way they made him behave, like someone who knew how to have a good time and wasn't worried about making the right impression, or obsessed with meeting the perfect boyfriend and settling down to a life of domestic bliss and dinner parties and dogs. With drugs, he could forget about Mr Right and make the most of Mr Right Now. With drugs, he lost all his inhibitions. With drugs, he didn't even know what inhibitions were any more. With drugs, even the word sounded alien to him. 'Inhibition.' What a strange word it was. 'In-hib-ition.'

'What did you say?' Mr Big Cock Brazilian's voice boomed in his ear.

Martin lifted his head and looked up at him. 'What?'

'You said something, just now.'

'Did I?' Martin thought for a moment. 'Oh, right. No, I was just going to say, do you fancy a drink or something? Or maybe a line of coke?'

Mr Big Cock Brazilian smiled and produced a bottle from his trouser pocket. 'I'd rather do K if it's all the same to you. I find it's better for sex. Coke just makes me want to shit. You want some?'

Martin looked confused.

'I meant, do you want some K?'

Martin laughed. 'Oh, right. Yes, sure.'

They spent the next few minutes passing the little bottle back and forth between them until finally the K kicked in and the desire to have sex as pornographic and as uninhibited as any early '80s, pre-AIDS, hardcore gay porn movie became almost too much for Martin to bear. He slid down onto the floor until he was kneeling between Mr Big Cock Brazilian's legs and slowly began unbuttoning his leather trousers. There was no telling exactly how long this task took, but once it was complete and Mr Big Cock Brazilian's cock was unveiled in all its tumescent glory Martin reached further down and began unlacing his big, black and really rather hard left boot.

'Let me do that,' Mr Big Cock Brazilian said, grabbing Martin's hand and pushing it away.

Martin tried to disguise the injured tone in his voice. 'Okay. I need to go to the loo anyway.'

He lurched into the bathroom, brushed his teeth, rummaged in the bathroom cabinet for some condoms and lube, and returned to the living room minutes later only to discover that Mr Big Cock Brazilian had mysteriously disappeared. Typical. The best-looking man he had managed to drag home in weeks, and he had gone and done a runner.

'I'm in here,' a voice called from up the hall.

Silently praying that his fantasy man hadn't climbed into Neil's bed by mistake – or worse, climbed into Neil's bed on purpose – Martin followed the sound of the voice up the hall, past the door to Neil's room and into his own bedroom. The bedside lamp was on and Mr Big Cock Brazilian was under the covers, his clothes arranged in a neat pile on the floor. Overcome by a mixture of relief, excitement, nervous anticipation and physical disorientation, Martin placed the condoms and lube on the floor next to the bed, quickly undressed and pulled back the covers.

Oh shit. There was something very wrong with this picture. It had to be some weird trick of the light, but right now, from this angle, Mr Big Cock Brazilian appeared to have a leg missing. Martin stared hard at the ten-inch stump where his left leg ought to have been and blinked several times. It must be the drugs. The K was making him see things that weren't really there. Or rather, it was making him not see things that were really there. Whatever, it was the drugs. It had to be. He would have noticed something earlier. And besides, what amputee in their right mind would go home with someone without once mentioning the fact that they had the best part of a limb missing? It didn't make any sense. Why spring something like that on somebody, when there was a very strong possibility that they might just freak out?

Mr Big Cock Brazilian's face was giving nothing away. 'Come on then,' he said, reaching up and pulling Martin towards him. 'Are we going to fuck or what?'

Martin was lost for words. Should he say something, mention that his eyes were playing tricks on him, try to relieve the tension with a joke? But what if the joke backfired? What if his eyes weren't deceiving him? What if this was real and rejection was something Mr Big Cock Brazilian suffered every day? Maybe if he just ignored the missing leg, it would go away – or come back, or whatever it was that limbs did in this situation. Carefully averting his eyes and vowing never to touch K again, Martin climbed into bed and switched off the light.

Caroline had watched Fernando's performance with a growing, inexplicable desire to jump up on stage with him and tear all of her clothes off. Never having met Fernando, she had no idea that he was in any way linked with Martin, although it would be fair to say that by the time the performance had ended she wasn't really aware of her own link with Martin and had certainly given up all thought of looking for him. The Ecstasy had lifted her up to a place she had never been to before, and she threw herself onto the dance floor with a feeling of complete abandon. She loved this place. She loved the music, and the lights, and the muscle boys with their oiled bodies and even the drag queen with her wonky tiara. And she loved Phil too. She loved him for standing up for her when the sour-faced queen was about to turn her away, and she loved him for administering the pill that had made her feel happier than she had ever felt before. But mostly she loved him for the way he felt, dancing close to her as he was now.

'Feel my skirt,' she said, and shivered with excitement as Phil responded by placing his hands on her hips. It felt so good, being with Phil like this, knowing that he was gay and that nothing sexual was about to happen, but still enjoying the feeling of his body pressed against hers. For years she had assumed that straight girls who hung out at gay clubs every weekend were simply afraid of straight men. They went to gay clubs to escape from all that male attention, all that testosterone. Now it suddenly dawned on her that, on the contrary, the reason they went to gay clubs was to get off on the testosterone, just as she was doing now. It made so much sense. It was physically stimulating without being overtly sexual, titillating without being threatening. And of course it was flattering that a man as gorgeous as Phil had chosen her as his dancing partner for the night, even if he had no intention of fucking her afterwards.

'Come with me to the toilet,' Phil said suddenly.

Caroline looked at him blankly. 'What for?'

'I've just remembered I've got a bit of coke in my wallet. We can't do it here in full view of everybody.'

Caroline smiled. All this and coke too. It was turning out to be quite a night. She took Phil's hand and allowed him to lead her across the dance floor, through the heaving mass of muscle and past the occasional girl in a glittery top, until finally they reached the men's toilets where, a couple of hours earlier, Martin had been given his first taste of K. Finding an empty cubicle, he ushered her in with him and locked the door.

'I can see you've done this before,' she said, as Phil tore off what remained of the toilet roll, wiped down the toilet seat and set about chopping two fat lines.

'There you go,' he said, standing up and handing her a rolled-up note. 'Ladies first.'

Caroline crouched over the toilet and snorted one of the lines. The sharp burning sensation took her completely by surprise. If this was coke, then it was like no coke she had ever tried before. What was it? Speed? As she struggled to her feet, she felt stranger still. Her vision blurred and suddenly she felt incredibly light-headed. 'My God,' she said, reaching out to steady herself. 'What the hell was that?'

Phil took her by the arms and smiled. Then, without a word of warning, he pressed her up against the wall and forced his tongue into her mouth.

She giggled. 'What are you doing? Oh my God! You're not supposed to be doing that. Naughty boy. Stop it. This is silly.'

But even as she protested, she was kissing him back. And when he reached under her skirt and peeled down her knickers she didn't raise any objections. As she felt him slide inside her, it suddenly struck Caroline that Phil wasn't quite the man he appeared to be.

Neil arrived home at 6.30 a.m., red faced and open pored from a visit to the all-night sauna in Waterloo. Before driving to the sauna he had spent a couple of frustrating hours at Crash, listening to John witter on about Fernando's impromptu stage performance and how he had never been so embarrassed in his life, except possibly for the time his mother caught him masturbating over the men's underwear pages in her Freeman's catalogue. When Fernando finally put in an appearance, shortly after three, he and John launched into a fight the likes of which Neil hadn't witnessed since *Dynasty* was taken off the air. Ignoring John's plea that he drive them all to Trade, he had made his excuses and left. 'I suppose you're off to be a floozie in a Jacuzzi,' John had said as they parted company.

In actual fact, Neil only decided to visit the sauna when he got into his car, drove up South Lambeth Road and spotted the leather men pouring out of The Hoist. Realising that his sexual frustration was about to get the better of him, he turned the car around and headed down towards Waterloo Bridge. As was so often the case, the pickings at the sauna had been pretty slim. There were the usual assortment of fat old men and young Orientals, plus the odd E head who had wandered in full of love and spunk, but who couldn't maintain an erection long enough to express much of either. Still, Neil had long since learned to make do with whatever was available. He also knew that, in the competitive world of gay casual sex, a plain face such as his could be forgiven provided certain rules were observed. In a fetish club, this meant appealing to the particular tastes of others by dressing in an appropriate manner or otherwise indicating his readiness to act out whatever fantasy was required. In a situation such as this, it meant making the most of his main asset – his body – and being prepared to take a few knocks before finding a willing partner, as he knew he would eventually. In this respect a gay sauna wasn't so different from a straight nightclub – in either case, a decent pair of tits went a long way. After several unsuccessful attempts to muscle in on a gang bang involving four

skinheads in the steam room, he settled for a skinny lad with
nervous eyes and an enormous cock who reminded him of
one of those dogs you saw being led around on a rope by a
crustie with a bag filled with copies of the *Big Issue* and a
kebab in their pocket. The sex had been adequate if a little
perfunctory. But at least he knew he would sleep better
tonight.

Creeping past Martin's door he made his way into the living
room, eager to check if there were any messages from Brian,
thanking him for driving him to Ikea this afternoon or enlist-
ing his help with some other errand that required an
ex-boyfriend with a set of wheels. Switching on the living-
room light, he was a little surprised to find an artificial leg
propped up behind the sofa.

Chapter thirteen

The first thing John wanted to know when he phoned on Monday morning was whether Martin had suddenly developed a passion for acrotomophilia.

'What's that?' Martin asked, although he had a rough idea.

John sniggered. 'I looked it up in the *Encyclopedia of Unusual Sex Practices*. Apparently, it means people who get a kick from having sex with amputees. I knew you were off your face on Saturday, but I had no idea you were planning to get quite so legless.'

Martin was at his desk, working on the packaging design for a new line of 95% fat-free desserts, and still feeling bloated from the pepperoni pizza with extra cheese, followed by half a carton of Belgian Chocolate Häagen Dazs, which Neil had encouraged him to tuck into the night before. All things considered, he was in no mood for John's sadistic sense of humour. 'It wasn't funny, John,' he snapped. 'If you must know, I found the whole thing quite traumatic. One minute he was just this normal-looking guy, the next minute he was in bed, waving his stump at me. He should have warned me. He could have said something.'

'No, you're absolutely right,' John said, stifling his giggles. 'There are some queens out there who should carry a public health warning. "I've only got one leg." Or "I live in Zone Three." It isn't right, springing surprises on people like that.'

Martin quickly changed the subject. 'You sound a bit blocked up. Are you sure you're not coming down with flu or something?'

'Just a little Colombian cold,' John replied dismissively. 'One of the few drawbacks of dating a coke dealer. Believe me it was a lot worse yesterday. I woke up thinking my nose was having a period. By lunchtime it was more like a miscarriage. Still, better out than in.'

'How are things with you and Fernando?' Martin asked, seizing an opportunity to give John a taste of his own medicine. 'Neil said you two had quite a falling out on Saturday.'

Now it was John's turn to come over all defensive. 'Neil doesn't know what he's talking about,' he sniffed. 'Anyway, I've got a bone to pick with Neil. Did she tell you she refused to drive us to Trade? Well, you'll never guess who was there. Only Tom Cruise.'

'Really?' Martin said doubtfully. Completely unverified rumours that Tom Cruise had been spotted at Trade circulated the London gay scene all the time, stirred up at regular intervals by people who firmly believed that *Top Gun* was a gay love story and that Nicole Kidman was a lesbian. In fact, the only rumour more persistent was the one which claimed that Madonna was booked to perform a surprise gig at Heaven. So far neither rumour had been confirmed.

'Yes,' John went on excitedly. 'You know Fernando's friend Roberto? Well, he was at Trade on Saturday and he says he saw him with his own eyes.'

'Is this the same Roberto who once claimed that he saw the Virgin Mary at Salvation?' Martin scoffed. 'And didn't it turn out to be some drag queen dancing with too many glow sticks? And what about the time he went to that swish party in Chelsea and swore that he saw Brad Pitt having sex with the host on the stairs? Or the time he said Jean-Claude Van Damme flashed his cock at him at the Oasis? Or how about that morning he was leaving the Dorchester Hotel after spending the night with that businessman, and Ricky Martin cruised him in the lobby? Don't you think it's a bit odd that the only famous people Roberto ever claims to have met are the ones he also happens to fancy? I suppose you'll be telling me "Tom Cruise" chatted him up next.'

'Well as a matter of fact he did say that Tom cruised him.'

Martin laughed. 'Honestly, John, you can't believe a word Roberto says. Anyone who does that many drugs is hardly a reliable source of information.'

'Maybe not,' John shot back. 'But I'm sure Roberto wouldn't have waited until he got home to discover that the hunk he had picked up for the night was one pin short of a pair. Anyway, never mind all that. I can't talk for long. You know what they say – life and Tom Cruise are too short. The reason I'm calling is that Fernando has some tickets for the Spice Girls' launch party tonight and I was wondering if you fancied coming along. The album's crap apparently, but it's at this really cool new place in Leicester Square called Red Cube. Plus David Beckham might be there and there's bound to be loads of free drink.'

'Hang on a minute,' Martin said, 'How come Fernando gets invited to record company parties all of a sudden?'

John slipped into his New York sassy black bitch mode. 'Er, hello? Honestly, daughter! I swear I don't know where you're coming from sometimes. Let's just say he has a lot of contacts in the music industry, okay? Now, do you want to come or not?'

'I suppose so. I mean, yes. Thanks.'

'Good. We're meeting in The Box at nine. Don't be late. Oh, and Martin?'

'Yes?'

'Don't get into a panic over what to wear. If you get really stumped, at least you know who to call.'

Caroline woke up feeling sick to her stomach. By the time she arrived at work, the sensation had crept down to her lower abdomen. By lunchtime, it had settled in her groin, which seemed to indicate that the nausea was in some way related to the events of Saturday night. Sitting with some of the girls from the agency in the local Italian, picking at her chef's salad and fielding questions about what sort of weekend she'd had, she could barely muster enough enthusiasm to make her lies sound even remotely convincing. The longer it dragged on, the more she regretted not having come up with a convenient excuse for skipping this week's female-bonding session. A long lunch with a particularly demanding client would have been less gruelling. Listening to Paula, Sophie and Tamsin as they swapped stories about romantic dinners and early nights and breakfasts in bed and brisk walks in the country, she felt every bit as much of a freak as she had felt at fifteen. It didn't matter that she no longer looked the part. It didn't matter that she had sweated, starved and shelled out vast sums of money to become the sleek, sophisticated woman she was today. Inside this carefully conditioned body there was the mind of a fat fifteen-year-old girl struggling to get out, and if she didn't get a hold of herself soon, that teenager was going to blow her cover once and for all.

Maybe it would be better if she did. At least it would take away the strain of all this pretending. And it would certainly make for a more interesting lunch. She tried to imagine how the conversation would go if she just cut through all the bull-shit and came out with the truth.

'So, how was your weekend?' Paula would say.

'Well, Paula', she would reply. 'First I was paid a hundred pounds by an ex-boyfriend to let him go down on me in the ladies' loo at the Sanderson Hotel. Have you been to the Sanderson? Oh, you really must. It's terribly chic. You'd love it, Paula, you really would. And after that, what did I do? Oh yes, that's right. Then I went to a gay club in Brixton where I took Ecstasy and watched a drag queen perform fellatio on half a dozen male strippers, before being led into the men's toilets by a gay man who actually turned out to be straight and proved it by fucking me senseless.'

'And is this something you do often?' Sophie would ask. 'Only I don't think my Justin would be at all happy if I got up to anything like that.'

'Quite often, yes', she would answer. 'When I'm not rolling around on crisp Versace sheets with my adoring boyfriend, planning our wedding day and debating whether to have the honeymoon in Bali or the Seychelles, there's nothing I like more than sex with strangers in public places. Toilets are a particular favourite. It's the smell, you see. That, and the fact that I could get caught at any moment. Turns me on like nobody's business. I think it stems back to my childhood, when the window cleaner caught me masturbating in the bath with a loofah. Luckily for me, Graham is very broad-minded about these things. In fact, we were thinking of cancelling our wedding reception and having an orgy instead. My gay boyfriend will be invited to attend, of course, along with Graham's latest bit on the side. It should be quite a night.'

'And did you make it over to Richmond to visit the in-laws on Sunday?' Tamsin would enquire. 'Or were you too tired after all that fucking?'

'As a matter of fact I *was* a little tired', she would say. 'But I usually find that if I shove half a gram of cocaine up my nose before breakfast, that pretty much sets me up for the day. And you know how Sunday lunch can wreak havoc with a girl's figure? Well, with coke it needn't be a problem. Just one little line before lunch is guaranteed to take the edge off your appetite. Then after lunch, another little line ensures that any nasty bits of food left in your stomach are flushed down the toilet in a matter of minutes, leaving you free to drink as many vodka and tonics as you want without worrying about the calories. It couldn't be simpler.'

Actually it could be – a lot simpler. She could joke about it all she wanted, but the truth was that right now her life was a complete mess. She only had to consider the evidence. First she had broken up with Graham because she had mistakenly believed that he was a gay man passing himself off as straight, and using her as a cover for his shameful existence. Then she had been taken advantage of by Phil, who had turned out to be a straight man passing himself off as gay, and used her as a receptacle for his shameless desires. Not that she hadn't enjoyed her brief coupling with Phil – in a dirty, druggy, 'If my mother could see me now she'd probably faint' kind of a way. But coming so soon after her equally dirty if not quite so druggy coupling with Dylan, it did make her wonder whether her sex life wasn't spinning ever-so-slightly out of control, and whether her mother's imagined response might not be entirely justified. Two casual encounters in two toilets in one night. George Michael was arrested for less than that.

'So what do you think?' Sophie said.

Caroline looked up. 'What?'

'About Sophie's proposal,' Paula said, widening her eyes and grinning madly.

Caroline looked blank.

'Justin has asked Sophie to marry him,' Tamsin explained helpfully. 'And they've already booked the church and everything. Isn't that just the most romantic thing you've ever heard?'

Caroline forced a smile. 'Yes, that's wonderful,' she said. 'Congratulations, Sophie. You must be thrilled.'

'Oh, I am,' Sophie cooed, all damp-eyed. 'And naturally you're invited to the wedding. And that mysterious boyfriend of yours. You know we're all just dying to meet him.'

Caroline barely skipped a beat. 'Of course,' she said. 'We wouldn't miss it for the world.'

Martin arrived home early from work to find Neil spread out on the living-room floor, watching an episode of *Ricki Lake* entitled 'I Want A Real Man, Not A Queen'. The studio was filled with some of the more outlandish examples of American gay manhood, namely those poor lost souls who would never make it into a Gap ad or a Madonna video and consoled themselves by plucking their eyebrows into oblivion and appearing on TV talk shows where they played to the cameras by snapping their fingers and calling each other 'girl-friend'. The audience's sympathies were clearly on the side of the long-suffering 'straight-acting' boyfriends, who in any other context would have come across as the hissy queens they clearly were, but who benefited hugely from the fact that their partners wore far more make-up than they did and weren't the least bit embarrassed about putting on a performance for the straight folks watching at home.

'I don't know why I watch this show,' Neil complained as Martin walked into the room. 'I thought Ricki was supposed to be on our side, but I don't see how a freakshow like this is meant to help anyone. It just gives them even more ammunition to throw at us.' Neil often referred to the gulf of understanding between gay and straight people as a simple matter of sides, a battle between 'them' and 'us'. This went some way towards explaining why he couldn't count a single straight woman or man among his circle of friends, which was mainly comprised of ex-boyfriends, fellow fetishists and a couple of guys from the gym. Neil's social circle was even considered a little strange by John, though for rather different reasons. John thought Neil's habit of remaining friends with former lovers was a sign that Neil was turning into a lesbian.

'John phoned earlier,' Martin said.

Neil didn't look up. 'Really?' he said quickly. 'And how is the Wicked Witch of the West End?'

Martin paused. 'He's fine. Only I do wish you hadn't told him about that guy only having one leg. You know what he's like.'

'Sorry,' Neil replied sulkily. 'I didn't realise it was such a big secret.'

'It isn't,' Martin said calmly. 'I just wish there were some things I could keep to myself, that's all.'

Neil's customary wounded look became positively pitiful, until it resembled something you'd expect to see on *Pet*

Rescue, rather than on the face of a man in his early thirties. 'If you want me to move out, you only have to say the word. I don't want to stay where I'm not wanted.'

Martin took a deep breath. 'I never said I wanted you to move out, Neil. I like having you here. All I said was that I'd like a little privacy.'

'Fine,' Neil said huffily, and turned back to *Ricki Lake*.

Martin hovered in the doorway for a moment, eager to avoid any unnecessary unpleasantness. Given the opportunity, Neil could sulk for days on end, and with his flatmate's midweek comedown still to come, Martin didn't want to start the week off on the wrong foot. 'I'm going to make some tea,' he said eventually. 'Do you want some?'

'No thanks,' Neil answered crisply. 'By the way, a package arrived for you this morning. I left it in the kitchen. I wouldn't want you thinking I'm prying or anything, but I've got a funny feeling it's from your dad.'

'Thanks,' Martin said, and headed into the kitchen. The large, oblong package was sitting on the kitchen table. He could tell straightaway that Neil's assumption had been correct. If nothing else, the wrapping paper was a dead giveaway. Who else would wrap a parcel with pages torn from the *Brighton Parishioners News*? Only his father, who was far more concerned with saving trees than saving souls, would see this as the proper recycling of natural resources. God knows he must have been leading the local parishioners a merry little dance over the past few months, because these packages had become as regular as church bells. The first one had arrived a week after Pride. Unaccustomed to receiving anything other than household bills and the occasional postcard through the post, Martin had torn into it with glee, and was a little disappointed to find the first of many self-help books, together with a packet of condoms and a brief note from his father thanking him for a wonderful day out and explaining the thinking behind his choice of gift. 'I hope you don't think I'm interfering', he had written, 'but I had the strong sense last weekend that you weren't very happy and I thought this might help.' Beneath the note was a book entitled *How To Be A Happy Homosexual*.

Since then the books had come thick and fast, and had built up into quite a library. There was *Out of the Closets – Voices of Gay Liberation*, which aimed to instill a sense of pride in the reader through the retelling of stories surrounding the Stonewall Riots and the subsequent birth of the Gay Liberation Movement. There was *Young, Gay and Proud*, which purported to tell young gay people everything they needed to know in order to find happiness in a homophobic world. There was a truly bizarre book entitled *Proust, Cole Porter, Michelangelo, Marc Almond and Me*, which seemed to suggest that the secret to a fulfilling gay life lay in claiming kinship with famous homosexuals from history (Martin noted that the likes of Dennis Nilsen and Jeffrey Dahmer were conspicuously absent from the list). There was *How To Survive Your Own Gay Life*, which offered 'An Adult Guide to Love, Sex and Relationships', whilst at the same time implying that gay men were often their own worst enemies. Finally, there was *Gay Shame and How To Beat It*, which took this theme further, with extensive chapters on the perils of 'internalised homophobia' and suggested exercises for overcoming feelings of shame and low self worth. Nowhere did it mention the kinds of exercises one could do at the gym.

Well intentioned as these gifts clearly were, Martin couldn't help but feel a little insulted by the implication that he was an emotional cripple in need of professional guidance. It wasn't as if he was still a teenager and had just come out. He had been an out and proud gay man all of his adult life, and had been on countless Gay Pride marches to prove it, not to mention the odd activist demonstration back in the days when such things were all the rage. More than once, he had considered writing to his father and explaining that, much as he appreciated the thought behind his little gifts, he really didn't need them. The fact that he hadn't yet got around to putting pen to paper merely showed that he didn't want to hurt his father's feelings, and was by no means an example of the crippling arrested development and complete lack of personal motivation described in some of the books.

Feeling rather like a child on Christmas morning, opening a present he already knows is going to be a chess set and not the computer game he had been dropping hints about for the past three months, Martin tore open the package on the kitchen table and was somewhat taken aback to find a copy of *The Joy Of Gay Sex*, together with a month's supply of multivitamins, a leaflet on safer sex and a packet of condoms. With them was a short note written in his father's familiar scrawl. 'See chapter on safe sex', it read. 'Very interesting.'

Caroline was working late at the office. Or rather, she was sitting at her desk, working through some personal problems which had been festering at the back of her mind all day. On the rare occasions that she wrote to her mother, her letters were always written on her computer, and laid out in bullet points. It may seem odd to compose a letter to a member of one's family in the same style used for addressing business clients, but relations between Caroline and her mother had never been intimate, and for some reason she had always found it the best way of articulating her thoughts. This was precisely what she was doing now, only this particular letter was addressed to nobody but herself.

At first she had considered writing a letter to Graham, but quickly abandoned this idea when it struck her that letters to ex's were rarely a good idea, especially when laid out in bullet points, and least of all when said ex had already moved on to a new partner and would in all probability be sharing the contents of the letter with her, whoever the hell she was. So instead Caroline had decided to lay her thoughts out on the computer screen, in the hope that this way she might be able to make a little more sense of them. So far she thought it was going rather well.

Reasons Why Breaking Up With Graham Was A Bad Move
- Graham was the best thing that ever happened to you
- Graham is kind and gentle
- Graham is very good looking
- Graham is very good in bed
- Graham doesn't mind you doing a bit of coke now and then
- Graham is easygoing most of the time, except when you listen to his answerphone messages, pick fights with him or accuse him of being gay in front of his friends
- Graham isn't gay

Indications That Life Isn't The Same Since Breaking Up With Graham
- Only having two orgasms in three months
- Taking too many drugs
- Becoming a prostitute

Reasons For Getting Back Together With Graham
- All of the above
- Sophie's wedding (not terribly important but would be nice)

Caroline scanned her eyes up and down the computer screen and smiled. This was easier than she had thought. Still, deciding that she should try and patch things up with Graham wasn't really the difficult part. In fact, the more she looked at what she had written so far, the clearer it became that getting back with Graham had obviously been what she had wanted all along. It was just reassuring to see it written there in black and white. But now for the hard part. It was all very well her deciding that she wanted Graham back, but how was she going to convince him?

Reasons Why Graham Should Want You Back
- You love him
- You're good in bed
- You're not fat any more

Shit, this wasn't going very well at all. If she was going to convince Graham that dumping his new girlfriend and getting back together with her was a good idea, she'd have to do a lot better than this. Maybe a little line of coke would help focus her mind. After all, she had done some of her best work under the influence of cocaine – written some of her most effective pitches, closed some of her biggest deals.

Caroline reached into her handbag for her Tiffany pouch and began chopping a line of coke on her mouse pad. Hunched over her desk, her mind firmly focused on the job at hand, she didn't notice her boss as he stepped out of his office and, spotting her still at her work station long after everybody else had gone home, walked towards her with a quizzical look on his face.

'Ah, Caroline,' he said, as he approached her desk. 'Glad to see that you're . . .'

Whatever her boss had been about to say next, something in his expression told her that 'chopping a line of cocaine' wasn't it.

Chapter fourteen

The atmosphere outside Red Cube was turning ugly. The seething crowd of tabloid photographers, teenage wannabes and clueless tourists pushed and shoved as Fernando, John and Martin brandished their invitations and breezed past the tightly packed security. John was sporting two days' worth of designer stubble on his chin, a diamond stud in his ear and a brightly coloured headscarf on his head. But if he had been hoping that someone might mistake him for David Beckham he was sorely disappointed. Not a single flash went off as they made their way past the banks of photographers lining the entrance to the building. As they approached the door, John looked back briefly over his shoulder and distinctly heard someone shout 'Wanker!', which was recognition of a sort.

Inside the club the atmosphere was no less frenetic. On the ground floor, swarms of PR girls in tops no bigger than John's headscarf buzzed around with clipboards, ticking names off various guest lists, and ushering the select few in the direction of the velvet-roped area at the far end of the otherwise empty dance floor. Upstairs where the majority of people seemed to be congregating, handsome cocktail waiters with broad smiles and narrow waists darted about with trays laden with glasses of red and white wine, vodka martinis and bottled beers. As for the other guests, for the most part they were the kind of people who gave music industry parties a bad name. Balding record company executives in flash suits flirted with simpering girls in micro-skirts and make-up an inch thick. Middle-aged rock critics with scruffy T-shirts and spiky hair-dos lectured their infinitely better-looking female companions on the meaning of 'Girl Power'. Tabloid gossip columnists with sweaty faces scoured the room in search of bona fide celebrities with a story to tell or, failing that, desperate wannabes who might entertain the idea of having sex with them in exchange for a line of coke and a mention in tomorrow's paper. Meanwhile, huddled next to the entrance, a crowd of young, female competition winners all the way from Switzerland waited expectantly for a glimpse of their heroines, oblivious to the adult games going on around them.

Much as John had predicted, it wasn't too long before Fernando was approached by one of his many record company contacts. A fat man with a few wisps of hair on top and a curly little pony tail that wouldn't have looked out of place on the rear end of a pig sidled up and whispered something in his ear, before leading him away from the main bar and through a door guarded by a bouncer with a walkie-talkie.

'Now do you see what I mean?' John said, helping himself to another vodka martini from a passing waiter. 'I told you Fernando was well connected.'

But Martin wasn't paying attention. His eyes were focused on a pretty boy standing a few feet away, dressed in vintage

'70s Wrangler jeans, a figure-hugging white T-shirt with studded sleeves and a pale brown cowboy hat over dark feathercut hair. His green eyes were rimmed with mascara and there was a dusting of silver glitter on his high cheekbones. Under normal circumstances, Martin would have assumed that any man wearing make-up must be straight, since most of the gay men he knew would sooner die than risk being seen as effeminate. Personally he hadn't applied make-up to his face since the age of fifteen, when he used to sneak out of the house on a Friday night with his mother's eyeliner smudged around his eyes in honour of Robert Smith, lead singer with The Cure. Come to think of it, practically every male pop icon he could think of who ever wore make-up had turned out to be straight, from David Bowie to David Sylvian. The obvious exception, of course, was Boy George. But then how many gay men wanted to look like him? If George had ever been a role model for anyone, it was for fat girls from the suburbs.

Despite all of this, something about this boy's appearance told Martin that he might just be in with a chance. For one thing, he had a red bandana threaded through the belt hoops on his jeans, which no straight man would even dream of wearing unless his belt had been stolen and his trousers were falling down. For another, he was surrounded by a gaggle of girls, any one of whom might conceivably have been his girlfriend were it not for the body language, which hinted at the kind of light-hearted intimacy enjoyed by a group of girls together on a night out, rather than anything even remotely sexual. Besides which, the boy was making it abundantly clear that he was not only aware of Martin's interest, but actually enjoying it. Every so often he would find an excuse to turn and stare in Martin's direction, with a look halfway between a smile and a challenge. 'Go on,' it said. 'Walk over here in front of all these people and talk to me. I fucking dare you!'

'What are you staring at?' John asked, following Martin's gaze. 'Oh, I see. Yeah, he's quite cute I suppose. But I'm really not sure about the make-up. And that cowboy drag is such old hat! Even straights are doing it now. I blame Madonna.'

'Well, not everyone can carry off a silk headscarf,' Martin replied sarcastically. 'Apart from you and David Beckham, obviously.' Then, staring dreamily across the room: 'Besides, I think the make-up suits him. It makes him look, I don't know . . . interesting.'

John sniffed. 'If he looks so interesting, why don't you just go over there and talk to him? Somehow, I doubt he'll be half as interesting when he opens his mouth. If you ask me, he looks pretty vague. Not that vague boys don't have their attractions, but there are limits. I'll bet if you shone a torch in his ear his eyes would light up.'

There was a pause while John waited in vain for some response to what he thought was a pretty sharp remark, and Martin continued to stare at the boy, who was evidently aware that he was the main topic of conversation and, judging by his self-conscious posturing and ever more frequent glances, seemed more determined than ever to prolong Martin's agony.

'Right,' John said finally. 'I'm bored. I'm going downstairs to see if I can spot anyone famous worth bumping into. Are you coming, or would you rather stay here and play cowboys and indians?'

Martin cast one last, lingering look across the room, before grabbing a drink and following John in the direction of the stairs, pausing once to glance back and check that the cowboy was still there and feeling slightly wounded to discover that he had already disappeared. He squeezed through the gang of giggling competition winners and caught up with John as he was about to head downstairs. Just then, two security guards came charging up the stairs towards them, waving their arms in the air and demanding that everyone immediately move back into the bar and keep the staircase completely clear.

'Quick!' said John, grabbing Martin's arm and elbowing his way into the middle of the competition winners. Moments later the screaming started as Posh entered the room, minus David Beckham but immediately followed by Mel B, Mel C and Baby, with some grinning children's television presenter trailing not far behind. The girls each waved half-heartedly as they were ushered through a door and quickly disappeared from view, with only Baby Spice pausing to say a few words to the waiting fans. The whole thing was over in a matter of seconds.

'What a cheek!' John said sourly as the door closed behind them. 'It wouldn't hurt them to spend a few minutes with the people who put them where they are today!'

'But you've never even bought a Spice Girls record,' Martin protested.

'That's hardly the point,' John said as a waiter carrying an enormous steaming tray of Chinese food swept past and disappeared through the door. 'I bet that's all for Mel C,' he went on. 'No wonder people are saying she looks like a big bull dyke. Still, at least nobody could accuse her of being too thin, or of having a coke habit.'

As John spoke, Martin suddenly became aware of a rather short, stocky girl with closely cropped hair standing directly in front of him. She turned to reveal an angry face covered with piercings and a T-shirt which read 'I Love Mel C'.

'Oh, for heaven's sake!' John said crossly, pushing his way through the crowd. 'This is supposed to be a bloody party! When are lesbians going to realise that it's okay to have a sense of humour?'

Caroline was obliged to take a taxi home when her boss insisted that she leave her company car in the all-night car park, rather than risk being stopped by the police and bringing the firm into disrepute by being exposed as a drug user. The fact that he had caught her at the preparation stage, well before any drugs actually entered her system, seemed to have passed him by completely. But considering that she had just narrowly escaped being given the sack, a taxi didn't seem like too great a sacrifice to make. She still couldn't quite believe that she had allowed herself to be caught in such a compromising position, or that her boss had been quite so understanding. She had been far too freaked out to take in every single word he said, but what it seemed to boil down to was that he didn't particularly care what she did in her own time, just so long as she didn't do it in his. Since their conversation had taken place well after 8 p.m. she had been sorely tempted to reply that, technically, it was her time, but thankfully her common sense had got the better of her and she had managed to bite her tongue. This left her feeling quite proud of herself. Her behaviour tonight may have resulted in her very nearly losing her job, but when it came to the crunch at least she knew when to shut up. She also knew that she had been extremely lucky. If her boss had any idea of the number of times she had taken coke at her desk he might not have been quite so lenient. When you took all these factors into consideration, it was hardly any wonder that Caroline left the office on a high. It was the kind of high often described by people who emerged unscathed from motorway pile-ups.

She arrived home shortly after nine and immediately fixed herself a large vodka and cranberry juice. She then spent a few minutes investigating the contents of the fridge and debating whether to cook herself some dinner or simply chop a quick line. Since the only remotely edible thing she could find in the fridge was a chicken breast which was already past its sell-by date, it didn't take her long to decide on the latter of the two options. 'I've earned this,' she told herself as she floated into the living room and saw the light flashing on her answerphone. The automated voice told her that she had three new messages, which sounded rather promising.

The first message brought her down with a bump. It was from her mother, which Caroline immediately took as a sign that she had been right to go with the coke and not the chicken breast. After all, who could rely on a chicken breast to deliver the kind of numbing pain control required when dealing with one's mother? Sure enough, the message personified her mother at her most manipulative.

'Hello, dear,' it began. 'It's your mother. I haven't heard from you in a while, so I thought I'd give you a quick ring to let you know that I'm still alive. Also, I wanted you to be the first to know that your brother and his wife are expecting a baby girl in the New Year. I don't know what names they're considering, but since when did anyone bother to ask my opinion about these things? Perhaps when you have children of your own you'll understand. Anyway, I can't talk for long. I'm meeting your Uncle Bill for lunch. He hasn't been himself since Auntie Pauline died. He's talking about buying himself a tombstone. He saw some programme on the television about that dreadful flu that's been going around, and now he's convinced that he's about to drop dead. I told him he'd outlive us all, but you know what he's like when he gets these ideas into his head. Anyway, perhaps you could give me a ring back when you get this message. If you can spare the time, that is. Bye for now.'

The second message was a little more uplifting. It was from Martin, inviting her over to his place for dinner on Thursday. That would be nice, Caroline thought, pressing the pause button on the answerphone as she flicked through her diary to check that she was free and happily pencilled in his name. It felt as if she hardly ever saw Martin these days. He was always at the gym, or busy doing something with his new flatmate, or out clubbing somewhere with John. She didn't begrudge the fact that he spent so much of his spare time these days with his gay male friends. He was still on the rebound from Christopher after all, and searching for a new boyfriend was probably a lot easier with other gay men for company. At the same time, it saddened her that she and Martin seemed to have drifted apart lately. There was a time, not all that long ago, when they spoke on the phone almost every day and made a point of seeing each other at least once a week, whether it was a quiet trip to the cinema or a big night out clubbing. That was why she had gone to the club on Saturday, to relive some of those wild nights. If she had only known beforehand that it would turn out to be a far wilder night than she was anticipating, with no sign of the person she had expressly gone to be wild with, she might have thought again. Still, Thursday would be a good opportunity to catch up, although quite how much she was prepared to tell Martin about what had been going on lately she had yet to decide.

She released the pause button and felt her heart sink as Dylan's voice flooded into her living room. 'Hi, Caz,' he said, sounding far too familiar for her liking. He knew perfectly well that she hated people calling her 'Caz'. She had told him as much only a couple of days ago. And now here he was calling her up at home, invading her privacy and winding her up with his 'Caz' this and his 'Caz' that. Well, she wasn't having any of it. She didn't have to listen to this. Before the message could play on any further, before Dylan completely contaminated her living room with his overly familiar voice and his deliberate misuse of the horrible nickname she had left behind her all those years ago, she pressed the delete button and wiped away all trace of him for good. She felt much better after that, and spent the rest of the evening slowly unwinding with several more vodkas and a late-night film called *The Net*. The film starred Sandra Bullock as a lonely computer programmer who accidentally taps into some secret government files and suddenly discovers that people are out to kill her. It was one of those silly thrillers that played on the fear that, in the age of e-mail and mass telecommunications, someone sat in front of a computer screen somewhere could learn everything there was to know about you. But Caroline had a soft spot for films featuring spunky career girls, even if they were played by someone as sickeningly winsome as Sandra Bullock, and she soon found herself suspending disbelief in the film's faintly ludicrous premise and rooting for Sandra to beat the bad guys.

It was a couple of hours later, just as she was drifting off to sleep, that Caroline suddenly remembered the document she had been writing at work when her boss walked in. The document in which she described breaking up with Graham. The document in which she described Sophie's forthcoming wedding as 'not terribly important'. The document in which she referred to herself as only having had two orgasms in three months. The document in which she admitted taking too many drugs. The document in which she confessed to becoming a prostitute. The document which, if her memory served her correctly, was still displayed on her computer screen, and from which her work colleagues could learn, if not everything there was to know about her, then certainly a lot more than she would like them to know.

'This party is so boring,' John said with a dramatic sigh. John had a sigh for every occasion, and quite a few put aside especially for those evenings he didn't deem worthy of the term 'occasion'. Martin was attuned to them all, and immediately recognised this as one of those special sighs. 'If this is Spice World, I'm not surprised Geri got out when she did,' John continued. 'I'd have a line to perk myself up, but it would be a waste of good drugs.'

'It's not that bad,' Martin insisted, sipping on his seventh vodka martini and feeling slightly the worse for wear. 'The cocktails are nice, and we've seen some interesting people.'

John, who had a far higher tolerance for alcohol but not for people, pulled one of his faces. 'You are joking! This is meant to be an A-list event, and the only remotely famous person I've spotted all night is Pete bloody Waterman! They'll be wheeling out Christopher Biggins next, followed by half the cast of *EastEnders*! Oh, hang on. Now I get it. By "interesting people" I suppose you mean people you'd like to take home and fuck. Where is your little cowboy anyway?'

Martin quickly scanned the room. 'I don't know. I haven't seen him for a while. Maybe he's already left.'

'Yes, well, obviously he's a lot smarter than he looks. I'd

leave too if I only knew where to find Fernando. I wish he'd hurry up. I've got a flight to New York tomorrow and I really can't see any point in hanging around here much longer. Oh fuck it, let's just go and have a discreet line. At least it'll give us something to do.'

Martin knocked back his martini and followed John to the toilets. There was an attendant keeping a watchful eye out for any illegal activities, so John ducked into a cubicle and chopped two lines of coke, quickly snorting one himself as he flushed the toilet, and leaving one on the seat for Martin. When Martin re-emerged, sniffing conspicuously and rubbing his nose, John was helping himself to the attendant's vast array of colognes and making eyes at the boy in the cowboy hat, who had just walked into the room and was standing with his back to them, studying himself in the mirror.

Much to Martin's embarrassment, John reached out and tapped the cowboy on the shoulder. 'We were just talking about you,' he said.

The boy answered without taking his eye off the mirror. 'Really?'

'Yes,' John went on. 'My friend was wondering, are you the midnight cowboy?'

The boy turned and stared at them both evenly for a moment, then glanced at his watch. 'Actually it's only half past eleven,' he said, looking directly at Martin with a cocky grin. 'You're a little early.' And with that he disappeared.

'It sounds to me like you've got yourself a date,' John said, nudging Martin in the ribs before pausing in front of the mirror to adjust his headscarf. 'Just think, tonight you could be giving a whole new meaning to the phrase, "ride 'em cowboy"!'

As they made their way back to the bar, it struck Martin

that the line of coke John had just snorted must have been substantially larger than the line he had left him, because suddenly John began talking incessantly about the various gay porn movies he'd seen in which cowboy hats, boots, chaps and stirrups were all featured heavily. 'I saw this great one once,' he said. 'There was this really cute blond guy who was supposed to be straight, but who was completely shaved all over, right down to his arsehole. I don't know about you, but I've yet to meet a straight man who shaves his arsehole. Most of the straight men I see at the gym can't even be bothered to trim their pubes. Anyway, this guy is the sheriff of this little town somewhere, and there are these outlaws stealing cattle and running around shooting at everybody, only not with their guns if you catch my drift. You can tell they're the bad guys because they're all dressed in black leather. So, the sheriff rounds them up one by one, and they have sex in haystacks and on black-jack tables and the backs of horses and all that kind of thing. And then finally there's this big group scene in the jailhouse where the outlaws all take it in turns fucking the sheriff, who is just wearing his chaps and is loving every minute of it. Anyway, you'll never guess what it was called.'

Martin, who had switched off at the mention of shaved arseholes and was busy surveying the room for the boy in the cowboy hat, turned and looked at John blankly. 'Sorry?'

'You'll never guess what it was called,' John said again. 'The porn film I was just telling you about. Guess what it was called!'

'I've no idea.'

'"Bunfight at the OK Corrall"!' John cried, and fell about laughing. 'Get it? "Bunfight"!'

Martin smiled weakly. 'Yeah, that's really funny.'

'Oh, just forget it then!' John said crossly. 'I was just trying to help pass the time. But if that's your attitude, I won't bother. I'm off to look for Fernando. If I don't see you through the week, I'll see you through the window.'

Martin looked confused. 'Window? What window?'

'It's just an expression,' John snapped, and flounced off.

Martin was about to run after him when suddenly the crowd parted to reveal the boy in the cowboy hat standing a few feet away at the end of the bar. He appeared to be deep in conversation with one of the girls from earlier, but when he spotted Martin he immediately stopped talking and gave a little grin. Still maintaining eye contact, he whispered something to the girl and sauntered over. Judging by the way he walked, Martin was pretty certain that he didn't have a wooden leg.

'Hello again,' the cowboy said. 'What happened to your friend? No, don't tell me. He's gone and found someone else to poke fun at.'

'Oh, John's all right really,' Martin replied, suddenly feeling much happier and more generous of spirit. 'He's just a bit full-on sometimes, that's all. I'm Martin, by the way.'

'Ben. But you can call me the midnight cowboy if it makes you happy.'

Martin blushed. 'I'm sorry about that. It's just John's sense of humour. I'm sure he didn't mean anything by it.'

Ben frowned. 'Really? That's a pity. I thought it was his way of getting us two to talk. I thought maybe you were hoping to get to know me a bit better.'

'It was,' Martin said quickly. 'I was. I mean, I am. What I mean is . . .'

'It's okay,' Ben smiled and placed a hand on Martin's arm. 'I know what you mean.'

'Yes, of course. Good.' Martin laughed nervously and tried

to think of something to say. 'So, what do you do?' he said finally.

'Well, I'm not a real cowboy. And to be honest with you, nothing bores me more than talking about work. Look, I know it isn't quite midnight yet, but what would you say if I suggested we leave this dreary party now and go somewhere more private?'

Martin grinned. 'I'd say that sounds like a great idea.'

Chapter fifteen

Martin woke up at 5.30 a.m. with a dead mouse in his mouth and no idea of where he was. Then he remembered. The sour, furry taste in his mouth was the hangover from all those vodka martinis, and he was at the cowboy's house, somewhere in the wilds of west London, possibly near Chiswick. The journey back last night was a blur. He vaguely recalled leaving the party and walking up to Shaftesbury Avenue to hail a cab. But after that it was just odd moments, a giddy collage of images like the view over the river, or the sudden glint of a front door key. Even the sex was a hazy memory of bruised lips and thrashing limbs, torn condom wrappers and pounding flesh. Had it really been that violent? The soreness of his nipples suggested that it had, but there must have been some tenderness too, surely? Or if not tenderness, then at least some contentment in the pleasure they had given one another, possibly even a little joy? Had they kissed before falling asleep? And when they drifted off, were their bodies still entwined, or at opposite sides of the bed? He couldn't remember.

He rolled over to find the cowboy still sleeping heavily. Martin had never seen anyone sleep quite so heavily, or in such an awkward position. He was lying face down with his neck twisted at an odd angle and his arms close to his sides, palms facing upwards, the way bodies were sometimes discovered in detective films. He was definitely breathing, which was a good sign. There was a trace of spittle in the corner of his mouth, and a blob of mascara on his cheek. His eyelids were shut tight. Beneath them, his eyes flickered and rolled, suggesting that he was dreaming – of what, Martin hardly dared imagine. It would be nice to think that he was featured in there somewhere – nice, but not very likely. The chances were he was dreaming of some previous encounter, or perhaps even some man who had walked into his life and turned everything upside down, the way Christopher had when Martin first met him. Maybe the cowboy had been hurt too, Martin thought. Maybe his cockiness was just a front, a way to disguise his fear of rejection. Maybe he was searching for someone too. It was a romantic thought, but then from where Martin was sitting, it was a pretty romantic picture. During the night, the glitter from the cowboy's cheeks had rubbed off onto the pillow, surrounding his face with a silver glow. In the strange half light, he looked pale, wounded, almost alien, as if somehow he had just landed there during the night – The Cowboy Who Fell To Earth. Ben – the cowboy's name was Ben. And as he lay there, white and fragile and clearly not the kind of person who would run off with a male prostitute, Martin had a strong sense that falling in love with him would be the easiest thing in the world.

Feeling the need to pee, he slid quietly out of bed and padded out into the hallway, looking for the bathroom. There was a shaft of light spilling through an open door at the end of the hall and he walked towards it, shivering slightly in his Calvins and feeling like an intruder. It was like that when you woke up in someone else's house, especially when it was someone you hardly knew. Without them standing beside you, talking you through the colour scheme for the living room or trying to lure you into the bedroom, you were divorced from your surroundings, out of context, completely alone. Even the photographs on the wall seemed to conspire to make you feel out of place. Faces you'd never seen before, people you'd never met, places you'd never been – each one reminded you that you didn't belong here, that this wasn't your natural habitat, that you were merely passing through. It was at times like these that Martin was grateful for the familiar gay trappings of tasteful watercolours, funky ethnic tat and track lighting. Sadly, Ben didn't appear to have any of these – just a plain white hallway with a few clip-framed photographs of himself posing with various friends and family, none of whom made Martin feel particularly welcome.

The bathroom was pretty disgusting. Whatever Ben did for a living, he clearly didn't believe in wasting his hard-earned cash on home improvements. There was a heavy build-up of limescale around the rim of the toilet and along one side of the bath. The linoleum flooring was worn through in several places, the bathroom mirror had a large crack running from top to bottom, and a solitary damp towel hung on the back of the door. Martin hesitated before gently flushing the toilet and then turning to examine his face in the mirror. He wasn't looking too good – not much better than the bathroom in fact. The hangover was etched deep into his features. That was the trouble with cocktails – the wider the variety of alcohol consumed the night before, the greater the damage in the morning. Far better to stick with vodka. He could wake up practically embalmed in vodka and not look nearly as bad as he did now. There were dark rings around his eyes, and his skin had the kind of deathly pallor usually associated with serious liver damage. Battleship grey, John called it.

He searched for some mouthwash to disguise the taste in his mouth, and wasn't the least bit surprised when he couldn't find any. He knew better than to use a stranger's toothbrush (these days it wasn't just rude but potentially dangerous), so he squeezed some toothpaste onto the tip of his index finger and ran it around his teeth and gums until his mouth tasted suitably minty. He did the breath-in-hand test and was relieved to find that the sour smell was barely detectable. There wasn't a lot he could do to combat the other effects of his hangover, except splash some cold water on his face and hope that the sudden shock would get his circulation going. As he patted his face dry with the towel, he recognised the faint smell of mould.

Hearing the creaking of bed springs from the bedroom, he padded back along the hall and opened the door. Ben was sitting up in bed, arms outstretched, mouth wide open, yawning silently like a cat. His eyes, when he opened them, were still glazed with sleep and slightly red. Seeing Martin standing at the bottom of the bed, he looked puzzled for a moment, then broke into a grin. 'Hello,' he said. 'Sorry, what's your name again?'

Caroline hadn't slept well. All night long she had been plagued by nightmares involving every authority figure she had ever known gathered around her desk discussing the contents of her document, the state of her mind and the chances of her ever finding another job with a good salary and a decent pension plan. Her boss was there, of course, together with her mother, her headmaster and the store detective who had caught her shoplifting from Woolworth's as a teenager. Her coke dealer was there too, which she thought was rather odd considering that, strictly speaking, he didn't really qualify as an authority figure. Theirs was a relationship based on shared interests and mutual trust. If anything, the balance of power rested more with her since she was the customer and the customer was always right. Then she remembered that when dealing with class-A substances the usual laws didn't always apply. Experience had taught her that, while her coke dealer wasn't always right, it was usually in everybody's best interests to act as though he was.

She climbed out of bed at 6.15 a.m. feeling completely drained, sleep-walked her way into the shower and had a brief panic attack over what to wear before gulping down a cup of coffee and setting off for the office. To make matters worse, her local minicab firm was having one of those mornings when the only driver who had turned up for work was the one who knew his way to Peckham but who so far hadn't been able to find his way back, and so she was forced to take the tube. It was years since she had handed over good money to London Underground in exchange for half an hour's chronic discomfort, and she resented each minute and every last penny of it. Standing in the over-crowded carriage, caught between a hatchet-faced woman with a rock-chick hairdo and a sweating businessman with a hard-on, she vowed to walk to work rather than catch the tube ever again. At the rate the train was actually moving, it probably wouldn't take her much longer anyway.

She alighted the train at Green Park and caught the Piccadilly Line to Leicester Square, where she left the station and headed up into Soho. Cutting across Berwick Street with its fresh vegetable stalls and piss-stained alleyways, she did her best to ignore the signs advertising live nude models. How much did those girls actually earn anyway? £50 an hour? £70? Whatever it was, it hardly compensated for having to lie down with men like that businessman on the tube, feigning pleasure while they poked away and the scorn in their mean little eyes showed that they considered themselves a million times better than the woman they were fucking. If anyone deserved performance-related pay, it was those girls. It made her feel sick just thinking about it. Was this how Dylan saw her now? Was this what her work colleagues would think of her if they saw that document, that she was some cheap hooker turning a few tricks in Soho after work? What would she do if they had seen it? What should her plan of action be? Try and pass it off as a joke? Claim that she was making notes for a novel, and had used real names as a simple matter of convenience? Insist that it was something she had accidentally downloaded off the internet, and that she had no idea where it came from or why it referred to a man called Graham who had recently broken up with his girlfriend and a woman called Sophie who just happened to be getting married?

Passing a sandwich bar, she quickly checked her watch before popping in and ordering a large cappuccino to take away. The silver-haired Italian man behind the counter winked as he handed over her change and she found herself blushing, imagining for one paranoid moment that he could somehow read her thoughts and knew exactly what she had been doing with her free time lately and why she was rushing into work so early this morning. Gripping the styrofoam cup in one hand and her briefcase in the other, she ran out of the sandwich bar and promptly collided with a man walking at a fair pace in the opposite direction, with his head buried in a magazine. As their bodies crashed together, the man's magazine fell to the floor, quickly followed by Caroline's styrofoam cup, which bounced once before breaking open and soaking both the magazine and the man's shoes with hot foaming coffee.

'Oh fuck!' she yelled, immediately dropping to the floor and picking up the magazine, which she noticed featured a rather lovely cover shot of a scantily clad Kylie Minogue, complete with a sticky brown stain spreading slowly across the lower half of her face and the best part of her cleavage. 'Fuck, fuck, fuck!'

'Caroline?' a familiar voice said.

She looked up. 'Graham!'

He smiled and helped her to her feet. 'I thought it looked like you. Then you started with all the "fuck" stuff and I knew it had to be.'

She blushed slightly, smoothed down her skirt and handed him the damp magazine. 'Sorry about Kylie,' she said.

'That's okay. I've got a dozen magazines with Kylie on the cover.' He grinned. 'Maybe I shouldn't have said that. I mean, I know how your minds works. I wouldn't want you getting the wrong idea.'

She frowned. 'What do you mean?'

'A grown man admitting to liking Kylie? I'd say that was pretty incriminating evidence.'

Caroline laughed nervously. 'Oh, that! Honestly, I don't know what I was thinking!'

He looked solemn for a moment. 'No, me neither. So anyway, how are things?'

'Oh, fine,' she lied. 'Working hard. Playing harder. You know how it is.'

'Not really,' he said. 'I don't seem to find much time for fun these days.'

I'll bet you don't, Caroline thought bitterly, instantly picturing him with the woman from the other night. Then her subconscious flashed up images of the kind of fun she'd been having lately, and she decided she was hardly in any position to judge. There was a long pause while she tried to think of something to say that wouldn't sound bitter, or desperate, or too keen, or not keen enough. 'So . . .' she said finally.

He smiled. 'I'd ask if you had time for a coffee, but you seem to be in quite a rush.'

'Yes,' she said, suddenly feeling terribly awkward and grateful for the excuse to make a quick getaway. 'Breakfast meeting. Must dash.'

If he was disappointed, he didn't let it show. 'Maybe another time then,' he said, still smiling impenetrably.

'Sure,' she smiled back. 'Another time. Why not? Great. Bye then.'

As she watched him walk away, she had the awful sinking feeling that fate had just offered her a helping hand and that she had foolishly gone and bitten it.

Martin was sitting on a busy District Line train with his back to the window, flicking through a copy of last night's *Evening Standard* and wondering how long he should wait before calling Ben and casually suggesting that they meet up for a drink. The sex this morning had been passionate enough to make the possibility of a repeat performance seem highly likely, and while Ben hadn't exactly jumped at the chance to offer Martin his telephone number, he seemed happy enough to scribble it down when asked. Playing it cool had never been Martin's strong point anyway, and since it was an unwritten rule of all relationships that one person was usually required to do the chasing, he couldn't see any reason why it shouldn't be him. At the same time, he couldn't help but wonder what would have happened had he not asked for Ben's number. Would Ben have volunteered it, or asked for his? Or would he have allowed Martin to leave without even a mention of the possibility of seeing him again? This didn't seem very likely. After all, they had got along pretty well. As enjoyable as the sex was (and it had been tender, he thought happily, it had definitely been tender), it was the whole business of getting dressed and eating breakfast together which had cemented the sense of real intimacy. Sitting in Ben's kitchen, avoiding looking at the pile of dirty dishes in the sink and listening to him talk about his job as a sales assistant at Versace and a part-time model, Martin was convinced that he had felt something significant pass between them. Sure, it was mostly small talk. But at the end of the day, wasn't that what most relationships were based on, at least some of the time?

He had turned down the offer of a bath, partly because the bath looked like a breeding ground for communicable diseases, but mainly because he wanted to savour last night's encounter for as long as possible. He could still smell Ben on his skin, still taste him in his mouth, still feel the warmth and the weight of his body. It was years since he had travelled home in last night's clothes after spending the night in somebody else's bed, and he had forgotten just how good it felt. He knew he wasn't looking his best today, but that didn't bother him in the slightest. He felt more desirable than he had felt in a long time. It was as if his night with Ben had brought out

everything in him that was attractive, so that now it was written on his face for everyone to see. And it wasn't going
unnoticed. The young city type in the pinstripe suit sitting
directly opposite had been staring at him for the past ten
minutes. And when the train pulled in at Earls Court, his
attention was drawn to a cute blond boy in jeans and a black
bomber jacket stood waiting on the platform, who made a
point of boarding the same carriage and squeezing through
the crowds until he was standing barely two feet away, peering over his newspaper in that casual yet significant manner
which Martin had never quite perfected but which often
seemed to make the gay world go around.

When he finally arrived home, half an hour later and with
half a dozen imaginary phone numbers in his pocket, the
front door was double locked, indicating that Neil had already
left. He thought this was rather odd. Neil rarely left for work
much before ten, and it was still only 8.15 a.m. He let himself
in quietly, and gently tapped on Neil's door. There was no
answer, and when he opened the door he could tell immediately that the bed hadn't been slept in. Perhaps Neil had got
lucky last night too, Martin thought. It seemed a bit churlish
not to be pleased for him, but he couldn't help but feel a
glimmer of disappointment. He was dying to give somebody
the full blow-by-blow account of where he'd been and who
he'd been with, to share the tiniest of details before they faded
into the dim recesses of his memory, just as the glitter on
Ben's pillowcases would inevitably fade with time, whether he
washed them regularly or not. Sharing it all with Neil would
make it seem more real somehow, even if he did miss out the
bit about the glitter and the eye make-up. Something told
him that these weren't the sorts of details Neil would find
particularly inspiring, although if John ran true to form it

probably wouldn't be very long before he heard about them anyway.

Closing the bedroom door behind him, he made his way into the kitchen and checked to see whether Neil had remembered to buy fresh milk. The fridge door was decorated with the kinds of campy magnets that were sold at popular gay shops such as American Retro in Old Compton Street. The magnets began appearing after Neil moved in, and in a few short months had multiplied to such an extent that these days the fridge door offered a comprehensive visual history of gay culture, from Michelangelo's David complete with an entire gay wardrobe to more recent gay icons such as Judy Garland and Peewee Herman. Attached to the door with David's leather shorts was a note in Neil's handwriting. 'Gone to collect Brian's mum from Euston', it read. 'Sorry about crack in toilet. Have called plumber who will come and fix it this evening. Told to turn water off. I'll pay for repair of course. See you tonight.'

Martin ran into the bathroom. Sure enough, there was a large crack in the toilet through which the water had obviously leaked at some point, creating a large puddle before Neil managed to locate the stopcock and turn off the water supply. Suddenly Martin wished he had taken up Ben's offer of a bath. Cursing the day he allowed Neil to move in, he stormed into his bedroom and packed a bag for the gym. If he was quick, he might just manage to squeeze in a shower before work.

Caroline's relief at finding her computer switched off and no trace of her document anywhere on the system was short-lived. Initially, she was simply grateful for the fact that she had managed to get to the office before anyone else arrived.

Greeting the security guard with a cheery 'Good morning', she had flown through the reception and up the stairs before finally landing at her desk. Laying her briefcase on top of the pile of papers littering the surface, she restarted her computer and looked around quickly to ensure that her boss wasn't about to spring out of his office or that Paula, Sophie and Tamsin weren't lurking by the water cooler. As the computer hummed into life, she was fully expecting to see the evidence of last night's ill-advised outpourings suddenly materialise before her eyes. When the screen came up blank, she was puzzled. Then, realising that her computer hadn't simply gone into sleep mode but had actually been shut down, she ran a search for her document and was surprised when nothing remotely resembling it was found. Oh well, she thought. At least if it had disappeared into cyberspace there was no chance of it getting into the wrong hands.

Then she had a truly terrible thought. Apart from her boss, she was the last person to leave the office last night. The cleaners had been and gone, and neither they nor the security guard were authorised to touch the computers. So if she hadn't closed the document, and she was pretty certain that she hadn't, the only other explanation was that her boss had closed it for her before shutting down her computer. And since he was her boss, and he had caught her chopping coke at her desk, it wasn't beyond the realm of possibility that he would have felt compelled to read what she had written. And if he had read it, it seemed highly probable that he would be feeling far less lenient about her little indiscretion. In fact, he had probably arrived at the conclusion that he was harbouring a drug-addicted prostitute and was preparing to give her the sack the moment he walked through the door.

This was all Dylan's fault, she thought. It was he who had insisted on paying her for sex. It was he who had suggested they meet at The Sanderson, and he who had waved her off in a taxi destined to stop at a traffic light just as Graham and his new girlfriend were passing by. It was he who had wound her up into such a state that she had gone to The Fridge and been molested by some pervert passing himself off as gay. It was he who had left her feeling so guilty and confused over Graham that she had sat down at her desk last night and written that bloody stupid letter to herself. It was he who had left that answerphone message for her last night, adding to the stress she was already suffering and ensuring that she didn't get a good night's sleep. It was he who had created the situation she now found herself in, waiting in anguish for her boss to arrive and give her the sack. It was all his fault.

Well, he wasn't going to get away with it. If nothing else, she wanted him to know exactly what he had done. She wanted him to take responsibility for all the damage he had caused. She wanted him to feel the full weight of her anger. Opening her briefcase, she pulled out her address book and searched for Dylan's telephone number.

If she rang now, she could catch him before he left for work. She dialled the number and sat quietly fuming with the phone tucked under her ear as she waited for him to pick up. It was then that she spotted the memo sticking out from under her briefcase, with her boss's signature written at the bottom. She pulled it out and began to read. 'Dear Caroline', it began. 'I hope I made myself clear last night, and that the little matter we discussed is now closed. Also, I should advise you that shortly after you left the office, the computer system crashed due to sudden power cut. I noticed that you were busy working on something, but I'm afraid it looks as though it may have been lost. If you would like some help trying to retrieve it, please let me know and I will ask one of the technical staff to come and assist you.'

Caroline couldn't believe her luck. The document had disappeared! She was saved! She wasn't about to be given the sack after all! Her moment of elation was suddenly interrupted by the sound of Dylan's voice. 'Hello?' he said. 'Hello? Who is this? Look, I'm standing here in a wet towel, so this had better be good.'

Caroline's first instinct was to hang up. Then, feeling a tiny pang of guilt for the way she had been cursing his name only moments ago, she relented. 'Hi, Dylan,' she said. 'It's Caroline. I'm sorry to call so early.'

'That's okay,' he replied. 'So, you got my message?'

'Yes. I mean no. Well, sort of. You got cut off.'

There was a pause. 'I see,' he said finally. 'Well, there's no easy way to say this, Caz, so I suppose I should just come out with it. The thing is, the reason I called was to tell you that I've just discovered I've got crabs.'

part three

Crash

Chapter sixteen

Wednesday was the day Neil went to see his therapist. Neil was one of those gay therapy junkies who spent far more time talking about his recovery programme than he spent actually pursuing it, and in the short time that they had lived together, Martin had learned everything about Neil's therapist that there was to know. Neil had been going to the same therapist ever since he and Brian had split up, and in almost three years he had never missed a single session. His therapist, Derek, was a gay man in his early forties with red hair and a friendly face covered in freckles. He was based in Euston, in a first-floor council flat with orange-painted walls and a view of the local recreation centre which Neil sometimes found distracting. Dotted around the flat were a selection of religious icons and other artefacts which Derek had amassed during his many visits to Morocco. In place of a couch, his clients were invited to unwind in a wicker rocking chair while he sat nodding in a similar chair directly opposite. The few remaining items of furniture reflected the Moroccan theme. The first time Neil entered the flat, he was over-whelmed by the range of herbal teas on offer, and asphyxiated by the smell of incense.

Derek was a recovering alcoholic and drug user who had been clean and sober for fifteen years, and who specialised in helping gay men with similar problems to overcome their addictions and avoid what he described as 'chaos living'. It was his belief that much of the excessive behaviour witnessed on the gay scene could be attributed to the impact of AIDS and the pressures of living through an age of immense grief and deep sexual anxiety. In a previous life he had been employed by one of the main AIDS organisations as an HIV counsellor, helping people to come to terms with their diag-nosis. These days he preferred to work for himself. The majority of his clients were drawn from the club scene, where HIV was rarely discussed and where the heavy use of drugs and alcohol often went unchecked. His client list included a DJ who had become addicted to ketamine and broke down whenever somebody left the dance floor during his set, and several club promoters who had developed serious cocaine habits thanks to all the freebies their security staff confis-cated at the door before passing on to their employers. It was no coincidence that Derek tended to screen his calls on Tuesdays, the day when most of his clients would be experi-encing their comedown from the weekend.

Neil had first heard about Derek from the transsexual who sold him his car, who woke up one Tuesday morning con-vinced that life wasn't worth living, and would have taken an overdose there and then had she not traded her prescription-strength pain killers for a couple of Es the night before. During his first couple of sessions, Neil was only prepared to discuss his break-up with Brian, but it wasn't too long before he began opening up to Derek about the other sources of pain in his life. Chief among these was his relationship with his father, who had been fairly violent when Neil was a child, and who reacted to the news that his only son was a bum bandit by removing everything belonging to him from the house and building an enormous bonfire at the bottom of the garden. Neil had already left home by the time this happened, and had often wondered whether his absence was all that prevented him from being burned along with his old school books and the bed in which he had masturbated regularly as a teenager. His attempts to come to terms with his father's actions weren't much helped by his mother, whose main concern seemed to be that her husband shouldn't have been building bonfires on a day when the neighbours had hung their washing out to dry. An unhappy marriage had long since driven her into the arms of the Catholic church, where she had found the comfort she needed, but learned very little in the way of tolerance or understanding. When Neil, laughing nervously, first told his mother that he was gay, she sniffed and scolded him: 'There's nothing funny about a prolapsed rectum!'

Although Neil regularly referred to Derek as his therapist, he was always at pains to point out that what Derek practised wasn't really therapy. 'He doesn't like the term "therapy",' Neil explained to Martin one day. 'He thinks it's too clinical. His approach is more holistic.' Martin suspected that it was really Neil who felt uncomfortable with the term 'therapy', but going on what Neil had told him he was forced to concede that Derek's methods were a little unusual. As befitted a man with a fondness for orange walls and camomile tea, Derek talked a lot about 'emotional clearing', 'co-dependency' and 'relationship training'. He was a firm believer in the power of personal healing and actively promoted rebirthing as a means of cleansing body and spirit of negative energies. Neil had taken to rebirthing like a baby to the bottle. Each week he would leave the flat filled with remorse about the various chemical and sexual addictions he had given into at the weekend and head off to Derek's flat for a spot of rebirthing. While Martin was the last person to criticise anyone for attempting to take control of their life in whatever way they saw fit, it did strike him as odd that each time Neil was reborn, he was reborn as the exact same person. Each Wednesday afternoon he would go to see Derek, and each Wednesday evening he would arrive home again, change into his leathers and go to The Hoist.

'Why don't you come with me?' Neil asked when he walked into the living room this particular Wednesday evening.

Martin, who was sitting on the sofa with a bowl of soup on his lap and his eyes glued to the television, barely looked up. *London Tonight* was about to show a report filmed at the Spice Girls' party. Besides, he was still angry about the damage to the toilet which, so he had discovered last night, had been caused by Neil sitting on it whilst trying to remove two fairly large steel ball-bearings which he had inserted quite a long way up his anus in an attempt to improve his bowel control. Clearly this hadn't worked, because a sudden fart had sent the steel balls shooting out of Neil's backside like bullets and ricocheting off the toilet bowl, cracking the porcelain in the process. The toilet had since been fixed and Neil had paid for the repair, but the knowledge that he was sharing his flat with someone who thought that inserting ball-bearings up their arse was a good idea still wasn't sitting too happily with him. His mood wasn't helped by the fact that he hadn't heard from Ben, despite leaving three messages and going to great lengths to ensure that his own answerphone was in perfect working order and hadn't mysteriously stopped recording messages just as he was on the verge of starting a new relationship.

'It's not really my scene, Neil,' he said, making no attempt to disguise the tone of mild disapproval in his voice.

'You're not still pissed off about the toilet, are you?' Neil asked. 'Because if you are, it's better to get it off your chest. Derek says that any negative energies we don't express can turn inwards and poison our whole being.'

'I really don't care what Derek says,' Martin snapped. 'My being is perfectly fine, thank you. Now if you don't mind I'm trying to watch this.'

'Is that the party where you met the cowboy?' Neil asked, ignoring Martin's attempt to brush him off and joining him on the sofa.

'Yes.'

'And do I take it from your tone of voice that he hasn't called?'

'As a matter of fact, he hasn't called yet, no.'

'And how many messages have you left?'

'Two. Maybe three.'

'I see,' said Neil gravely.

Martin turned to face him. 'What do you see, Neil? Because right now all I can see is you doing your best to wind me up.'

'Excuse me for showing an interest,' Neil said, rising from the sofa with an injured look. 'I just thought a night out might help take your mind off him. Sorry if it came out wrong. I'll try to remember to keep my suggestions to myself in future.'

Martin felt a sudden pang of guilt. 'No, it's me who should be saying sorry. I'm just disappointed he hasn't called, that's all. He seemed really nice. I liked him. I thought he felt the same way about me.'

'Maybe he's just busy,' Neil offered.

Martin forced a smile. 'Yes, and maybe he's just like all the others.'

'Maybe. Or maybe he's been tied up and he'll call you tomorrow. In the meantime, the last thing you should be doing is sitting here on your own waiting for the phone to ring. It never rings when you watch it. Take it from one who knows.'

'No, you're right,' Martin said, switching off the television, picking up his empty soup bowl and disappearing into the kitchen, returning moments later with a peace offering in the shape of two large vodka and tonics. 'I suppose I should go out,' he said, handing Neil a glass. 'I don't know about The Hoist, though. I'm really not into SM and leather and all that heavy stuff. Besides, I haven't got the right clothes.'

Sensing victory, Neil smiled. 'Most of the guys who go to The Hoist aren't into anything heavy. It's not like Fist. You won't see people pissing on each other or anything like that. It's just a dress-code club, that's all. And you needn't worry about what to wear. You can borrow something of mine.'

Qualada was not a product Caroline had ever had cause to purchase before, and she sincerely hoped that it was one she would never have to ask for again. The Asian girl with the one eyebrow and the black headscarf serving behind the pharmacy counter at Boots couldn't have looked more disapproving if she had asked for a home pregnancy kit and an extra large knitting needle. When Caroline tried to make light of the situation, joking that it was a teensy bit embarrassing to be suddenly infested with pubic lice at her age, there wasn't so much as a glimmer of a smile. Maybe good little Asian girls saw crabs as a symbol of Western decadence, Caroline thought, rather like homosexuality or plucked eyebrows.

Not that she regarded it as a laughing matter. On the contrary, the moment she put the phone down after talking to Dylan she had been consumed by the urge to strip off all of her clothes, pile them up on the floor and set fire to them. Since she had been sitting at her desk at the time, this didn't seem like a particularly advisable course of action. Instead, she had hot-footed it over to Boots, eager to take whatever steps were necessary to rid herself of Dylan's little surprise gift as soon as possible. Never having contracted crabs before, she had no idea what to expect. She hadn't even dared to peek inside her knickers, for fear of what she might find. But the mere thought of the tiny bloodsucking creatures roaming freely around her nether regions was enough to make her skin crawl. It was bad enough picturing them nestled among her pubic hair, without imagining them wandering off like ants in search of fresh food supplies. She had heard reports of pubic lice spreading to people's armpits and even eyebrows, which only served to confirm her faith in Immac and eyebrow tweezers. Never mind diamonds. Forget vibrators. When it came right down to it, depilatory products really were a girl's best friend.

The first thing she did when she arrived home the previous night was to take a shower. Then she opened the bottle of Qualada and, following the instructions on the label, applied the first coat of milky solution to her poor itching body. The label said to leave the solution on for a full twenty-four hours, before washing it off and following this up with a second application. For Caroline it had been twenty-four hours of physical discomfort and mental torture. How could she be expected to sleep knowing that some parasite was literally feeding on her? All night long she tossed and turned, convinced that her body was under attack by some alien life-form. In her nightmares, she was the unwilling protagonist in a David Cronenberg movie. She woke up several times during the night, half expecting to find that her fingernails had fallen out and that she was on the verge of sprouting wings, like Jeff Goldblum in *The Fly*. Getting ready for work this morning, she caught a faint whiff of the strange solution on her skin and wondered how long it could possibly be before someone at the office commented. Before leaving the flat, she sprayed herself with half a bottle of her favourite perfume and popped the remaining half-bottle into her briefcase for good measure. It must have worked, because nobody said a thing.

And now it was that time again. Easing herself into the bath, she smothered her skin with Clinique foaming body wash and lay there for a good half-hour, relishing the warmth and cleanliness of the water and resisting the temptation to explore her pubic area for evidence of dying parasites. She knew she was probably over-reacting. She knew that, as venereal diseases went, crabs were child's play. She also knew that, despite what some people might say, there was nothing immoral about contracting pubic lice, any more than there was something immoral about catching head lice as a kid. They were two very similar, naturally occurring parasites that happened to take up residence on different areas of the body, that was all. But she couldn't help herself. She felt dirty. As far as she knew, nobody in her family had ever needed to seek treatment for any form of venereal disease, with the exception of her grandfather who had grown up on a farm in Ireland and who announced after his third brandy one horribly memorable Christmas afternoon that he had once caught crabs off a prize pig.

Still, this time tomorrow she would be free of the shame and the itching and looking forward to dinner with Martin and the chance to absolve herself by sharing a joke or two with a trusted friend about some of the scrapes she had got herself into these past few days. In fact, if there was one positive note in all of this, it was the pleasure of knowing that, whatever nasty little surprise Dylan had given her, she had more than likely passed it on to the slippery Phil.

The first time Martin had ever set foot inside a leather bar was in 1992. It was the year that Madonna kindly offered to teach the world how to fuck with her *Sex* book and *Erotica* album. Suddenly, sadomasochism was all the rage as black leather outfits came out of the closet and were paraded around on Paris catwalks and daytime TV. John was never one to let a fashion craze pass him by, least of all when it met with the approval of the world's most ambitious blonde, so naturally he insisted that he and Martin should give the West End a miss for a night and pay a visit to London's most famous gay leather bar, The Coleherne, which as luck would have it was situated just around the corner from his flat in Earl's Court. Martin had never shared John's interest in fashion. Nor, for that matter, was he a particularly big fan of Madonna. However, he did have a more than passing interest in Tony Ward, who had last been seen cavorting with the pop queen in her 'Justify My Love' video and whose lean, tightly muscled torso was exhibited to good effect in the *Sex* book, and so he agreed to go along with John's plan. Of course he wasn't seriously expecting to bump into Tony Ward on a wet Friday night in Earl's Court. But since it was common knowledge that Madonna had found many of the models featured in her book by scouring New York's leather bars, it seemed highly possible that there might be someone equally desirable just waiting to be discovered at The Coleherne.

Or perhaps not. The first thing that struck Martin as he and John stepped into The Coleherne that night was the number of men there who bore an uncanny resemblance to his father. It wasn't simply that many of them looked as though they might be the same age as his father. That he could cope with. It was the fact that they were dressed in the exact same biker's garb his father had worn when Martin was a child, although he could tell just by looking that most of them had probably never ridden a motorbike in their lives. To say that this dampened his spirits somewhat would be putting it mildly. He felt as if he had wandered into strictly forbidden territory – not in the 'Oh my, aren't we all so queer and radical' sense, but in the 'Oh my God, I've just walked in on my parents having sex' sense. It was by far and away the most unsettling thing that had ever happened to him, so much so that when John suddenly drew his attention to a man with his penis poking out through a strategically placed hole in the front of his trousers, Martin experienced what could only be described as a panic attack of Freudian proportions.

Compared to that ill-fated foray into the world of leather and latex, tonight's visit to The Hoist wasn't going too badly. Neil had been telling the truth. There was nothing here to suggest the kind of heavy sexual antics Martin associated with a full-on fetish club like Fist, where it was widely reported that no holds were barred and no holes were too small to take a well-greased arm if that happened to be the order of the day. So far, Martin had seen no evidence of people pissing on each other, no sign of anyone being fisted and most importantly nobody who looked too much like his father. Instead he had watched a steady stream of men, mostly in their thirties and above, pour through the door and either position themselves at the bar where they chatted idly about opera, or disappear into darkened corners where no doubt there were other more serious pleasures to be had.

'So what do you think of this place?' Neil asked. He had given his leathers a break tonight and was dressed head to toe in rubber. A black rubber biker's jacket hung open to reveal a white rubber vest with a plunging neckline emphasising the expanse of his large, shaved cleavage. A pair of black rubber shorts with a single white military stripe down each side reached down to his knees. Black boots with white laces came up to meet them, leaving an inch or two of calf muscle exposed. The whole ensemble was topped off with a rubber biker's cap worn at a jaunty angle. The overall effect was to make him look strangely sexless, like a giant inflatable penguin.

'Yeah, it's okay,' Martin replied, still getting used to the feel of Neil's leather chaps, which made his packet look enormous but rubbed the insides of his thighs, leaving him barely capable of walking and terrified of running in case he crushed his testicles in the process. He wondered how he would cope in the event of a fire. Come to think of it, a fire in a place like this would be a total disaster. The venue was housed in a converted railway arch that left few avenues for escape. He could just picture the fire brigade breaking down the doors and scratching their heads as they tried to identify individual bodies from one solid mass of molten black gunk. He looked around for the fire exits and was relieved to see that there was one only a few feet away.

'Those chaps look really great on you,' Neil said. 'A lot of guys you see wearing them don't carry them off properly. But you fill them out really well.'

'A bit too well, I think,' Martin joked. 'I can barely move.'

'Oh, they'll soon loosen up,' Neil said. 'That's the great thing about leather. It stretches. Not like rubber, which is hell to get into every time, even if it is worth it in the end.'

Martin could certainly vouch for the first half of this statement, even if he couldn't quite bring himself to endorse the second. Before leaving the flat tonight he had experienced the dubious pleasure of assisting Neil as he levered himself into his rubber vest – an item of clothing which ought to have come with detailed instructions and a health warning, and which if handled incorrectly was quite capable of dislocating an arm. The whole procedure, which involved half a tin of talcum powder and a lot of tugging, had taken almost half an hour. And that wasn't all. Then there was the added bother of spraying the vest with a special silicone spray to bring up the shine, all of which convinced Martin that rubber was not a look he would be experimenting with any time soon.

'It's my round,' Neil announced. 'What will it be? Another pint?'

While Neil walked over to the bar and waited to be served, Martin stood quietly fingering the tops of his chaps and surveying the room for someone to take his mind off Ben, if only for the next few minutes. He was focused on a pretty blond boy with a bare chest leaning against a pillar at the far end of the room when suddenly his view was obstructed by a man dressed in full leather, with what appeared to be a gas mask covering his entire face. As Martin leaned sideways to get a better view of the half-naked blond boy, the man in the gas mask slowly turned to face him. Then, just as Martin was thinking things couldn't get any more surreal, the man walked over and stood directly in front of him, his masked face only inches from Martin's own. Martin half expected him to say something like 'Take me to your leader'. But he didn't. He just stood there, breathing deeply through his gas mask, before slowly extending a leather gloved hand.

Martin stared at the shiny black hand held out to him, nervously wondering if this silent, strangely formal greeting was part of some sadomasochistic ritual to which he wasn't accustomed, and which carried with it an unspoken agreement to engage in sexual acts the likes of which he could barely begin to imagine. Then he stared at the gas mask, trying to decipher the face behind the glass and seeing nothing but his own worried expression reflected back at him. He was about to move away when a muffled voice echoed from behind the mask.

'Uhum,' it said. 'Uhumm hmm?'

'What?' Martin replied. 'I can't hear you.'

Seeming slightly agitated, the man shook his head and repeated his series of unintelligible grunts before reaching up and lifting the mask away from his mouth. 'Hello,' a now vaguely familiar voice said. 'How are you?'

Martin frowned. 'I'm sorry. Do I know you?'

'It's me,' the man said, lifting his mask up until finally Martin could make out the lower half of his face. 'It's me, Matthew!'

Suddenly recognising the man in the gas mask as the same man who had given him a blow job the last time he visited a sex club, Martin blushed and wondered if Matthew made a habit out of this kind of thing. 'Sorry,' he said, shaking the gloved hand and trying to avoid looking at the gas mask. 'I didn't recognise you.'

Matthew laughed. 'You look different too. I didn't know you were into all of this.'

'I'm not,' Martin said quickly. 'I'm just here with a friend.'

'Pity,' Matthew replied, and readjusted his gas mask. 'Oh, well. Nice seeing you again.' And with that he turned and walked away.

Just then Neil reappeared. 'Who's your friend?' he said, handing Martin a pint glass of lager. 'Darth Vader?'

'Oh, nobody,' Martin shrugged, watching Matthew melt into the crowd. 'Just someone I used to know, that's all.'

'It seems to be filling up a bit,' Neil said as a fat man in fishing waders squeezed by. 'Shall we move over there? I think there's a bit more room.'

Clutching their drinks in their hands, they made their way over to an empty space towards the back of the room. High above them, on a metal grate that served as a viewing gallery, a few people milled about in search of sexual partners.

'Feel free to wander off and have fun if you want,' Martin said, taking a gulp of his beer and looking around to check that Matthew and his gas mask weren't hovering near by. 'I'll be okay on my own.'

Neil grinned. 'Are you sure? I wouldn't want any harm to come to you.'

'Very funny!' Martin laughed. 'Really, I'm fine. There's nothing here I can't handle.'

The moment the words were out of his mouth, something appeared in the air directly above his head, fell down in front of his eyes and landed with a gentle splash in his glass.

Martin stared in horror at the white suspension floating in his beer. 'Some bastard just spat in my drink!' he said, looking up at the gallery for the culprit and spotting two men huddled together in what looked like a fairly compromising position.

Neil peered into Martin's glass and clasped his hand to his mouth. 'I hate to tell you this,' he said, stifling a laugh. 'But I don't think that's spit.'

Chapter seventeen

Ben hadn't called by the time Martin arrived home alone from The Hoist and eased himself out of Neil's leather chaps. Nor had he called by the time he arrived back from work the following evening and rushed eagerly into the living room to check the answerphone. Martin dialled 1471, and felt his heart sink as the automated voice confirmed that the last incoming call matched the only message on the machine, left by John at 11.23 a.m. precisely, inviting both him and Neil to 'a small, surprise party' at his place on Saturday night. Martin could tell from the tone of John's voice that he had something to celebrate, although his words gave little away. He simply said that there was going to be an announcement of some kind and requested that they each brought along a bottle of something bubbly. Maybe John had finally been given that promotion he was always talking about, Martin thought, and tried not to feel too resentful at the prospect. John already cleared a couple of thousand a month. Then there were the various bonuses the airline awarded to him in the form of premiums and free flights, not to mention the other little extras Fernando gave him in the form of free drugs and, if John was to be believed, sex more or less on demand. It wasn't as if John actually wanted for anything these days. He already had it all – the smart flat, the hot boyfriend, the invitations to celebrity parties, the place on the guest list, the free drinks tickets, the complimentary drugs, everything. In fact, the only thing Martin could imagine John regularly paying for was food, and since his diet appeared to consist mainly of pills and powders supplemented by the occasional takeaway, it seemed pretty safe to assume that his monthly food bill wasn't about to break the bank.

Martin's mind had been on money all day. Since collecting the post this morning and making the mistake of opening his bank statement, he had been trying to get to grips with the sorry state of his personal finances. Try as he might, he couldn't work out where all his money went each month. It wasn't as if he squandered his earnings on fancy clothes or flash restaurants. He rarely went to the cinema, never visited the theatre, and hardly ever went to clubs where he couldn't bluff his way in without paying or count on a free lift home afterwards with Neil. He didn't smoke particularly heavily and only did the bars once or twice a week at most, which he thought showed remarkable restraint for a single gay man in pursuit of a boyfriend. At home he drank cheap, supermarket-label vodka, and when he was out clubbing he tended to last the night on a single bottle of water which he refilled at regular intervals from the tap, unless John was feeling especially generous with his drinks tickets in which case he might treat himself to the odd vodka and Red Bull. Unlike John, he was usually required to pay for his drugs. But a couple of Es and the odd gram of coke could hardly account for him being overdrawn by the middle of each month, could it?

Despite having no money in the bank and two weeks to go until his next pay cheque, he arrived home this evening with another dent in his credit card and his hands weighed down by three carrier bags full of groceries, the contents of which were intended for tonight's dinner with Caroline. For the first course, he planned to make a salad of spinach, Pecorino cheese and almonds, served with a sherry vinegar dressing. For the main course, he had bought some lean sirloin steaks, new potatoes and sugarsnap peas. For dessert, he had fresh blueberries and frozen yoghurt. This would be followed by freshly ground coffee, and the whole lot washed down with a bottle of red wine and as many vodka and tonics as seemed appropriate. The bill for this orgy of culinary delights had come to just over £40. When push came to shove, Martin's attitude towards debt was rather like Quentin Crisp's attitude towards dusting – once a certain amount piles up you might as well ignore it completely because, relatively speaking, it doesn't get any worse. And besides, it was ages since he had entertained anyone at home, and while Caroline would be eaten up with guilt if she thought for one moment that he was feeding her with food he really couldn't afford, the truth was that she was hardly the kind of person you could invite over for dinner and present with a bowl of pasta smothered in a cheap, ready-made sauce. Caroline had what Martin's mother would describe as 'champagne tastes'. The fact that his income barely seemed to stretch to beer was beside the point.

Maybe it was the idea of Caroline and her champagne tastes which planted the thought in his head, but as he was rinsing the spinach for the salad he suddenly remembered that he had half a gram of coke left over from last weekend.

Turning off the tap and drying his hands with the tea towel, he headed into the bathroom. It was John who always said that a wise queen hides his drugs in the bathroom. That way, if the police ever came knocking at the door, you simply locked yourself in the bathroom and flushed them down the toilet. Martin had taken this advice to heart, and kept his drugs hidden inside an empty condom box in the bottom drawer of the bathroom cabinet. But when he opened the drawer and took out the box, it was completely empty. Thinking this was odd, he went into the bedroom to check that he hadn't accidentally left the wrap tucked safely inside his wallet, or lying open for all to see on the bedside cabinet. Again, nothing. It was then that an unpleasant thought began to form in the back of his mind. Could Neil have stolen his coke? Martin had left Neil at The Hoist last night, chatting away to some guy in a leather chest harness. Hours later, he was half asleep in bed when he heard Neil arrive home, talking in muted tones with a man with a high voice and heavy boots. It wasn't beyond the realms of possibility that either Neil or his piece of trade had gone into the bathroom looking for some condoms, found the coke and decided to help themselves. At least that would help explain how they had managed to keep going for most of the night.

Remembering that Neil was working late and wouldn't be back for hours, Martin decided to take a quick peek inside his bedroom. Opening the door, the first thing that struck him was the smell of poppers. Living with Neil was a bit like sharing a flat with a teenager – you never knew what manner of disgusting surprises were in store for you when you ignored the warning signs and entered his bedroom unannounced. Looking around the room, his eye was drawn to a copy of *QX* lying on the floor next to the bed. The cover of the magazine showed a bare-chested black man with enormous nipples, but this wasn't what caught his attention. Scattered across the man's chest was a sprinkling of white crumbs and, lying next to the magazine, a screwed-up piece of paper. So, his suspicions had been right all along! Neil had stolen his coke! In fact, it looked as if there was barely a line left! First the toilet, and now this. He could see that he and Neil would have to have a serious talk.

Carefully lifting up the magazine so that none of the precious white powder fell onto the floor, Martin carried it gingerly into his own bedroom, where he arranged the crumbs into a surprisingly large line and quickly snorted it before returning to the kitchen and the task of rinsing his spinach.

John was having a Britney moment, dancing around his living room to an extended dance remix of 'Oops! I Did It Again'. His body was still on New York time, and his mind was mulling over an incident which had taken place a few nights ago in the city that never slept, possibly because a fair number of its inhabitants were addicted to crystal meth. John had tried crystal once, three years ago at a gay club in Los Angeles. It was a bit like speed, only the effects were far stronger and it didn't make his dick shrink. He took several lines and was awake for two days and horny as hell, which he quickly learned was the best way to enjoy West Hollywood. Every gay man John met in LA seemed to be permanently wired, whether they were on drugs or not. If they weren't telling you how they planned to break into the movies, they were working the room in search of film producers, casting directors, talent scouts or anyone else who might be persuaded to help make them a star in return for a discreet blow job. Most claimed to know someone who knew someone who had slept with David Geffen and hadn't looked back since. The name of a certain Hollywood heart-throb with short legs and a winning grin came up in conversation a lot.

John hadn't arrived in New York on Monday evening planning to repeat the crystal experience. After a quick shower at the hotel, he headed straight for the Splash bar in Chelsea, hoping to score some coke but quickly falling for the charms of one of the barboys, a beefy, corn-fed blond in a pair of black Calvin Klein trunks called Jamie. The bar staff at Splash were required to undress for work right down to their underwear, which helped explain why the bar was always full and why most of the customers were happy to throw in an extra dollar or two here and there as tips. John must have tipped Jamie twenty dollars in total that night, the tips becoming more generous the more drunk he became and the more Jamie dazzled him with his sweet white smile. One thing John had noticed during his many trips to New York was that the locals didn't really drink in the way that Londoners did. Even on the gay scene, the excessive consumption of alcohol was generally frowned upon. So when he wandered off in search of the toilets and practically fell down the stairs, it was inevitable that he would attract attention. As luck would have it, attention came in the form of a slightly pudgy queen who was clearly accustomed to having to buy friends in gym-fit Chelsea, and who tried to win John over by offering him a line to help sober him up. John accepted his offer before quickly losing him in the crowd and returning to the bar to continue drooling over Jamie. It was only then that he realised that the line he had been given wasn't coke but crystal meth.

John's subsequent attempts to charm the Calvins off Jamie hadn't met with much success. He quickly learned that Jamie didn't have a boyfriend, which was good, only to be told an hour later that he did have a girlfriend, which obviously wasn't so good. At one point, their conversation was interrupted by an older queen with his arm in plaster, who assured John that Jamie wasn't quite as naïve or quite as straight as he made out, insisting that the barboys at Splash were encouraged to invent girlfriends and pass themselves off as straight in much the same way that porn stars were required to butch it up in gay porn films. John didn't find this the least bit comforting. By the time the bar closed and Jamie bade him a fond but firm farewell, he was high on crystal, fuelled up on testosterone and desperate for sex. He caught a cab and told the driver to take him to the meatpacking district, where he had been reliably informed there was an after-hours jack-off club.

His recollection of what happened after that was pretty fragmented, but filled with moments of alarming clarity, the way memories of mad, drug-fucked nights often were. He remembered finding the club, paying his entrance fee and ordering a Diet Coke at the bar. He remembered someone grabbing him from behind and smothering him with beery kisses. He remembered leaving and being led across the street to an apartment building that looked like something out of the film *Seven*, but without the added attraction of Brad Pitt or Gwyneth Paltrow's head in a box. He remembered having clumsy, unsatisfying sex on a mattress on the floor with the daylight streaming in through a bare window and onto a bare Puerto Rican who looked far less appealing in the cold light of day than he had first appeared in the darkness of the club. He remembered waking up several hours later, discovering that the door was locked and arguing with the Puerto Rican to let him out. He remembered suddenly feeling very, very afraid for his life and promising to come back later before finally being released and stumbling out of the building and into a cab.

John remembered all of this, and for the past three days all he had really wanted to do was to forget it all as quickly as possible. Guilt was not an emotion John was overly familiar with, but when he thought about Fernando and Jamie and the Puerto Rican, it was definitely guilt that he felt. Six months ago, what happened in New York wouldn't have bothered John in the slightest. He would have joked about it with his friends, or written it off as one of those crazy things that happen from time to time, and which provide the raw material for entertaining anecdotes to be polished and trotted out at regular intervals for years to come. But if someone had told John six months ago that he would be in a relationship which meant more to him than any he'd had before, he would probably have laughed in their face. Something had definitely changed since he'd met Fernando, which was why he had arranged a little party on Saturday, where he planned to surprise everyone by demonstrating his commitment to the man who had brought him so much happiness and for whom he was willing to mend his ways once and for all.

Of course, when John promised faithfully to have sex with nobody except his boyfriend for the foreseeable future, he didn't foresee cybersex as coming within the bounds of the agreement. Earlier this afternoon, he'd had a nice long session with 'CuriousCute28'. If asked to justify his behaviour, John would have insisted that he had only gone online in order to check his e-mails, and that he was as surprised as anyone when, half an hour later, he found himself sitting at his keyboard with his briefs around his ankles and a blob of semen drying on his thigh. The truth was, try as he might, John couldn't give up these illicit meetings in cyberspace. In their own way, they fulfilled a need in him that wasn't being met by his sexy, strong, but not very verbal boyfriend. He needed 'CuriousCute28' almost as much as he needed Fernando, which was why he planned to continue his dangerous liaison after Fernando moved in.

But for now it was just him and Britney. Pop music was the one thing guaranteed to lift his spirits at times like these. And what could be more appropriate than Britney making light of the fact that, oops, she did it again? Somehow, the contradiction of knowing that she was a self-proclaimed virgin, and that she was making excuses for the kind of bad behaviour she had probably never even indulged in, made this particular dose of pop therapy all the more comforting. Turning up the volume on the CD player, John turned to face the mirror and sang along at the top of his voice: 'I'm not that innocent!'

Caroline set down her dessert spoon, took a sip of wine and stared at Martin across the table, trying to gauge his reaction to what she had just told him and not getting very far. 'So,' she said finally. 'What do you think?'

Martin frowned. 'Let me get this straight. You saw Graham with another woman, which confirms what I said all along, that he is in fact heterosexual and not the closet case you always insisted he was. Then you bumped into him in the street, and he invited you for coffee, and you said no.'

'Yes,' Caroline said, already feeling guilty for editing out the part about Dylan and Phil and the fact that she had spent the past forty-eight hours smothered in Qualada.

'Well, I don't get it,' Martin said. 'I thought you said you wanted him back. So why say no?'

'It was a bit awkward at the time,' Caroline mumbled. 'I was rushing to get to work. And he is seeing someone else.'

'He's only seeing someone else because you drove him away with your wild accusations,' Martin said, and was immediately taken aback by how accusatory he sounded. There was a long pause.

'Yes, well, I fucked up,' Caroline said finally. 'Anyway, what's been happening with you? Met anyone nice recently?'

'There was this one guy . . .' Martin began, then trailed off. 'Look, I'm sorry for snapping just now. I didn't mean to sound so unsympathetic.'

Caroline smiled to show there were no hard feelings. 'No, it's okay, really. I was stupid. I've been kicking myself ever since.'

'Well, don't kick yourself. Just call him and tell him you'd like to meet for a drink or something. What's the worst that could happen?'

She shrugged. 'He could tell me to piss off, I suppose. Anyway, enough about me. Tell me about this guy.'

So for the next ten minutes Martin talked about Ben, and the night they had spent together, and how it was the closest thing to real intimacy he'd felt in a long time, and how he'd left several messages and how Ben hadn't returned any of them. When he finished, he poured himself another glass of wine and forced a smile. 'And that's about it,' he said, staring into his glass. 'Another one bites the dust.'

'Well, it's his loss,' Caroline said gently. 'I think you're really strong.'

He blushed. 'Strong, why?'

'Because you don't play games. Because you aren't afraid to let your feelings show.'

He laughed. 'Hang on a minute! This isn't like you – the queen of denial! I thought hiding your feelings and playing hard to get was all par for the course.'

She shrugged and lit a cigarette. 'A girl can change her mind, can't she? Actually, I've changed my mind about quite a few things lately. And trust me, playing games is a waste of time. If you know what you want, the best thing you can do is just go for it.'

'So why don't you?'

'Maybe I will,' she said, pushing her plate away and reaching for the ashtray. 'Well, that was a lovely meal,' she added brightly. 'But I'm afraid the after-dinner speeches are getting a bit morose. How about a line of coke to liven things up?'

'I had one earlier,' Martin said, clearing the plates and carrying them into the kitchen. 'I didn't feel a thing. Maybe I've done too much and it just isn't working any more.'

'You can never do too much coke,' Caroline shouted, reaching into her handbag for the final gram purchased with the proceeds from her date with Dylan. The crabs had already been obliterated. By the time this gram was finished, there would be no link with him left.

Martin reappeared with the bottle of champagne Caroline had brought, which had been chilling for the past hour and a half. 'What about when your nose caves in?' he said. 'Like that girl from *EastEnders*?'

Caroline grinned. 'That will never happen to me. At the first sign of trouble, I plan to have the insides of my nostrils lined with solid gold. Believe me, cosmetic surgery has an answer for everything.'

Twenty minutes later they were deep in coke conversation, each feeling the urge to confess things they had previously held back from mentioning, and ranting at one another without even realising it.

'The problem with straight men,' Caroline said, 'is that they're never really straight with you. They don't know what they want half the time. And even when they do, they're afraid of telling you in case you trample on their fragile little egos. It's no wonder so many women are willing to give lesbianism a try. I don't think I could, though. Women are too emotional. We analyse things too much. Put me in bed with another woman and we'd probably end up discussing our relationships with our mothers for hours.'

'Gay men are exactly the same,' Martin said. 'If anything, they're probably even more uptight than straight men because they feel like they've constantly got to prove something. I mean, I like men to behave like men. But some of them take it far too seriously. You should see some of the personal ads in the gay papers. It's all "straight-acting" this and "straight-looking" that. And some of the photos! Half of them look as if they're constipated. What's wrong with smiling? Is it only women who are allowed to smile? Actually, I wouldn't mind being a lesbian. Although, having said that, a lot of them don't smile very much either.'

'Maybe *we* should just get it together,' Caroline joked. 'You never know, it might be fun.'

'Forget it,' Martin said. 'Madonna and Rupert Everett tried that and look where it got them.'

Caroline laughed. 'I'll bet he never gave her crabs though.'

'Maybe not, but he didn't do her acting career any favours. They should have called that film *The Next Best Thing To A Telemovie*. It was awful.'

'Did I mention that I caught crabs?' Caroline asked, knowing full well that she hadn't.

Martin stopped and stared. 'Crabs? Seriously? Who from?'

'Well, you remember Dylan?' she began, and proceeded to tell him the entire story, beginning with the meeting at The Sanderson, moving on to the encounter at the Fridge with

Phil and the crisis at work, and ending with the irritating indignity of the past two days.

'No wonder you were freaked out when you bumped into Graham,' Martin said, before telling her the tale of the one-legged man – partly to make her feel better, and partly out of a compulsion to get it off his chest and solicit a little sympathy into the bargain.

'We're a right pair, aren't we?' Caroline said when he'd finished. 'Still, it could be worse.'

'Really?' Martin asked. 'How?'

'Well, we could be all out of coke for a start,' she replied, and began chopping another line.

By the time Neil arrived home shortly after midnight, Caroline had left and Martin was sitting in front of the television, wired to the eyeballs and watching a late-night movie without really concentrating.

'I see you finished off your coke, then,' Neil said as he walked into the room.

Martin looked up. 'What do you mean?'

'Your coke,' Neil repeated. 'I found a wrap last night when I came in, on the floor outside your bedroom. I guess it must have fallen out of your wallet. I put it back in the drawer in the bathroom. Anyway, I'm going to make myself a cup of tea. Fancy one?'

'Please,' Martin said, and waited for Neil to wander off into the kitchen before dashing into the bathroom and searching through the bathroom cabinet. Sure enough, the wrap was there, not in the bottom drawer where he usually kept it, but in the second drawer down.

'Have you seen my copy of QX?' Neil shouted. 'I thought I'd left in my room but it doesn't seem to be there.'

'I'll just go and get it,' Martin called back, running into his room and returning with the magazine. 'I was having a quick flick through it earlier,' he explained, handing it to Neil.

'Thanks,' Neil said. 'There's a personal ad I thought I might reply to. It's in under the Tongueworks' section. Sounds quite promising.'

'Great,' said Martin. He paused. 'Um, Neil, I'm really sorry about this, but the thing is, when I took the magazine from your room, well, I think some coke might have fallen onto the floor when I picked it up. I hope you don't mind. It was an accident.'

Neil thought for a moment, then laughed. 'That wasn't coke. That was just me filing my toenails this morning. I was going to tip it down the toilet, but then someone phoned from work and I forgot. Stop looking so worried. There's no harm done. I'll just hoover it up in the morning.'

Martin forced a smile. 'Good,' he said. 'That's a relief.' Then he ran into the bathroom and threw up.

Chapter eighteen

Caroline had arranged to meet Graham at a tapas bar in Camden Town at eight. Camden wasn't a part of town Caroline frequented very often. For her, it would always be the stomping ground of solemn student types with green hair and blue Doc Martens. Nor was she particularly fond of tapas bars. Tapas was for people who liked to eat between meals, which invariably meant people who didn't have to watch their weight. But she wasn't about to question Graham's judgement. She was surprised that he had agreed to meet her at all, especially at such short notice, and was amazed when he turned down her initial suggestion of an afternoon coffee in favour of a potentially more intimate arrangement. The fact that he was free to meet her on Saturday night, when she would have expected him to be spending quality time with his skinny new girlfriend, meant that Caroline spent much of Saturday afternoon fantasising that Graham and his mystery woman had already split up. The fact that she was meeting him at eight, and not three as she had first suggested, meant that she spent the rest of the afternoon slowly working her way through the various beauty products cluttering up her bathroom shelves, finally emerging with barely an hour to go and a face that bore witness to the power of Clarins.

She took a taxi into Camden and arrived at the bar twenty minutes late to find Graham already seated at a table. It looked as though he'd spent a fair amount of time getting ready himself. The red shirt he was wearing was one that she had helped him pick out, and he was sporting a fresh haircut, complete with a fresh razor rash on the back of his neck. He looked happy to see her and, if she wasn't mistaken, slightly nervous. He stood up to greet her with a polite peck on the cheek while all around them Camden couples snuggled together over candle-lit tables.

'You made it, then,' he joked as she sat down.

She smiled. 'Yes, sorry I'm a bit late. The traffic was terrible.'

There was an awkward silence as she puffed away furiously on a cigarette and he scrutinised the wine list, before finally settling on a bottle of Chilean red. Caroline made a mental note that a bottle of wine would take far longer to drink than a couple of glasses and wondered how long Graham was expecting this meeting to last, and whether she should waste time with small talk or cut straight to the chase.

'You look good,' he said, pouring the wine.

'You too,' she replied brightly, and they both laughed.

Caroline took a sip of wine followed by a deep breath. 'Look, Graham,' she began. 'I know you're probably still angry about the way I behaved before, which you've every right to be, obviously. And I'm sure you've probably got other plans tonight. So, if I can just say what I . . .'

'Hang on a minute,' he said. 'Why do you say that?'

'Say what?'

'That I've got other plans tonight.'

Caroline hesitated before answering. 'Well, I just assumed that you'd be seeing your girlfriend later.'

'Girlfriend? What girlfriend? I haven't got a girlfriend. What makes you think that?'

'I saw you,' Caroline said quickly, and immediately regretted the way the words came out, like an accusation. Now he was going to think that she'd been spying on him again. 'I think it may have been last Saturday,' she went on as casually as she could. 'Anyway, I was in a taxi, on my way home after a few drinks with . . . a friend. I think it might have been somewhere around Edgware Road, or possibly Baker Street, somewhere like that. And I just happened to see you. With a woman. You looked pretty close, so naturally I assumed . . .'

Graham looked confused for a moment. Then he broke into a smile. 'That must have been Charlotte!' he said, laughing. 'Of course! Wait till I tell her about this. She'll wet herself. Believe me, Charlotte is just a friend.'

Hating the thought of Graham and his new female 'friend' sharing a joke at her expense, Caroline felt her temper rise. 'Really?' she said. 'I don't remember you ever mentioning a friend called Charlotte before.'

'That's because I only met her recently,' he said, still chuckling quietly. 'Trust me, even if I was looking for something more than friendship from Charlotte, which I'm not, I don't think I'd get very far. I'm not her type. For one thing, she's a lesbian.'

Now it was Caroline's turn to look confused. 'But . . .' she began. 'But . . .'

'But what?' Graham asked. 'But she doesn't look like a lesbian?'

'Well, no. As a matter of fact, she doesn't.'

'And how many lesbians do you know exactly?'

Caroline thought for a moment. 'I've met a few,' she said finally. Then, sensing that she was digging herself into an even bigger hole than the one she was in already, she tried to bluff her way out. 'Anyway, that's not the point.'

'No,' Graham said with a smile. 'It's not the point. The point is that you have an uncanny habit of jumping to the wrong conclusions about the kind of person I am and the kind of people I sleep with. But that's partly my fault, so why don't we just agree to let it go for now? There's something I'd like to clear up first. I wish I could have done this three months ago, but I needed more time to get my head around it first. The reason I suggested we meet tonight and not this afternoon is that there's something I've been wanting to explain to you, and I think the best way to explain it would be to just show you. So, will you come?'

'Where to?'

'You'll see,' he said, looking at his watch. 'It's still a bit early yet. Why don't we get a bite to eat, finish our wine and then go? Don't worry. It's not very far.'

It was barely even ten, and already John's party had reached that point where people were starting to wonder whether it was time to make their excuses and leave. The host clearly wasn't in the best of moods, largely due to the non-appearance of his boyfriend. And without Fernando there to provide them with drugs, some of the guests were beginning to get into a panic over where their next chemical high was going to come from. It was Saturday night after all, and nobody wanted to wind up at a club two or three hours from now, devoid of artificial stimulants. Most of them wouldn't have the first clue how to behave.

'Fernando is coming, isn't he?' Camp David asked as he followed John into the kitchen, hoping to find a line to tide him over until the serious dealing began and he could avail himself of other people's generosity as they entered into the party spirit.

'Of course he's coming!' John snapped, removing a bottle of champagne from the fridge and attacking the foil with a kitchen knife and a ferocity that was enough to warn off all but the most determined of coke whores.

'Do you have any idea when?' David enquired, standing his ground and smiling innocently. 'Or is that all part of the surprise?'

John glowered at him. 'Your guess is as good as mine,' he said sharply. 'Now if you don't mind, I do have other guests.'

He swanned back into the living room, where Martin and Neil were deep in conversation with the two Steves while an assortment of John's friends, colleagues and mere acquaintances milled about with half-empty glasses and pained expressions. Martin had already exchanged a few words with Shane, John's friend from the airline, and was a little taken aback to find that Shane seemed to know far more about his break-up with Christopher than he did. He was about to get to the bottom of this when Shane's boyfriend Yuichi appeared, chattering hysterically about something he'd overheard in the bedroom and leading Shane away with a firm grip.

'No word from Fernando yet, then?' Neil said as John made his way towards them.

'No, Neil,' John replied. 'Though judging by those blocked sinuses of yours I'd say you've shoved quite enough coke up your nose for one week.'

'It's just the start of a cold,' Neil protested.

'You should try euthanasia,' John said, snatching Neil's glass and refilling it with champagne.

'I think you mean echinacea,' Neil laughed.

John smiled icily. 'I know exactly what I mean.'

'I had a chat with Shane earlier,' Martin said. 'He seems to know an awful lot about me and Christopher.'

John's face gave nothing away. 'Really? I can't think why. Maybe they have a friend in common. Anyway, I wouldn't worry about it. Nobody takes anything Shane says seriously. You only have to look at his taste in men to see why.'

'Who are those two over there, John?' Neil asked, gesturing towards a rather overweight, not terribly attractive man in an orange T-shirt with the word 'Massive' emblazoned across the chest, standing huddled in a corner with a far younger, far prettier boy in a white vest.

'The one in the T-shirt is a DJ,' John replied. 'I forget which clubs he works at. And before you ask, yes the other one is his boyfriend.'

'What's a boy like that doing with him?' Martin asked. 'He's not what you'd call a catch, is he?'

John looked at Martin as if he were mad. 'Er, hello? Didn't you hear what I just said? He's a DJ! Anyway, from what I hear you've been getting more than your fair share lately. First that cowboy, then allowing Neil here to drag you to a bar full of leathermen. What are you trying to do? Sleep your way through the Village People?'

Before Martin could come back with a smart reply, Shane and Yuichi reappeared, followed by David. All three were clearly wired on coke and giggling hysterically.

'We've been admiring your computer, John,' Shane said. 'Don't tell me you're one of those sad queens who spends all day looking for sex on the internet.'

John scowled. 'Of course not. In case you hadn't noticed, I have a boyfriend.'

'Me too,' said Shane, sliding his arm around Yuichi's narrow waist. 'The only difference is, mine is actually here.'

'Don't knock it until you've tried it,' David said, wagging a finger at Shane. 'The only sex I ever get these days is with people I meet on the internet. And at least in cyberspace nobody can scream at you for not being safe.'

'You mean you don't actually meet these people?' Martin asked, confused.

'Oh, no,' David replied, happy for an opportunity to discuss his sex life. 'It all happens right there on the screen. The secret is to think up a good screen name, one that will get them going. Having the word "Muscle" in there helps. Or you can always do what I do, and pretend to be straight.'

John laughed. 'Straight? You? I can't believe anyone falls for that.'

'You'd be surprised what people will fall for,' David said, narrowing his eyes. 'For example, tell them that you're twenty-eight, cute and curious about gay sex and they're soon hooked. There's this one queen I have a wank with fairly regularly. He says he works as a security guard for an airline, which I assume means he's a trolley dolly. Maybe you know him.'

John bared his teeth in what just about passed for a smile. 'I don't think so,' he said. 'I'm choosy about the kind of company I keep.' And with that he flounced off in the direction of the bathroom.

'Don't take any notice of him,' Neil said. 'He's just pissed off because Fernando hasn't turned up.'

Shane nodded. 'I wonder what's happened to him?'

'Maybe he's been stopped by the police,' the first of the two Steves suggested.

'Another dealer we know was busted last week,' the second Steve added mournfully, shaking his head. 'It totally ruined our weekend.'

'Well I hope Fernando isn't sitting in a police cell,' Neil said. 'Aside from the fact that it would make John even more of a nightmare than he is already, I've ordered a gram of coke, some K and four Es for later. I assume we are still going to Crash?'

'I suppose so,' Martin replied. 'But we should probably wait and see if Fernando shows up.'

They didn't have to wait very much longer. Martin was about to resume his earlier conversation with Shane about his break-up with Christopher when there was a sudden flurry of activity. The buzzer rang and John came dashing out of the bathroom and ran towards the door to greet his rather late and already much-missed boyfriend. There was the sound of the front door opening and voices being raised. A few minutes later John reappeared, closely followed by Fernando who as usual seemed prepared to let John do all the talking.

'Okay, everybody!' John said, raising his voice to be heard over the general murmur of conversation, most of which involved at least some degree of speculation as to the reason for Fernando's late arrival, and whether or not he was fully equipped to deal with all the requests that were about to be made of him.

'I hope he's got my drugs,' Neil whispered to Martin. 'After this, I've got a feeling I'm going to need them.'

'Can I have a bit of quiet please!' John shouted, glaring at Neil, who returned his gaze with a frosty smile. 'Thank you. Now, I asked you all here tonight for a reason, and now that Fernando has arrived, I can reveal what that reason is. I'm sure most of you know that Fernando and I have been seeing each other for just over three months now, which is practically a year in gay time. And I'm sure there are some people here who might be a little surprised that this relationship has lasted as long as it has, given my track record.'

This prompted a ripple of laughter, together with shouts of 'tart' and 'slapper'.

'Yes, very funny,' John said impatiently. 'Believe me, nobody is more surprised than me. But the fact is that it has lasted, and I think the time has come for us to acknowledge that in some way. And it's for this reason that I've decided to ask Fernando to move in with me.'

The room fell silent. All eyes were on Fernando, who simply stood there saying nothing, with a shell-shocked look slowly spreading across his face. He reminded Martin of a trapped animal, suddenly realising that the cage he has been lured into doesn't have an exit.

'Well?' John said, turning to him with a slightly worried expression. 'Aren't you going to say something?'

Fernando stared back at John, then gazed around the room at all the open-mouthed guests. 'Hmm,' he mumbled finally, turning to face John and shrugging his shoulders. 'Erm, maybe.'

Caroline stood outside the busy pub on Camden High Street and watched in disbelief as Graham pushed open the door. This had to be some kind of joke. The Black Cap was one of the oldest, most famous gay pubs in London. She knew this because she'd walked past it one afternoon with Martin, and remembered him telling her that Lily Savage performed there before making the leap into television. Caroline couldn't understand it. After all that she and Graham had put each other through over the past few months, after all the things she'd accused him of and all the confusion he'd caused with his secret meetings and his funny phone calls and his mysterious lesbian friends, Graham was actually taking her to a gay pub. Just what the hell was going on? Was he about to turn around and tell her that he was gay after all? Was he trying to orchestrate a situation whereby she and Charlotte somehow met and got it on together and he was given the chance to fulfill the ultimate straight male fantasy of watching two women having sex? Was it all an elaborate wind-up designed to make her see the error of her ways? Had he wandered into the wrong pub by mistake?

'Are you coming in then?' Graham asked, holding the door open with one hand and waving at her with the other.

Caroline stared back at him. 'Graham, would you mind telling me just exactly what we're doing here?'

'All in good time,' he said. 'Now, come on. I think the show is about to start.'

He led her through the busy front bar, which was filled with men who looked nothing like those she'd seen the previous weekend at Love Muscle – partly because they had their shirts on, and partly because the shirts they happened to be wearing didn't look particularly fashionable. A few heads turned as they squeezed their way through the crowds and entered the noisy rear bar, where attention was taken off Caroline and focused onto a stage at the far end of the room. As they found an empty place at the bar and Graham ordered the drinks, the music suddenly stopped, and a chorus of shrieks and whistles announced the arrival onstage of an ageing drag queen in a red curly wig and a dress that was probably once white but which a combination of sweat and beer had turned a pale yellow. It didn't take long for Caroline to form a pretty good idea of how the beer stains might have got there. As the drag queen proceeded to mime away inexpertly to a series of Shirley Bassey numbers, the crowd's enthusiasm waned considerably, until finally the cries of 'Off!' threatened to drown out even the Welsh warbler's amplified vocal performance. By the end of the show, the only person who still appeared to be enjoying himself was Graham, who never took his eyes off the stage for a moment, and whose applause never dwindled.

As the drag queen wandered off, still smiling bravely and blowing kisses to the baying crowd, Graham turned to Caroline and asked her what she thought of the show.

'I thought it was terrible,' she said.

Graham grinned. 'Yes, it was pretty bad, wasn't it? Still, it's only his third time on stage. It's probably just nerves. I'm sure he'll get better with practice.'

Caroline stared at him incredulously. 'Do you mean to tell me that you actually know that person?'

Graham hesitated, then turned to wave at the drag queen, who waved back as he made his way through the crowd towards them.

'Graham,' Caroline hissed. 'Would you please tell me what's going on?'

'Just a minute,' Graham said, and stepped forward to greet the drag queen. Then, placing a hand on the drag queen's shoulder, he turned back to face her. 'Caroline,' he said, smiling awkwardly. 'Allow me to introduce you to my father.'

The drag queen winked and offered Caroline a hand the size of a garden spade. 'Pleased to meet you,' he said in a gruff voice. 'Graham has told me a lot about you.'

Caroline stared back at him in disbelief. 'Really?' she said, suddenly remembering her manners and shaking his hand. 'He's told me absolutely nothing about you.'

*

Saturday nights at Crash were always busy, and tonight was no exception. Elbowing their way through the mass of wide-eyed muscle queens packed like veal calves and swaying in time to the music, Martin, Neil and John queued for ten minutes with their coats and finally made it onto the dance floor in time for the E to come up. Fernando had long since disappeared. He and John had barely spoken to each other since leaving John's flat and climbing into the back of Neil's car for the drive across town. By the time Neil found a place to park a short walk away from the club, the atmosphere inside the car had taken a turn for the worse, resulting in Fernando shouting something in Portuguese before leaping out and disappearing into the club ahead of the others. That was the last anyone had seen of him.

As the sudden rush of the E blended with the buzz from the coke he'd had earlier, and Neil began passing round the bottle of K, Martin concentrated on clearing his mind of negative thoughts. Given the situation with Fernando, he hadn't said anything to John about the conversation he'd had with Camp David moments before the party ended. But based on what David had told him, he certainly intended to have his say once tonight was over. According to David, the reason Martin's father had been bombarding him with self-help books and free condoms for the past three months was that John had taken him aside at Gay Pride and expressed concern about his son's emotional and physical well-being, even going so far as to suggest that Martin should probably be persuaded to go for an HIV test. What possible motive John could have for planting such ideas in his father's head Martin couldn't begin to imagine. But the knowledge that John had spoken out of turn in this instance left him in little doubt that John was also the person responsible for Shane being so well informed about his break-up with Christopher. Frustrating as it was, Martin knew that now was not the best time to take any of this up with John who, judging by the dopey grin spreading across his face, was in a far happier place than he had been for the past couple of hours.

'I think I'm getting my second wind,' Neil said suddenly. Earlier in the car, Neil had complained of feeling nauseous. Evidently this was no longer the case. Watching as he took out his bottle of K and jammed it in his right nostril, Martin took it for granted that Neil would be up for a third, fourth and possibly even fifth wind before the night was out.

'Do you remember when we only used to take one type of drug on a night out?' Neil asked, handing Martin the K bottle.

'I can remember when I didn't take any drugs at all,' Martin replied, and laughed at how ridiculous it sounded. Hovering next to him, two men locked together in a sweaty embrace with their tongues firmly lodged down one another's throats suddenly came up for air and gazed longingly at the bottle he held in his hand.

'This is fantastic!' John announced, throwing his head back and flinging his arms wide open. 'Can you feel it? This is the best feeling in the world! Can you feel it? It's amazing!'

Realising that John probably wasn't ready for a bump of K just yet, Martin turned to return the bottle to Neil, who had his hand clasped tightly over his mouth. His eyes were watering and he was making a strange hacking sound, like a cat coughing up a furball. 'Are you okay?' Martin said, touching Neil's shoulder.

Neil nodded and spluttered, before gently lowering his hand from his mouth and staring at the tiny puddle of vomit that lay in his palm. 'I think I just threw up my E,' he said, studying the contents of his palm some more and then lifting his hand back to his mouth and gobbling the whole lot down again. 'Better to be safe than sorry,' he said, grinning happily and reaching out for the K bottle. 'I wouldn't want some queen finding an E on the floor that I paid good money for, even if I did have the first bite at it.'

Martin handed Neil the bottle and turned away in disgust. Maybe it was the effects of the K, or maybe it was the shock, but suddenly everything seemed to go into slow motion. Seeing the look of horror on John's face, Martin stared at him quizzically before turning and focusing on the spot where Neil had been standing only moments ago. Only now he wasn't standing. He was lying flat on his back on the floor. His legs were thrashing about, his eyes were wide open in a glassy stare and blood was foaming out of his mouth. He looked like a fish that had just been hooked, which Martin thought was a strange thing to pop into his head at a time like this, and which added to the general sense of unreality. A few people had stopped dancing and were staring blankly at the man gasping for air on the floor in front of them. Most carried on as if nothing remotely unusual was happening.

'Oh, my God!' Martin cried, and looked around in desperation for someone to step in and tell him what to do. He reached out to John, who was backing away slowly, mouthing something about needing to find Fernando. Suddenly a woman appeared from nowhere and knelt down beside Neil, turning him over on to his side, forcing her hand into his mouth and pulling out his tongue. 'Help me!' she shouted at Martin, who fell to the floor next to her and followed her instructions to pin Neil down while she tried to clear the obstruction in his throat. People were beginning to move away now. A path cleared and two men in white uniforms appeared, lifting up Neil's limp body and carrying him off across the dance floor. Martin stood frozen to the spot, wondering why the music was still playing and watching as Neil's white face and wide lifeless eyes bobbed along through the parting crowds and finally disappeared from view. There was a brief moment of hesitation as people exchanged puzzled looks and then everything reverted to normal. Within a matter of minutes it was if Neil had never even been there.

Martin looked around for John, who was nowhere to be seen, then started wading through the crowd until he reached the entrance to the club. 'I'm looking for my friend,' he shouted at the security guard. 'They just carried him off.'

Someone tapped him on the shoulder and he spun round. Suddenly everything froze. Standing there in front of him was the man Martin had lived with and loved for the best part of four years – Christopher. He looked exactly as he had done the last time Martin saw him, that night on the dance floor at Heaven – shirtless and handsome and, judging by the size of his eyes, pumped full of happy pills. The only difference was, he didn't have Marco's muscular arms wrapped around him. Tonight, in this club, for this moment at least, Christopher was on his own. And the strangest thing was, as Martin stared at him and tried to figure out what, if anything, to say, he suddenly realised that he felt no emotional connection with this person at all. There were no sudden stirrings in his stomach, like a small animal turning over in its sleep. There was no flush of love, no anger, no pain, no bitterness, nothing. That was all so far in the past, it was almost as if it had never happened, almost as if Christopher and he had never been anything more than casual acquaintances. It felt odd, and at the same time it made complete sense. They weren't the same people they were before. The man he used to be in love with no longer existed. In his place was this person Martin barely even knew. And in place of the life they had once shared, there was a new life full of new experiences, new possibilities and new friends.

'I'm looking for my friend,' Martin said finally.

Christopher frowned, then turned and pointed him towards the front office. Just then the door to the office opened and a man Martin recognised as a DJ from one of the cheesier clubs in the West End walked out carrying two large record boxes.

Martin rushed up to him. 'They took my friend in there,' he said, grabbing the DJ's arm. 'Is he all right?'

The DJ rolled his eyes and mimed someone having their throat cut. 'Sorry,' he said with a spiteful little smile and promptly disappeared.

Chapter nineteen

It took another fifteen minutes for the ambulance to arrive and for Martin to digest the fact that Neil hadn't actually died, but was already semi-conscious and was being taken to a local hospital to have his stomach pumped and to check that there was no permanent damage. Sitting in the back of the ambulance, watching as Neil was fitted with an oxygen mask and feeling that he was somehow being held responsible for what had happened, Martin responded to the nurse's urgent calls for information as quickly and as fully as he could.

'What's his name?'

'Neil.'

'What has he taken?'

'Ecstasy.'

'How many pills?'

'I don't know. One. Maybe two.'

'Anything else?'

'Some coke. A few lines I think. And some K.'

The nurse clutched Neil's hand and peered into his face. 'Can you hear me, Neil? Squeeze my hand if you can hear me.' She turned and looked at Martin with a wry smile. 'You boys don't do things by halves, do you?' she said. 'Don't worry. I think your friend is going to be all right.'

By the time they arrived at the hospital, Neil had spared himself the indignity of having his stomach pumped by spewing up the contents of his belly, and was sitting up and cracking jokes.

'It isn't funny, Neil,' Martin said as they wheeled him into the accident and emergency department. 'For a while back there I thought you were dead.'

Neil smiled up at him. 'Sorry about that,' he said. 'What happened to John?'

Martin shrugged. 'What do you think? At the first sign of trouble he decided it was time he looked for Fernando. I haven't seen him since.'

'And how are you feeling?'

'Me? I'm fine. Why?'

Neil laughed. 'Because you don't look fine. Your eyes are like saucers. You look like shit.'

The nurse who helped Neil into his temporary bed and left him to produce a urine sample while she jotted down some details was a no-nonsense type with permed, plum-coloured hair and a smoker's cough. 'So, where've you two been tonight?' she asked Martin.

'Crash.'

'Oh, they're all posers there,' she said with a wink. 'I live near The Fridge. They're all posers there too.'

Martin smiled. 'Where do you go out then?'

She laughed. 'I don't. I get enough excitement here. Your friend's the fourth one we've had in tonight. Must be some dodgy pills going round. Still, I don't suppose that will stop you.'

Martin stared at the floor.

'You might as well go home,' she added gently. 'The doctor won't be free to see him for a while yet, and then he'll have to wait for his test results. I'll tell him to call you when he's ready.'

'He'll be all right, won't he?'

She gave a crooked smile. 'I should think so. Until the next time.'

'Why didn't you tell me before that your father was gay?' Caroline asked. It was the early hours of the morning and she and Graham were sitting at her kitchen table, talking in circles as their coffee went cold.

'I only found out myself about six months ago,' he said. 'Timing was never Dad's strong point. Thirty-two years of marriage and suddenly he decides he can't go on living a lie. Mum was devastated. I'm still getting used to the idea.'

Caroline shook her head. 'I can't begin to imagine what your mum must be going through.'

Graham smiled. 'Really? I would have thought you'd have no trouble putting yourself in her place.'

She looked away. 'You seemed pretty cool with your Dad earlier.'

'Well, the group has helped.'

'You mean C.L.A.G.?'

'Yes. Children of Lesbians and Gays. Dad put me onto them. They've been great. That's where I met Darren, the guy whose message you overheard. His father was arrested in a public toilet and tried to hang himself. Compared to what he's been through, I've had it easy.'

'And Charlotte?'

'Charlotte's having other problems. She's always known that her mother was a lesbian. But now her mother has started blaming herself for Charlotte turning out gay too.'

'What about you?'

Graham grinned. 'Well, contrary to popular opinion I'm not following in my father's footsteps. Besides, I can't walk in heels.'

Caroline blushed. 'I meant, do you blame him?'

'I'm not ashamed of him, if that's what you're asking.'

'But you must have been embarrassed, or you'd have told me earlier.'

'I suppose I was a bit embarrassed at first, yes. But who isn't embarrassed by their parents sometimes?'

Caroline pictured her mother and was forced to agree. 'I'm glad you took me to meet your dad,' she said finally.

'Me too,' Graham said. 'His act needs a bit of work though, doesn't it? And he could probably do with one of your makeovers.'

Caroline laughed. 'It could be worse. At least he wasn't up there having sex.'

'What?'

'Oh, nothing,' she said. 'Just some other drag act I saw once. Anyway, it's getting late. Shall I call you a cab, or would you like to stay over?'

He smiled. 'I thought you'd never ask.'

Before leaving to collect Neil from the hospital the following morning, Martin phoned his father.

'It's a bit early for you on a Sunday, isn't it, son?' his father asked with a slightly anxious tone. 'Nothing wrong, is there?'

'Not really,' Martin said. 'Well, not in the way you think anyway. The thing is, Dad – I know what John said to you, about how he thought I should go for an HIV test. He had no right saying that. I'm fine, really. I don't know where he gets some of his ideas from.'

'Well, I'm sure he didn't mean any harm,' his father said, somewhat charitably. 'He is your friend, after all.'

'Yes, so he tells me,' Martin replied flatly. 'Anyway, that's for us to sort out. I just wanted you to know that there's nothing for you to worry about. I'm fine. I know how to take care of myself.'

His father chuckled. 'I'm sure you do. You always did.'

'What do you mean?'

'Even as a kid, you were always the strong one. It was your brother I worried about. Especially after the divorce.'

Martin took a moment to take this in. 'Really? You never told me that before.'

'Perhaps I should have done,' his father replied. 'It isn't always easy being a parent, you know. There are a few things I'd do differently if I had my time again.'

'You did okay,' Martin said gently. 'Oh, and there's just one other thing, Dad. Those self-help books you keep sending. I know you mean well, but I honestly don't need them. I hope you're not offended.'

'Of course not,' his father assured him. 'I'll tell you what. The money I save by not sending those books I can put towards coming up and seeing you again sometime soon. How about that?'

Martin smiled. 'That sounds great, Dad.'

When the taxi pulled up at the hospital half an hour later, Martin was surprised to find Neil waiting outside. He looked a little pale and his pupils were like pin-pricks, but other than that he seemed fully recovered.

'The doctor says I should avoid taking drugs for a while,' Neil said as he climbed into the back seat.

'Maybe you should think about giving them up for good,' Martin replied, amazed that Neil would even consider taking drugs ever again. 'What happened last night wasn't just some minor mishap. It was serious.'

'I know that,' Neil said sulkily, and turned to stare out of the window. 'Maybe it's something I should talk over with my therapist,' he added quietly. 'What do you think?'

Martin gritted his teeth. 'I think that would be good idea, Neil.'

They continued the journey in silence, and when the taxi finally pulled up outside the flat, Martin took a few minutes to persuade Neil that now was not a good time to go and collect his car before ushering him inside.

'I think I'll go and lie down for a bit,' Neil said as they entered the flat. He stopped outside his bedroom door and turned to Martin. 'Thanks for everything. You've been great.' And with that he disappeared into his room.

Martin hung up his jacket and drifted into the living room. The answermachine was winking to indicate that there were two new messages.

The first message was from Caroline.

'Hi, babes,' she said. 'I'm just calling to say that I took your advice and called Graham and that we've sorted everything out. I've got loads more to tell you. Honestly, you won't believe some of what's been happening. Call me as soon as you can. Lots of love, and thanks for the other night. Oh, and I've left a message on your mobile too, so if you hear this one first, just ignore it. Okay, bye.'

The second message was from John.

'Hello, daughter,' it began. 'Look, I know you're probably a bit pissed off with me after last night, but I just wanted to ring and check that Neil's okay. I saw the ambulance arrive, so I assume he didn't die or anything. Also, Fernando's a bit worried about the police getting involved and his name being mentioned, but I told him he could trust you to keep him out of it. Anyway, I'm in all day, so call me when you get this message.'

Martin reached for the phone, then thought better of it. Some things were better said in person. Creeping about the flat so as not to disturb Neil, he put on his jacket, picked up his mobile phone and slipped quietly out of the door.

John and Fernando hadn't said more than two words to each other all morning. There was one very good reason for this. Ever since they left the club together last night and came back to John's flat, all that seemed to concern Fernando was whether or not his name would be mentioned in connection with Neil's apparent overdose on the dance floor. As he explained to John, it wasn't just the police he was worried about. If word got out that it was he who had supplied Neil with drugs last night, his business would suffer terribly – at least for a week or two. Much to John's annoyance, Fernando had been so preoccupied with Neil's little misadventure that he appeared to have completely forgotten about the whole point of last night's party. Having risked public humiliation by inviting Fernando to move in with him, John was still waiting for an answer.

To make matters worse, Fernando's silence on this particular subject seemed to have coincided with a sudden lack of interest in other departments. Despite the fact that they had arrived home last night high on a combination of E and K, and had then proceeded to work their way through a gram of coke, they hadn't fallen into their usual routine of pouring a stiff drink and having wild, druggy sex on the living-room floor. Instead, they had fallen into bed, where Fernando promptly passed out. And when he nudged John awake this morning, it wasn't sex he wanted but further reassurance that Martin wouldn't mention his name to the police. Finally, after persuading John to phone Martin and leave a message, Fernando had gone out to clear his head.

He had been gone for the best part of an hour now, leaving John to clear up the mess from last night's party and gradually work himself up into an indignant rage. He was elbow deep in soap suds and practically foaming at the mouth when the buzzer rang. Expecting it to be Fernando armed with a bunch of flowers, an apology and possibly even a suitcase or two, John dried his hands and ran to open the door.

'Hello, John,' Martin said.

John made little attempt to disguise the disappointment in his voice. 'Oh, it's you,' he said. 'I thought you were Fernando.'

'I need to talk to you,' Martin replied. There was a steely quality to his voice John hadn't heard before.

'What about?' John said, suddenly panicking and peering over Martin's shoulder. 'Oh my God, the police aren't with you, are they?'

'Of course not!' Martin snapped. 'And in case you're wondering, Neil is fine.'

John blushed ever so slightly. 'Oh, I see. That's great news,' he said, stepping back from the door. 'Well, I suppose you'd better come in.'

Martin didn't move. 'There's no need,' he said. 'This won't take long. I just came here to tell you that I know what you've been saying behind my back. I know what you told Shane

about me and Christopher. And I know what you said to my
dad about how I should go for an HIV test. I couldn't believe
it at first, but then it all sort of fitted together. I don't know
why I was surprised. I've always known you could be a spiteful little queen. I just never imagined that you would be so
disloyal. Now that I know, I'm really not sure I want to be
your friend any more. Anyway, I think that's all I came to say.
Oh yes, one more thing. I bumped into Fernando on the way
here. He was sitting in that café next to the tube station. I hate
to be the one to tell you this, but I got the distinct impression
that he won't be moving in. He said something about going
back to Brazil.'

For the first time in all the years that they had known each
other, John found himself completely lost for words. He
simply stood mouth agape as Martin turned and walked away.

Martin left Stockwell tube station and was turning into his
street when his mobile phone rang.

'Hi, baby,' Caroline's voice said. 'It's me. Where've you
been? I've been trying to track you down all day.'

'There was something I needed to do,' he replied. 'Sorry I
didn't get back to you before. I got your message about you
and Graham. That's great news.'

'You sound a bit strange,' she said. 'Are you okay?'

'I'm fine. I had a bit of a drama last night. Neil ended up in
hospital, but he seems all right now. And I ran into
Christopher. It was weird seeing him again, but I feel kind of
okay with it.'

Caroline sounded doubtful. 'Are you sure you're okay? You
don't sound it.'

'I'm just tired, that's all. I'll tell you all about it later. Look,
I'm almost home now. I'll call you back in a little while, okay?'

'Okay. I'll be at home. But make it quick. I'm worried.'

Martin laughed. 'Not you as well. I've had enough of that with my dad. I'll call you back in half an hour, I promise. Now can I please go? I have to find my keys.'

He let himself into the flat and padded quietly past Neil's door and into the living room. The light on the answer-machine was flashing. It would be John no doubt, phoning with some tart response to their earlier conversation. Maybe it would be best to leave it until later. He really was feeling incredibly tired. Then again, if it was John on the machine Martin didn't really want Neil hearing whatever nasty little speech John had composed as his rejoinder. He hit the play button.

'Hi, Martin,' a voice said. 'It's me, Ben. Sorry it's taken me so long to get back to you, but I've been out of town for a few days and I only got back last night. If you're still interested, I'd really like to see you again. Maybe we could go for dinner or something. I think you've got my number, but just in case you've thrown it away or something it's . . .'

Suddenly Martin didn't feel quite so tired any more. As he reached for the phone and dialled Caroline's number, something stirred in his stomach and his face broke into the biggest smile he'd smiled in a long time.

Acknowledgements

This book could not have been written without the assistance, encouragement and shameless behaviour of a number of people. Thanks to:

Marcello Almeida; Marc Almond; Elaine Burston; Georgina Capel; James Collard; Nichola Coulthard, Chris Hemblade, Judy Kerr and all at *Time Out*; The Lady Denise; Aruan Duval; Alex Erfan; Elaine Finkeltaub; Lorraine Gamman; William Gibbon; Chris Headon; Sophie Hicks; Karen Krizanovich; Clayton Littlewood; Projit Mallick and Andy Theodosiou; Alison Menzies; Carl Miller; David Parker; Wayne Shires, Kerry Chapman and all at Crash; Carl Stanley; Martin Thompson; Andrew Wille.

Special thanks to Deborah Orr for sound advice, Frances Williams and Rachael Underhill for always bringing out the party monster in me, Pedro for some great lines, and my family for taking it all in their stride.

Thanks also to Miguel Cid, whose encouragement helped enormously, and to Russell T. Davies and Will Self for their kind words.

Last but not least, a big thank you to Antonia Hodgson, the best editor a boy could wish for.

QUEENS' COUNTRY

Paul Burston

'The gay community.'
For years Paul Burston has heard talk of this fabled people, but he's never been quite sure who they were. So he decided to set off and try to find them for himself. His travels around gay Britain take in a wide cross-section of people and places, from his own childhood in South Wales to middle-aged gay men enjoying a beach party in Bromley, from the gay couple running their own massage parlour in Bristol to the men cruising Edinburgh's Carlton Hill, from gay youth groups in Belfast to gay Young Conservatives in Derbyshire. Witty, irreverent and fiercely intelligent, *Queens' Country* presents the rich diversity – and occasional cultural poverty – of the forces shaping gay life in modern Britain.

'Such fun to read . . . an entertaining and topical book'
Independent

'A cracklingly irreverent snapshot of gay life . . .
a funny, thoughtful read'
The Face

'Challenging, fearless, funny and micro-detailed –
his British trek adds up to a portrait of Britain
which is complex, rich and satisfying to read'
Time Out

'Funny, provocative, thoughtful and spiky . . .
Burston is incapable of writing a boring sentence.
This book screams out to be read'
The Big Issue

Abacus
0 349 11178 2

ME TALK PRETTY ONE DAY

David Sedaris

Welcome to the wonderful world of America's foremost
humorist David Sedaris, where learning French, like life, is
littered with idiosyncratic delights . . .

'The Italian was attempting to answer the teacher's latest
question when the Moroccan student interrupted, shouting,
"Excuse me, but what's an Easter?' The teacher called upon
the rest of us to explain. "It is a party for the little boy of God
who calls his self Jesus." "He die one day and then he go
above of my head to live with your father." "He weared of
himself the long hair and after he die, the first day he come
back here for to say hello to the peoples." "He nice, the Jesus."'

'A humorist who puts the grin in chagrin'
Independent

'A comic gem to savour . . . if only our everyday
lives were this much fun'
Daily Mail

'Possibly the sharpest and funniest observer of human
weakness at work today . . . seriously addictive stuff'
The Times

Abacus
0 349 11391 2

SEX AND THE CITY

Candace Bushnell

Wildly funny, unexpectedly poignant, wickedly observant, *Sex and the City* blazes a glorious drunken cocktail-trail through New York, as Candace Bushnell, gossip columnist *par excellence*, trips on her Manolo Blahnik kitten heels from the Baby Doll Lounger to the Bowery Bar. An Armistead Maupin for the real world, she has the gift of assembling a huge and irresistible cast of freaks and wonders, whilst remaining faithful to her hard core of friends and fans: those glamorous, rebellious, crazy single women who are trying hard not to turn from the Audrey Hepburn of *Breakfast at Tiffany's* into the Glenn Close of *Fatal Attraction*, and are – still – looking for love.

'Irresistible, hilarious and horrific, stylishly written . . .
Candace Bushnell has captured the big, black truth'
Bret Easton Ellis

'Jane Austen with a martini, or perhaps
Jonathan Swift on rollerblades'
Sunday Telegraph

'Hilarious . . . a compulsively readable book, served up
in bite-sized chunks of irrepressible irreverence'
Marie Claire

Abacus
0 349 11186 3

FOUR BLONDES

Candace Bushnell

With its uncensored observations
of the mating rituals of Manhattan's elite, Candace Bushnell's
Sex and the City created a sensation. Now, with *Four Blondes*,
Bushnell triumphantly returns to the playgrounds of the
beautiful and powerful – once again capturing the essence of
our era, like no other writer.

Four Blondes charts the romantic intrigues, liaisons, betrayals
and victories of four modern women: a beautiful B-list model
scams rent-free summerhouses in the Hamptons from her
lovers until she discovers she can get a man but can't get what
she wants; a high-powered magazine columnist's floundering
marriage to a literary journalist is thrown into crisis when her
husband's career fails to live up to her expectations; a
'Cinderella' records her descent into paranoia in her journal as
she realises she wants anybody's life except her own; an artist
and ageing 'It girl' – who fears that her time for finding a man
has run out – travels to London in search of the kind of love
and devotion she can't find in Manhattan . . .

Studded with Candace Bushnell's trademark wit
and stilleto-heel-sharp insight, *Four Blondes* is dark,
true and compulsively readable.

Abacus
0 349 11403 X

LIKE PEOPLE IN HISTORY

Felice Picano

Flamboyant, mercurial Alistair Dodge and steadfast, cautious Roger Sansarc are second cousins who are both gay and whose lifelong friendship begins when they first meet as nine year old boys in 1954. At crucial moments in their personal histories their lives intersect, and each discovers his own unique – and uniquely gay – identity.

Felice Picano chronicles and celebrates gay life and subculture over the last half of the twentieth century. From Malibu Beach in its palmist surfer days to the legendary parties at Fire Island Pines in the 1970s, from San Francisco during its gayest era to AIDS activism in Greenwich Village in the 1990s, *Like People in History* presents 'the heroic and funny saga of the last three decades by someone who saw everything and forgot nothing' (Edmund White).

'A hugely ambitious and engrossing saga . . . gloriously camp and also acts as a critique of America in general'
Guardian

'The gay *Gone With the Wind*'
Edmund White

Abacus
0 349 10838 2

Now you can order superb titles directly from Abacus

☐ Queens' Country	Paul Burston	£6.99
☐ Me Talk Pretty One Day	David Sedaris	£7.99
☐ Sex and the City	Candace Bushnell	£6.99
☐ Four Blondes	Candace Bushnell	£6.99
☐ Like People in History	Felice Picano	£6.99

The prices shown above are correct at time of going to press. However, the publishers reserve the right to increase prices on covers from those previously advertised, without further notice.

—————————————— (ABACUS) ——————————————

Please allow for postage and packing: **Free UK delivery.**
Europe: add 25% of retail price; Rest of World: 45% of retail price.

To order any of the above or any other Abacus titles, please call our credit card orderline or fill in this coupon and send/fax it to:

Abacus, PO Box 121, Kettering, Northants NN14 4ZQ
Fax: 01832 733076   Tel: 01832 737527
Email: aspenhouse@FSBDial.co.uk

☐ I enclose a UK bank cheque made payable to Abacus for £ . . . .
☐ Please charge £ . . . . . . to my Visa/Access/Mastercard/Eurocard

Expiry Date ☐☐☐☐   Switch Issue No. ☐☐

NAME (BLOCK LETTERS please) . . . .

ADDRESS . . . .

. . . .

. . . .

Postcode . . . . Telephone . . . .

Signature . . . .

Please allow 28 days for delivery within the UK. Offer subject to price and availability.

Please do not send any further mailings from companies carefully selected by Abacus ☐